NIGHT AS IT FALLS

JAKUTA ALIKAVAZOVIC

Night as It Falls

Translated from the French by
Jeffrey Zuckerman

faber

First published in 2021
by Faber & Faber Ltd
Bloomsbury House
74–77 Great Russell Street
London WC1B 3DA

Typeset by Typo•glyphix, Burton-on-Trent, DE14 3HE
Printed in the UK by CPI Group (UK) Ltd, Croydon, CR0 4YY

A CIP record for this book
is available from the British Library

ISBN 978-0-571-34226-6

2 4 6 8 10 9 7 5 3 1

Contents

Paul was with Sylvia when he found out what happened to Amelia Dehr. In bed with Sylvia, who was sleeping, or pretending to, as blurred glimmers from outside, from the *bateaux-mouches*, bathed them, sweeping nonchalantly over their bodies, across the sheets, up to the ceiling. He mulled over how they might just blend into the space, into the surroundings, and maybe that was happiness, or the closest thing to it. Camouflage, really, Paul thought.

There was a phone call, she was between life and death, and Paul knew there could only be one outcome. Amelia Dehr wasn't the sort to hold back. This precarity, rather, betrayed just how fragile, how frail she now felt – must have felt – not in going through with it but rather in failing, with an imprecision wholly unlike her. An imprecision that convinced Paul that at the moment she had set to ending it all, she was no longer the woman she had been. She had ceased to be Amelia Dehr.

The other possibility or interpretation – the idea that something in her was clinging to life, refusing to die; that the true Amelia Dehr, the one he had known, loved, yearned for, hated, this Amelia Dehr was now battling against death; the idea she was on the losing side, and was losing everything – was unbearable to Paul. He would rather believe that for ages now the woman about to die, the one struggling, had not been the real Amelia Dehr, that the relationship she bore to Amelia Dehr was the shaky one connecting a leaf to the tree from which it had fallen.

She had sunk into insanity, Paul thought, she who at twenty had been resplendent, lively, wildly imaginative; she who, lying in the grass, seemed to be an extension of the grass, no, even more than that: its continuation, its tenderness – she who, lying in the grass, seemed to be the wisdom of the grass, its vivid essence. The last time he saw her, he had been shocked to see her unkempt. Worse than that; listless. Lacklustre, even. She was sure she was being watched. She had called him and asked him to come meet her in the courtyard. She trusted him to tell her; as he stood down there, could he see her at her desk? He hadn't understood the question. He would rather not have understood, had been tempted to brush it aside. Out of tact, or cowardliness. Or a tact that was also cowardliness. Why don't you go back up, he said, that'd be easier, that way I can tell you whether you can be seen. Or not. The look she gave him wasn't blind, strictly speaking, not so much blind as unseeing. It was a gaze that simply took him in amongst other things. As if Paul himself were somewhere beyond his body. And he felt himself drifting away. His spirit or personality or soul was just floating off, away, towards this place where he wasn't, couldn't be, but where Amelia Dehr's gaze fell. This was the kind of power she still held over him. She had clutched his hand and, in a rush, before her pride (because she had been so proud, it was so much a part of her) forced her to hold back her words, she had let out: No, I want you to tell me if I'm sitting there *right now*, you have to tell me, Paul, please.

She was one of those people who destroyed everything and called it art.

*

At that time it seemed inconceivable to them that a young woman, a student just like them, could live in a hotel. It wasn't even a particularly fancy hotel. On the contrary, it was one of those ever-sprawling American chains; but the mere sentence *She lives in a hotel* was provocative, explosive. An eighteen-year-old girl in an American hotel. Everyone thought she would become a writer, everyone except for her; it was her mother who was the writer, and the fact that her mother had been dead a long time didn't change a thing. *The writer* meant her mother. And she, Amelia Dehr, was a character, and, as far as they could tell, determined to remain one. And whether she was the author who dreamed up that character, or merely a character in someone else's story, nobody could quite say, and the question was never answered.

hotel nights

I

Paul couldn't believe that she lived in a hotel. Better yet, or worse, he had known it, then forgotten. They talked about her on campus, rumours had preceded her, so much that her body already existed in whispers, but Paul didn't care about gossip. He cared about girls, and women. Their mouths, their flesh. He was eighteen years old, and living multiple lives. By day he went to university, he stared at huge blackboards or whiteboards, he traded and compared notes with his classmates; it was odd how sometimes they would swear they couldn't possibly have gone to the same lecture, until they landed on one or two identical sentences and had to concede that they had indeed both been listening to the same professor, but aside from those fixed points each of their notebooks meandered, diverged. The ones who understood best were the ones who understood nothing and, terrified by their own ignorance, had written everything down verbatim.

They spent hours gathered together at the café: girls running their fingers over his scalp and stroking it, cold fingers probing the waves of his hair, exploring the topography of his cranium, light fingers slipping across the back of his head as if momentarily, unwittingly breathing life into long-forgotten theories, as if the bumps they found could reveal the secrets of his personality or his soul through the old, discredited markers of amativeness or acquisitiveness, or benevolence, or adhesiveness – even though the mystery these eighteen-year-old girls ever so gently touching his head were trying to decipher was simply that of their own desire, the desire they felt for this young man in particular or the desire they felt for young men in general. All these fresh-faced students were happy; they talked too much, their breaths forming small clouds in the cold air, they smoked too much, drank coffee in quantities that set their hearts racing. Deep down, they scared as easily as deer, even the boys, especially the boys, and so they shied away from open contact – would never have dared to lock hands, much less lock lips. Yet they were all so close together that just one of them had to catch a cold for all the others to catch it as well.

In the evenings, at night, there were long, drunken, anonymous parties where Paul lost his friends in the crowd, intentionally lost them, because everybody swooned over him with his swimmer's torso and his long lashes. Nights when people handed him glasses full of clear or cloudy liquids that sometimes plunged him into extraordinary slowness where everything flowed as if underwater and where gestures were never quite completed, where they barely got nine-tenths of the way through. Nights on rooftops or in basements or at mansions or in abandoned métro stations. Nights full of smoke. Nights when he lost sight of his friends then found them again, but sometimes it wasn't them, sometimes it was just his face, just his own reflection caught here or there. Nights when people tried in vain to get him into bed. Nights when he was obsessed with sex because at that time Paul was under a curse or a spell, *he just couldn't get rid of his virginity*, every time, the girl disappeared or he left or someone showed up or they had to go; but stranger still, even when he had sex, and whatever the definition one gave the act, whether it was ordinary or pornographic or legal or none of the above, even when he inserted his genitals into someone else's, even when he came with an uncontrollable shudder and the deed had finally been done, he thought, *finally!* – the next day or a few days later, it was as if nothing had happened. He was a virgin again, and resigned to it. It was a nightmare for him.

He slept little but slept well. Wherever he was, at the university or at the café, in an unknown house or at home, most of the time, just a few feet away would be a screen with flickering images of murders and investigations or funerals and tears or collapses and escapes or questions and answers, or only questions. And he, impervious to all these tragedies, slept peacefully. But that was before Amelia Dehr. That was before the hotel.

There wasn't much money. His father had been blunt: the classes were fine, the rest wasn't. He took the first job that came his way, distractedly, without even realising what he was agreeing to; indifferent or inattentive, because what he cared about was beginning a new life. Security monitoring – or rather, simply monitoring – during the off-hours at the hotel. In the evening; at night. He got bored there. And he

9

offset that boredom by watching the women. Watching them at a remove. He looked for them. Sometimes he found them, sometimes he lost them. In any case, it was a game he played without any of them knowing. This one leaving her room and immediately disappearing, vanishing. Only to reappear, somewhere he hadn't expected, as if by magic, slipping from one small window to another, almost at random. There were nine cameras and just as many squares on the monitoring screen, Paul's screen. He waited for surprises; he could only anticipate their trajectories to a certain degree, because that didn't account for random stops, sudden about-faces. He stared at all those bodies walking around and thinking thoughts he couldn't see on the screens. He couldn't see what had been forgotten in the rooms, on the nightstands, in the bathrooms; and he had no hope of seeing any lingering afterthoughts. And every so often came one of Paul's favourite moments: rare, unexpected, evasive embraces in the emergency stairwells. All he ever saw was a fire door slowly – lazily – closing.

He couldn't really say that he enjoyed his job, which he didn't think of as a job so much as an accident – less than that in fact, an incident, nothing more: a casual thing. But he could say that he enjoyed watching women. That he enjoyed looking down at them, playing at (or so he told himself) looking down on them – and only at the hotel, only at night, was that possible for him, specifically because of the cameras, aimed so sharply downward that he was positioned high up, like the sun, like some god. If the warmer air – the sighs they exhaled as they redid their make-up in the elevator's infinite mirrors, the seismic heat their warm flesh exuded as they stood in these empty, thoroughly ventilated spaces – and these exhalations rising up, accumulating beneath the ceiling, could see, then that vapour's gaze would be the gaze Paul now had. So dreamed Paul.

When the women weren't going in and out much any more or he wasn't watching them much any more, he tried to study. He liked university but more than that he liked being a student, it exhilarated him, as did the pride his father felt – which didn't keep him from being, deep down, a bit jealous of Paul, just a bit, in those little crannies of his heart of which he himself was unaware – actively, insistently unaware, in total denial. He would rather cut off his arm than admit it, because he was a good man, as proud of his goodwill as he was of his son, and a good man doesn't envy his only child. But, at the construction site, he sometimes thought of that university and spat in the drywall, and sometimes pissed in the drywall, as people have always done – general hygiene notwithstanding – to bind the components, to (this Paul knew, even if his father didn't) alter the pH, the acidity, the stability; and to (this his father knew, even if Paul didn't) leave something of oneself in someone else's space, in walls that construction workers laboured to build with no hope of ever living there. To secretly, silently spit or piss on other people's comfort.

Their origins were modest and they took nothing for granted, especially not university education; they lived, had lived, Paul thought, as if nothing under their feet was certain. As if they were on water – but that image didn't occur to him then; he would only think it much later, after finally meeting Amelia Dehr.

He tried to study but needed to take in far more than just his architecture classes, which sectioned off various eras, areas, and approaches. He had cut off – or so he thought – all contact with his past, which he didn't think of as a past so much as an incident, more than that, an accident. The first eighteen years of his life had given him a particular body, and this body had a particular relationship with space, with others. He sensed that he didn't quite belong. At the outset, he had observed. And imitated. First the clothes, which he stole. Then the haircut, which he'd had to adopt a whole new language just to describe, to ask for. It was a challenge he had never faced before, as complex as an international expedition, the greatest of conquests. Finally, he mastered the delicate art of talking. But this drained him. Some nights in the dorms he stayed in his bedroom, in the dark. Listening to the noises in the hallway, and all the other students' chatter made him seasick; and if someone knocked on his door, he wouldn't answer, the idea that it might be a mistake horrifying him just as much as the idea that it might not. He was terrified that it would never end and, even though it never did quite fade away, not really, still it only lasted two weeks, maybe three, and then it didn't matter any more. He was already feeling at home, or so he thought. He had closer friends than ever, whom he loved intensely, for whom he sometimes thought he would have given an arm, a kidney, even. But sometimes he forgot their names. Or their faces. At three or four in the morning he would realise that all he retained of this friend, this guy or girl, was just a blurry shape. And sometimes it was just his face, just his own reflection caught here or there. Maybe deep down some part of him still lived in darkness. And maybe, worse still, he had gone on to think of this darkness, in bleak terms – all the bleaker given that he was an eighteen-year-old man with a swimmer's torso, with long lashes, who now had a new self – as *real life*.

*

For some people, the Elisse hotel seemed to be not just where but how crimes were committed. It was the kind of place that stood in for reality, if reality was, first and foremost, disappointing. It was, in any case, no place for lovers of literature or even plot. Some member of an older generation might end up there on occasion, and Paul didn't even try to disguise how he stared at them as worry and sometimes, rarely, death took root in their souls the same (thankfully) brief way they settled in a bedroom exactly like all the others for the night. It was a place that killed not by beauty or ugliness but, really, by indifference. Somehow, this no-man's-land quality accounted for the chain's immediate success: it was exactly what people were looking for here when they had some choice of *here*. It boasted every modern comfort, and the secret to this comfort was its neutrality, its anonymity. Nothing was more like an Elisse hotel than another Elisse hotel and so it was almost possible for someone staying there to wake up as someone else. Or, better still, as no one at all. Yes, in these mid-range spots it was possible to be oneself and someone else, oneself and no one at all. The windows were perfectly square and did not open; the air conditioning circulated microbes and distributed them equitably. All these forms of contagion mixed together. People were so scarcely themselves there that the coughs they coughed were those of strangers. Paul was bored stiff, and after enough time had gone by, gently swivelling his chair in front of the surveillance video screens, all alone in an empty lobby, some sort of trance came over him. The fountain's unceasing flow did not help. He wasn't lonely so much as he was feeling the cumulative effect of certain physical phenomena; not so much a state as an environment, like certain altitudes or depths, and eventually he started breathing differently, in a new rhythm. Sometimes his ears buzzed. He waited for something to happen and sometimes, out of sheer isolation, something did, just not in the way he hoped.

For two or three hours, the usual clientele for this type of establishment would come and go: young and not-so-young executives, individuals passing through, here for a function or a mission, for union committees or academic colloquia. Some, oddly enough, seemed to have taken a shine to the place. Paul didn't care about them, and they cared even less about Paul. This didn't keep them from polite conversations or the occasional joke, but the moment they turned away, smiles faded from faces and faces faded from memory. Some nights there was a dead calm: nobody walked past for hours on end, Paul's heel swivelled the chair left and right unthinkingly, no human sound rose above the flowing water which created what the hotel's architects designated a climate – on those nights, something did happen. Paul didn't realise it because he was waiting for something to happen in front of him, something he might see with his own eyes. Something outside him. What did happen, however, took place inside him. He sat amongst the monitor screens displaying empty elevators and deserted hallways and the television channel playing the news bulletin on a loop, and time went by, always slower than he liked, and suddenly, at the pinnacle of his boredom, something would happen. The sliding doors, for example, might sigh open, activated by the movement of a body nowhere to be seen. Or someone might walk past one of the nine monitor screens. Or, very specifically, he might suddenly insist that he could see a woman sitting, her hair damp, on the edge of the fountain where she's just washed her hair. He knows she's there, just as he knows the door's just opened and someone's entered – he'd swear on it, it's a fact, an indisputable fact – until he looks up. The water dripping from her hair onto her shirt seems to darken her hair and her clothes, her eyes meet his, she takes her time, he does as well. In that moment he could almost foresee exactly where her eyes would be. But he'd look up and, sure enough, see nobody there.

Paul dismissed these impressions as if they were figments of his imagination, the effects of exhaustion, the artificial light. He didn't think of these moments, these mistakes, as events. He waited. He waited but, one night after the doors were locked – in the wee hours, guests buzzed at the door to be let in – he saw Amelia Dehr on his monitor screen, standing in the street like an apparition, and he panicked. He had never imagined that he might see her there, at two or three in the morning, at the place where he worked.

Honestly, he wasn't impressed. She struck him as a bit ridiculous. Or rather, what everybody said about her struck him as a bit ridiculous. On campus, he had never said a word to her and saw no reason to. But everybody else there thought differently, it was a thrum of childish delusions: her beauty was bewildering, her soul was black; *whenever she walks into a room, someone runs out crying*; her father was rich or dead or rich and dead; she was an heiress; she was the Elisse Hotels heiress; she had lovers by the dozen; she was this, she was that, a proliferation of clichés. The first time he saw her, when someone pointed her out in the cafeteria, where she was scanning the room, as if looking for a friend or the emergency exits, Paul wasn't impressed at all. He found her, unsurprisingly enough, smaller than he'd imagined. Smaller and less symmetrical, her features less *legendary*. Whatever he had expected, it wasn't that, certainly not a redhead. She had the sort of hair that, when it was backlit, seemed to be ablaze – but to actually touch it would be underwhelming, just as it would be for anyone wondering what it would be like to catch a fox, to grab it with their bare hands and stuff it in their coat. But what a silly idea that would be, what strange, dark eroticism, and of course, Paul thought, if this girl had such a reputation it was because liking her, liking her red hair, in fact meant liking a certain sort of danger, a danger that had real teeth; and courting it, and complaining bitterly after about having been bitten. Oh, *that's* Amelia Dehr? Paul had said with a rather unconvinced grimace, and his scepticism had made half the table's occupants quiver with relish and something verging on fear, as if he were questioning something far greater and far more fundamental than that girl right there. As if the uncertainty he had just breathed into this seemingly unambiguous fact – that Amelia Dehr was worthy of being looked at – could spread to other things that everyone at the table would prefer to stay stable and clear-cut.

And now she was once again standing at the threshold of a place where he was sitting; but this was nothing like that day at the university when the presence of his friends had been a bulwark. This time, he was alone, as was she – her outside and him inside. So, he realised, it was true after all: she lived in a hotel. He contemplated not letting her in, leaving her outside all night. Yes, all night if he had to. She buzzed again, and Paul finally pressed the button for the sliding doors, which opened to let in Amelia Dehr. And then Paul did something he had never done before: he hid. He slipped down, calmly, as if his body had lost all form and his clothes were now drifting down, and he huddled beneath the desk. He heard Amelia Dehr's heels clacking on the black-green marble tile that blurred all the silhouettes reflected in its sheen. He heard her pause at the front desk before walking on to the elevators. All this time, he was crouching beneath his desk, discomfited by how shameful it was to work where she lived, how horribly close that felt to working *for her*. His pride was so essential to him, so much a vital organ, that he could not accept this; if Amelia Dehr's gaze

17

ever met his, he and his pride would both burst. In his head, that made sense, but honestly, if anyone was to feel ashamed here, it ought to be those who lived where others worked, it ought to be Amelia Dehr who felt that shame. Paul did not realise this truth, but Amelia, to her credit, did. His sense of shame overpowered him. It wasn't just that he was poor; he also felt guilty for being so. Yet when he wasn't at risk of being seen by Amelia Dehr, he felt as if he lacked for nothing; and so he would rather be folded up, curled up, wedged into a crevice, would rather be under the desk than sitting upright in his chair in her line of sight, humiliation eating away at him.

And so a haphazard two-step played out between Paul and Amelia, more specifically between Paul and the Amelia he saw on the screens, the Amelia he imagined, an Amelia who bore little connection to the real one. And young and not-so-young men came and went, waiting in the lobby, on the seats in front of the reception desk and in front of Paul, as he watched Amelia on her floor above leaving her room and coming down, unhurriedly, sometimes running her neat fingernails along the wall, almost gliding. He watched her redo her make-up in the elevators. Her motions seemed unexpected, almost violent to him. But as she peered into the mirror, bit her lips, pinched her cheeks, there was no way for the black-and-white video to show how the blood rose and gave her skin a healthy, attractive flush. And just as the elevator door opened, scarcely a few feet away, Paul would suddenly think up some urgent task he needed to deal with in the back room or he would become absorbed in an apparently lively conversation with one or two of his colleagues. Or he would simply, awkwardly turn his back for as long as it took Amelia to cross the hall and wave to her suitor (where did that word come from, Paul wondered; these men were utterly unsuitable for her). She would leave with him or maybe the man would follow as she turned and led the way upstairs. Paul would then spend far more time than he realised staring at the screen that showed the empty third-floor hallway, waiting for someone there who never did come out. Maybe they're still all in there, Paul mused as he finished his shift. Maybe it's one of those rooms you walk into and never leave again.

Sometimes he saw her going down to the basement, to the gym; other times she came to sit in the empty restaurant. He wondered what she was doing in the half-light – there, or in the deserted meeting rooms. He watched as she tried the door handles to see if one was unlocked, which there always was since the staff were often careless, or not so much careless as rushed, and forgot to lock them after business meetings and industry conferences and all those deathly boring talks that went on there. Paul would sometimes go down, and, even though there was no one else to watch the monitor screens, anyone who did look would have thought he was locking all the doors, when in fact he was using the hotel key to make sure that one of them remained unlocked should Amelia Dehr feel the need for a meeting room.

Once or twice there were disturbances, rowdy parties, smoke alarms going off, and once or twice there were screams. I don't know what's happening next door, said the worried guest whose name Paul never did learn; I don't know what's going on, but it sounds like something being broken. Maybe furniture? There are voices. Paul's face remained impassive. She wasn't deterred: what if it's *bones*? That night Paul had no choice but to go up, this woman hot on his heels, and knock on Amelia Dehr's door, even though they couldn't hear anything from the hallway. He had no choice but to bang on the door, and Amelia finally opened it, slightly breathless yet steady – though her lips, Paul thought, seemed to have been bitten recently, bitten by someone else? As if by tacit agreement, they acted as if they didn't know each other, as if each had never seen the other before. Is everything all right, miss? Paul asked, and Amelia replied: Thank you, sir, yes, everything is all right. Her eyes were unsmiling. He tried to look past her, into the room. An unmade bed. A lampshade, slightly askew. Nothing.

*

They were nothing to each other and then they were friends. Later on, they would be lovers – or they were lovers, and later on they would be friends. But before all that, before any kind of relationship, Paul and Amelia Dehr were rivals. Secret, stubborn rivals. She came out the victor. Paul saw this as a tragedy; later on, he would see it as a blessing. At the time, the undisputed celebrity of their university, of *all* universities (or so they thought) was Anton Albers; crowds of students thronged in front of the lecture hall at dawn, long before their class started, in order to snag a spot. The wait, Paul would say much later, was part of the class. The wait, Amelia would say much later, *was* the class. He disagreed adamantly, but he would come to feel that it was under Anton Albers's auspices that he had become who he was. Amelia, by all appearances, hadn't become who she was then. Amelia already was who she was. Paul saw this as a blessing; later on, he would see it as a tragedy. Now, she only had to unbecome herself.

Anton Albers was internationally renowned, but Paul had no idea of that. There was so much he didn't know when he arrived: he got lost in the streets, in the hallways and even in his own thoughts. It took him two weeks just to find the lecture hall for Albers's class and when he finally walked in, he walked right back out, because the classroom was packed. The emergency exits were blocked; students sat in the aisles, on the steps, against the doors. They were listening to a woman, when it seemed perfectly clear that this professor he was looking for was a man. This was how deeply ignorant he had been. A wisp of a woman whose age was impossible to guess even though she did not hide it: she had been born in Buenos Aires, right after World War II, the daughter of a German engineer turned Nazi sympathiser, a regular correspondent with the architect Albert Speer and Wernher von Braun, the father of rocket science who had been welcomed to the United States with open arms. Albers's father went to Argentina, where he met his wife and where their daughter Antonia Albers would be born, then to Chile, where the girl would lead a dreamy childhood, and she soon left on her own, as a minor, for Mexico, and the next chance she got, she was on her way to the United

States. She had been a fleeting figure, if not necessarily a flee-ing one; and only ever alluded to her earliest years in vague terms which, even though she mentioned no real particulars, made it seem all the more concrete: a father, a mother, sun-shine on the patio. A dog. Notwithstanding her family's past, it was her first name that she changed, lopping off the fem-inine suffix that was its final syllable. Antonia became Anton; the few photographs of that time showed what appeared to be a slim young man with fine lips and finer hair.

Would you say, Madame Albers, that it was more diffi-cult to have a feminine present, a present as a woman, than a chequered past? was one of the questions she was most fre-quently asked, and one she never answered. I'll let you draw your own conclusions, she usually replied. It was hard not to admire this commitment to ambiguity. Other people were unimpressed by her refusal, of course, and considered it cow-ardly or simply unacceptable. Her biography was nebulous and spotty: she seemed to have studied on every continent and in just about every time zone. She had authored theses in history and law and urbanism on the topic of the night – or were they all the same unpublished text that her biographical note always alluded to? By the time she had become the icon she now was, equal parts revered and reviled, the bound manuscript was long gone from the dusty shelves at the Uni-versity of California, Berkeley. When people asked about it, Albers's only answer was a shrug and a mischievous smile. Her beauty had left with her youth, but she radiated a particular charm all the same; ever since her early thirties Albers had looked the way she did when Paul shouldered his way into the lecture hall, a sexless, impish, ageless mien reminiscent of a hermit or a nun. When exactly she had stopped trying to pass as a man wasn't clear; maybe during graduate school, maybe later. In the sixties and in the American Southwest, she had hung out with artists, the sort who dug immense pits in the dust and called it art; the sort who bought craters from which to watch the sky and called it art; and who, without exception, ended badly. 'Ending badly' was a running theme amongst Albers's closest acquaintances, or those who warranted the slightest bit of interest. Then came a surprise of sorts: somewhat late for the time, she gave birth to a daughter whose father's identity she didn't disclose. The child did not live.

At that point, Albers's work had already swerved towards a poetics of risk. The future of cities she believed to be the future of the world. From that point on, her career veered away from the traditional academic path and became something else: a philosophy, a vision. She taught all over the world, she lectured about lost cities and pirates, she delved into emotions that had been relegated to history books as well as those yet to come. She talked about the seal of Tutankhamen's tomb, a knot that lasted 3,245 years. In the late eighties, she asserted, in answer to a question about the creation of post-war Europe, that the Europe to come would resemble nothing so much as a besieged city. When she was asked how she envisioned the twenty-first century, she responded, in painstakingly precise French, *In the twenty-first century, everybody will be in security,* which the journalist had relayed as 'in safety,' a misinterpretation that would inspire, Anton Albers suggested with her perpetually indecipherable smile, the labour of the next decade.

In and of themselves, her lectures were strange and riveting. Her words were clear yet impenetrable; nobody else could speak such sentences. It was like watching someone foretell the future, not unlike those shows in which some clairvoyant made contact with souls from the hereafter, except Albers seemed to be in direct communion with the West to come, the future of capitalism and industrialism, whereas the people Paul thought of while listening to her were all, to a man, impostors. The semester's lecture was called 'The Cities of Tomorrow', but so far it seemed she had only talked about fear. Hour by hour, week after week, she slowly assembled a history of the feeling. As they got deeper into autumn and icy rain pounded the skylight of the lecture hall, she still hadn't made any mention of cities, much less of tomorrow, and so the rows thinned out. Paul continued to go, but he was not attending a class so much as a secret ceremony. Every sentence Albers uttered seemed to signify more than the words themselves, but this *more*, this subtext, kept escaping him. It lay on the tip of his tongue, always just out of reach. He couldn't shake the feeling that, if he could catch it, it would have made sense of the days and nights and betrayals soon to be inflicted.

Albers spoke of cities now gone, cities of single or double or triple outer walls, with underground tunnels capable of sheltering troops of a hundred knights, and she read out, in Old French, detailed protocols for locking the city's gates at

nightfall, and quarantining travellers who had had the mis-
fortune to arrive at twilight and were left to wait for daybreak
in limbo between two barriers of stone. And then she spoke
of the city-dwellers' fears, their fears of wolves, their fears of
Turks; she drew bird's-eye views from the ramparts, diagram-
ming how, as she insisted, terror spiralled outward. What she
meant to say, in this vein, about cities and about tomorrow,
about the cities of tomorrow, remained unclear, but the first
exam took the form of a single question: *Can a city die of fear?*

The rows thinned out but, in the second term, when it was
time to sign up for further seminars, both Amelia Dehr – who
only ever seemed to show up on campus for Albers's lectures,
but was at every single one – and Paul were quick to put down
their names for Anton Albers. She showed no hint of approval.
Whether she simply didn't know them yet, or whether she
knew them better than they realised, there was no change in
her demeanour: a vague look of detached contentment, or of
contented detachment. She was a woman slowly (very slowly)
doing what she had to do. Paul and Amelia jockeyed like precocious schoolchildren. They were besotted with their own
intelligence, because it was finally being put to the test. Albers
was the reason they were exploring areas that they otherwise
might not have considered, or not until much later, excavat-
ing dangerous realms despite their dread of what they already
knew, or began to sense, of the world – and despite their dread
of coming across a sentence or idea that would prove the limits
of their intelligence. Not unlike the retrograde fears of those
who, believing the earth to be flat, set sail for its edge while

terrified they might in fact discover it. They fought to be the first to read something; their intellectual tug-of-war played out through the gaps on library shelves, each missing volume an affront to Paul, a further proof not only of Amelia's existence but of her potential superiority. All that was straightforward enough, but their simmering rivalry also played out on another battleground – although it was anything but a ground: it was an instability, a dark ocean. When it came to Albers, they competed the way only two motherless children could. And it was perfectly clear that Amelia had the upper hand, which very nearly broke Paul, but he resigned himself to that reality, as if he'd known from the very beginning that disappointment lay in store for him. The two women seemed very close; he tried to grin and bear it in class, but he was genuinely annoyed and kept wondering: why *was* Albers so taken with that girl? (The answer: Amelia's intuition for disaster, her instinct for catastrophe.)

One evening, during the February break when everybody seemed to be away, skiing or with their families – or worse still, skiing *with* their families – and he was stuck in the freezing, damp city, he discovered just how close his beloved professor and Amelia Dehr were. The entire month had been tough; money was so tight that he'd had to sign up with a temp agency and take on some night-watch work. He paced up and down dark warehouses and car parks amidst the echoes of his own footsteps. The uniforms he was given were a failed attempt at semantics, at a language of sorts, drawing inspiration from the gear of riot cops, exuding something almost military but coming up short. Every part was designed to evoke municipal troops, but not quite, and Paul was never more unhappy than when he wore his laced-up combat boots and reinforced nylon jacket, a truncheon swinging against his hip.

Lonely and cold, he saw them coming down the underground ramp of a car park, a spiral burrowing into the city's core. Really, he saw their silhouettes on a monitor screen. He panicked. A German car. Albers in the passenger seat, perfectly recognisable, her black bangs just starting to turn grey – although he couldn't see that – and, slamming the driver's door shut, a willowy woman a full head taller than her. They made an almost comical pair; one tall and one small, one young and one not so much. They could have been fox and hen. He watched with dread as the two women headed towards the exit and towards him. He had never contemplated what Albers might do with her spare time, outside those two hours during which she gently addressed Paul's own fears, led him ever so patiently through deep-rooted, embarrassing anxieties, until she could show that he was in good company, demonstrating that these feelings were not his alone, were in fact shared by all – and a worthy object of study. Fear of the dark, fear of others, as well as the murky, abstract memories of widespread plagues, widespread purges retained in his bones and marrow – memories of things his body hadn't experienced but which all the same had shaped him. People huddled in the dark, a communal terror circulating amongst them, through points of contact, shoulder against shoulder, palm against palm, hand against mouth – a huge, collective body of fear. Never had it occurred to him that the woman tracing the genealogy of this feeling might some day end up eliciting it in him.

He heard their footsteps long before he saw them. It took them forever to reach his booth, like in some drawn-out horror flick, although one of the least horrible parts. The two women were talking, Amelia was carrying a cardboard office-supply box, the kind made to hold five reams of copy paper. Twenty-five hundred blank sheets that had meaning, or perhaps none – in a box rather like the ones some teachers filled with class materials, booklets, photocopies. Paul felt a sudden urge to yank the box out of her hands and run with it, as if digging through its contents could offer him some hint of the future that might otherwise remain painfully out of reach. Impulsively he hid (*not again!* he thought), sliding down in the sentry booth, and waited ages, pins and needles in his legs, until he was sure they were gone. Mercifully, they hadn't seen him.

Yet that night, at the hotel, the front-desk phone rang, late but not that late, some time around ten or eleven, and it was Amelia Dehr, suggesting that he come up and eat with her. At first, Paul said nothing. His instinct was to hang up. Then he found his words and said that he was sorry, but he couldn't leave the desk. Amelia said, Of course, gracious but not fooled, perfectly aware that, in fact, he left his desk all the time for any excuse at all and sometimes even without one. In that case, she said, I'll come on down.

And in this way Paul and Amelia became friends – if that's what they were.

2

After that, Paul kept waiting in the underground car park for the German car to reappear. He didn't really expect to see it again, and when he did, he suspected it had appeared by sheer force of will, of desire. Once she was done parking, Amelia Dehr stayed in the car for a long while. Far too long, really. The camera's angle kept him from seeing much, but he sensed that she was crying. He suspected that she was punching the steering wheel, struggling, trying to escape something inescapable. Staring through his small screen at the car no one had got out of, Paul felt a growing fear that he thought he had buried for good. A childish fear that rose up in him like sap. His world was now reduced to a rectangle that Amelia Dehr, by not stepping out of the car, stayed within; a frozen image on the screen that stayed unchanged. When the car door finally opened partway, he knew his weakness. He couldn't look at the person stepping out of the car, the person who would be *his* Amelia but would not be; would be some other version of her; and he knew just as well that he could not look away. He had no choice but to look and not to look at the same time. My heart's going to explode, Paul thought. My eyes are going to burst. She stepped out of the car, one long leg following the other. And then nothing. There was nothing to see on her face, nothing but a closed-off, sullen expression that would become familiar to him but which, for the moment, he considered unpleasant. This time, he did not hide. He stayed at his desk. She did not look at him and he decided that she was trying not to see him, that her indifference was feigned. He did as she did. But when he saw her later at the hotel, she was herself again, or rather she was that version of herself that he considered more consistent with her own nature (or with his own desire), and they ate popcorn together while watching the news on a loop, watched until the short bulletin began again, then a third time, until they knew it by heart and could recite it from memory. She did not mention the car park, and he did not ask.

In the seminar, Albers's digressions continued – the digressions, Paul would say much later, *were* the class, his eyes brimming with tears at her funeral; those words supplanted the flesh that no longer lived. Her meandering meditations on the cities of tomorrow led to a single end point: even though space can't be extended infinitely, night can and does create many cities within one. Paul was transported. He was a disciple of Albers, and at eighteen, he saw very clearly the three or four or five decades to come: he would be at Albers's side. He would become the architect of nights, of their light. His life's work would amount to a footnote, an appendix to his professor's missing thesis: he would shed light on the night. He would enshrine the night, and the night, he realised, would enshrine him in turn.

At some point in the class, each of them seized on something destined for him or her alone, something that sparked their deepest obsessions. For Paul, it was cities in darkness – a particular strain of darkness that now only existed, in the cities, to be eradicated. He was especially drawn to Albers's digressions on night-time, and when he had to give a presentation, having never spoken in front of an audience before, he did so on the topic of urban lighting. The rise of gas and then, later on, electric street lamps; light as a new tool in the fight against crime. However, he said, inequalities remained. The nation's unification in light might never come about. In the nineties, blue lights had been installed in his hometown; they were meant to look futuristic, although the future they sought to usher in was already outdated – a thing of the past. Like everything else in that city, a former industrial hub that was trying and constantly failing to rebuild itself, it had proven to be a dead end. Besides, he'd always heard – and still remembered, so well and vividly that it had become the very reason for his interest in these issues – that the blue light of the city centre kept junkies from finding their veins. They would pull up their sleeves to inject themselves – and nothing: turning their arms uniformly blue was how to clean a neighbourhood up and clear it out.

Light was a wordless language that the body understood. There are as many neurons in the human stomach as in a cat's cortex, Paul said; evidently he wanted to convey the intelligence of feeling something in your gut – a saying that science was only just starting to verify, as if the most hackneyed clichés were in fact mechanisms for sidestepping appearances and getting to the root of reality. There were a few laughs but he felt Albers's benevolent eyes upon him, he knew that she understood, which to him was intoxicating. Amelia Dehr, sitting at the end of the first row, did not laugh either. She peered at him as if she were assessing their chances in bare-knuckled combat.

Amelia was more reticent, or rather, her passion manifested itself in a more nuanced, strained way. She never missed a class, never skipped a sentence, but she refused to simply go along: the passion she felt for Albers was the sort a swimmer feels for the current against which she swims. Her resistance was proof that she understood. And what she understood was that fear extends the city. Doubles it. A city is forged out of its struggle against fear but fear seeps in, and so the city becomes the site of what it is supposed to keep at bay, outside its walls. There won't be any fear in the cities of tomorrow, Paul replied, fear is to be eradicated, just as darkness has been. There hasn't been real darkness since the nineteenth century. Amelia said: fear adapts. She pronounced that phrase once, distinctly, but never said it again; either she was too proud to repeat herself, or she wasn't as self-assured as she claimed to be. Often, Paul realised, Amelia's vehemence disguised a secret wish to be proven wrong. Often, Amelia Dehr was sorry to be right.

Soon, without any apparent discussion, they started sitting together in class, not looking at each other, slipping each other pens and sheets of paper. For lack of money, Paul couldn't buy all the books, and so he read with her, turning the pages as one might for a musician, sensing instinctively when she had finished. There was almost nothing to see there, but what there was to see was beautiful. That was how it was, at the beginning: almost nothing. One day, as Paul's friends, the friends he was slowly abandoning, watched on in collective disbelief, Amelia, without turning her head to Paul, without showing any sign of particular attachment, nonchalantly draped her own coat across his too-wide shoulders. She apparently knew without looking at him that he was cold – and he knotted the sleeves around his neck without a word or a look, confirming her intuition, but not showing any kind of gratitude. This icy, blind consideration being invented there and then was rather erotic. In public they never touched each other, but this curt vigilance, amongst young people who played at brushing up against one another, was so effective as to be almost obscene, almost pornographic; and all the same they themselves almost weren't even aware of it. They experienced this, of course, in a wholly contrary way: paralysed by timidity. But for someone with more experience than them, say, Albers – even if Albers never let on that she had the least opinion here – it was clear that they would be perfect lovers for one another. And this more experienced someone, whether Albers or somebody else, would have also foreseen something worrying, that their pleasure would inevitably grow almost mechanical and would, at some point, for the two of them or at least one of them, turn nightmarish.

But at the hotel things were different. The hotel was where they could be together, where they could look at each other, walk up to one another, shy and aloof, until they could sense, before even touching, the radiant heat of the other's skin, eager to be stroked. In the beginning it was Amelia who came down. They ate side by side at the front desk. Nobody in room service had ever seen such a thing; Paul was putting his job on the line and pretending not to know it. They watched the monitor screens and the hallway screens that played the news bulletin on a loop. After a while, a few weeks, a month or two – Paul was stubborn – he finally came upstairs. This room that he had imagined and obsessed over for so long – a room where things were breaking – turned out, when she finally opened the door for him, to be a room where everything was in its proper place. The blackout curtains. The bedspread, which she claimed (lying on it, propped up on her elbows, gazing at him sleepily or suggestively) emitted chemical vapours, having been sprayed with flame retardants – in case of fire, she said – and he nodded at her though he had never heard of such practices at the hotel. Their conversations moved circuitously from the most prosaic things to the most intimate, and so what was impersonal entwined with what was profound – all questions of favourite beverages or films or songs now freighted with vital importance. All the two of them needed of this ritual, this esoteric language, was for it to bring them closer together. Maybe, as they lay on the bed, they were each already holding the other's hand, or maybe one of them brushed a leg against the other's by sly accident: not yet a caressing gesture but still an act of bravery. The television was off, they didn't talk, their minds were empty of everything except the other's warmth – nothing to remind them of time's passage. For them, the world had momentarily stopped, or rather it was pretending to pause. A moment of grace, perhaps, or the quiet before a storm. Soon one of them, the boy or the girl, would get up on an elbow, kiss the other; kiss the other until they couldn't feel the arm they were leaning on, and they'd keep doing so anyway, one hovering above the other still lying on their back, until a limb gave way and their bodies realigned, but in the moment, time would be frozen. It was an unexpected blessing to be there, simply there, wholly ensconced in the anticipation, like the smallest animals in their sleep. All was now motionless. For once, they were outside the evil that flows in and permeates the heart of everything.

*

They loved each other. Paul would have said that. He did say that; his world hadn't been defined by fiction. In his world nobody read books, and so he had been protected from novels and what novels did to young hearts in search of reflections. He was swayed by imagination, of course, by an intuition of the unreal, but the thoughts he had in this realm were wayward, frenetic, almost instinctual; what he saw was at odds with the trappings of grand sagas and as such, at twenty, he saw himself on equal footing with Amelia Dehr. The commonalities they shared were yet to be discovered. She, of course, concealed herself behind an aura, a kind of glow, of romance. She embodied all the clichés: dead mother, absent father, money, all this money that so often turns out to be the true subject of books, its subtext – the money between the lines, the money one misses and covets, the money that puts the words on the page – the money that kept people from being so quick to insist she was insane.

Paul, however, wouldn't have come to the conclusion that she was insane. Their minds were too similar for that, even if their thoughts and the products of their thoughts were wholly dissimilar. He put words together painstakingly, like a young man who knows that the language he's speaking isn't the one he actually dreams in; she more fluidly, due to the excellent education she had received and which led her to disdain any lines that came to her effortlessly. Her sentences were swift and perfect and elegant; form and content were inseparable. Paul was left in awe. Everyone was. She herself saw that grace as the result of violence, of being tamed and trained like a circus animal, her spirit demeaned and tamped down. I'm a little monkey, she said sometimes, a clever little monkey. He laughed. She bounced on the bed, letting out small inarticulate shrieks, a language beyond words that spoke to him.

They loved each other. All the other men disappeared, at least from the hotel. He cast off his friends with relief, the way he might have pulled off clothes that were now too small or too heavy or soaked from a long run in the torrential rain, clothes so wet they would never be dry again, their fibres utterly ruined. What Amelia hated about herself – being domesticated, being subjugated – he now saw everywhere except within her.

The curse was lifted, the nightmare was over. So Paul believed. He wasn't a virgin any more. Sex entered another phase, one that better suited him. It was simply that so far he hadn't had the chance to learn what a woman liked, nor – back then this seemed like a minor consideration but it was clear now that it mattered – what he himself liked. They had sex all the time. She didn't say *have sex*, she said *fuck*. He didn't say anything, he would just look at her in a particular way, and she would understand immediately. They didn't hold back, or rather the way they held back was in the moment, of the moment: there was always a screen somewhere, a screen turned on somewhere. He fell asleep while in her, or he came on her, on her stomach or her breasts, and then carried her to the bathtub, where he washed her scrupulously, and the faith he felt in his own gestures aroused him anew, and she laughed and sucked him off or he stepped into the water with her. Sex defined everything about their relationship. Even when they read side by side or face to face, it was sexual, even when he was stuck pacing warehouses or car parks or darkened stores for the night and she was having dinner with her father.

This was an absent father, whose name rarely crossed her lips, a man who only ever existed when she, putting on makeup for the occasion, applied lipstick to the mouth that formed those words. Afterwards she and Paul came back to each other; he was exhausted and sad, and she consoled him, sucked him off again. She washed the crud of his night shift off his body and the red of her lipstick off his cock, and he wondered if it was the same lipstick she'd had on the night before, when she'd gone out, or if she'd redone her make-up some time that evening or early in the morning. How she'd redone it, in which reflective surface, in front of whom.

Their teachers (Albers excepted) resented her for anything and everything, for being provocative or aloof, sarcastic or indifferent, or simply difficult. At the hotel, however, things were different. At the hotel (which, to Paul, meant *where they could be together*), Amelia was passionate and attentive and funny. She was also reclusive, but she still welcomed his company eagerly, gratefully, as only children did. Until they'd had enough and absolutely had to get away, out of sight. This did not bother Paul in the least, because nothing about Amelia bothered Paul in the least.

She hid her books and papers under the bed, as it was the one spot the maid service always skipped; Paul knew, however, that they were perfectly aware of this habit, and expected it. She drove her professors crazy. They were exasperated by how she could look at anything and see exactly where that thing stopped being itself and shifted into another state, another realm. She upended the concepts they tried to instil just as unintentionally as someone might knock over a glass of water. Paul believed her intentions were pure. Yet, she wasn't clumsy. She was something else; she seemed to detect limits and sense shortcomings, she craved instability, and had a vaguely destructive streak that no one but Albers managed to see properly for what it was: a fascination with catastrophe.

Her brief stint in higher education was a long run of debacles. One revolved around monuments: from under her bed, Amelia pulled out a stack of Soviet photographs in which specific individuals had been removed and more or less successfully replaced with walls or plants; she presented these before-and-afters as examples of future monuments: not edifices but erasures, disappearances that had been wilfully planned out and executed. A history that erased people. A history that itself was erased. This was the truly monumental aspect that monuments – cast-iron pedestals, statues, commemorative plaques – hid from us. This was the architecture that she insisted be noticed. Not the way power makes itself seen, but the way it makes itself unseen.

In this presentation, titled 'The Astronaut in the Rosebush and the University in the Forest,' she started by projecting retouched photographs, lingering on the one that Paul liked best, from around 1960, commemorating the seven applicants who had gone through a rigorous selection process to be named the pioneers of the Soviet space programme. Seven candidates, Amelia insisted, her hair blazing in the projector's backlight, yet only six were visible. They stood in more or less triangular tiers like school sports-team photos, and maybe this vague, headless triangle hinted at the trajectory of a pilot's career, akin to 'climbing one of those ancient Babylonian pyramids made up of a dizzy progression of steps and ledges, a ziggurat, a pyramid extraordinarily high and steep.' In this photograph of the Sochi Six, incidentally, there was indeed a staircase, a rather insignificant one – although, Amelia said, architecture should never be purely a matter of scale – and in fact, the staircase turned out to have actually been a man.

Disappeared as thoroughly as comrades Trotsky or Kamenev had been; he had vanished outright. It took fifteen years to identify the missing man, Grigori Nelyubov, who had been assigned to an orbital flight but was exiled to Siberia after a drunken brawl by the space centre. To add insult to injury, he was subsequently erased, pure and simple, from the first class of cosmonauts. In this way the delicate art of dematerialisation had (in Amelia's words) counterbalanced the monumentality asserted by Soviet architecture; in another version of this same photograph (an image that further proved her point), the unloved Nelyubov had been turned into a rosebush. We imagine, Amelia said – and this simple word, *imagine*, was so alien to academia that all her listeners shivered – we imagine that the second censor told to doctor this photo, the one who chose flowers over stairs, loved the unloved Nelyubov, or poetry, or both. We imagine that in disappearing the astronaut, in obeying the order to retouch the image, he added his own twist by choosing to incarnate one of the saddest, stubbornest lines of Ronsard: *that in death as in life thy body may be roses.*

She paused theatrically and without any segue turned to a photograph of the Bois de Vincennes that Paul distinctly remembered her having taken during one of their walks. Trees, grass. This is what's left of free revolutionary discourse, she said. This is what's left of another way of thinking. There's *nothing* left: it is by design that we have been circumscribed within what is, as if only what has already come to be could ever exist in the future. It is by design that such possibilities have been erased. What we see here, this outgrowth, this rewilding, is what we need to reach for. This alone will free us. These oaks here. That cedar there. Soon the forest will descend upon us. Soon the forest will meet our minds.

And Amelia left the room. Everyone wondered what to do now. Nothing, apparently. The lights were turned on, and the photograph of the forest that she had left up went on haunting the class, the harsh fluorescent lights leaving it just barely visible.

At an oral exam, she decided to recite a list of car bombings, and was given a fail. It didn't bother her; she wasn't like Paul, she didn't want a diploma; she didn't seek recognition or stability. She didn't need to convince anyone, she didn't need to earn money, she didn't need to secure a future. Paul, on the other hand, played by the rules and wanted to win; she didn't hold that against him. He was too young to wonder who these defiances were supposed to impress, what language these monuments of disappearance were meant to articulate, these cars on fire, what aphorisms and poems these restrained acts that were not yet events were meant to express.

＊

They loved each other and time went by and several things came about. Slowly, without meaning to or even realising it, Paul became a rumour. This might have made him smile, or even laugh, had he been the least bit aware of it. It began at the hotel, since the comings and goings between room 313 and his desk were widely, almost collectively known – and yet this knowledge was fragmented, short-lived, just as fleeting as the seasonal hires. Paul, being in the flush of first love, did not consider how risky *this* – the nightwatchman with a hotel guest – might be. Both consenting adults, yes, but so young. The way his colleagues talked to him shifted, as though a rift in space and time had opened up and he was now so invisible that he could only be found in what people said about him.

Another thing happened over time: Paul's relationship with Albers deepened. He thought Amelia Dehr had won over Albers while he hadn't; in fact Albers's heart was capacious enough for both of them. He and Amelia would go to dinner at their professor's, and he had never imagined, never dreamed of such a connection. Still pedagogical, yes, but in a different way: Albers stood on her tiptoes to kiss his cheeks (hovering, barely touching his skin); she brought out heaps of books, which she handed them with a few well-chosen, charming lines that gave them both the desire to read them all there and then as well as the impression, somehow, of having already read them; she offered them wine and laughed at Amelia's jokes, or what she called Amelia's jokes, and maybe she shouldn't have. Maybe later on she regretted doing so. Paul, who wasn't afraid of authority so much as aware and respectful of it – or so he thought – was perplexed that, after what would come to be known as the car-bombing incident, Albers wasn't angry; on the contrary, she seemed to have been fully aware, before the fact, of the twist the exam would take. She simply shook her head, smiling, ever so amused, while Amelia, in a pale tunic with blue embroidery, a tunic that made her eyes sparkle and that gave Paul, who knew each inch of her veined body, the impression that she was not only naked but more than naked, that she was vitally *there*, bared, gorgeously so, snickered as she recited the list she had regaled the jury with. The rue Saint-Nicaise attack on 24 December 1800 that was intended to bring down General Bonaparte; the farmer Andrew Kehoe's dynamiting of the Bath School in 1927; the Stern Gang's booby-trapped trucks in Haifa in January 1947 and those of the National Liberation Front in Algeria, followed by the gory attacks the reactionary OAS carried out. In the 1950s, in Vietnam, the booby-trapped vehicles of choice were motorbikes; in August 1970, a van exploded in front of the physics department at the University of Wisconsin–Madison, its target being the Army Mathematics Research Center. They cut me off right around then, Amelia explained. She had taken off her shoes and her foot was nestled between Paul's legs, under his thigh, right by his crotch and arousing wholly unambiguous thoughts.

Before leaving, they went into Albers's room to grab their things. Paul had been wearing a duffel coat, Amelia a dark-red raincoat and, in the street, he had been too hot and she too cold. Amelia lingered in Albers's dim room, looking at the art on the walls, at the photograph above the bed of a woman and a bird, the woman holding the bird to her lips for a kiss. It was a photograph that the artist had given Albers. It had never been reproduced anywhere so it existed solely in this room, a strange and warm and, come to think of it, perhaps even threatening image. It looks like you and me, Amelia said, not bothering to say who was the woman and who the parakeet. The smile on her face was a teasing one, but maybe there was something to her words, considering that one day Albers would gift the artwork to Paul. That night they didn't dwell on it; instead Amelia turned to the green marble mantelpiece – a sickly, repulsive colour, Paul thought – and pointed at a slightly overexposed photograph in a frame noticeably older than the print, older even than the people in it: a young man in a badly tailored tuxedo and a young woman in Mountbatten pink. The young man was not a man but Albers, and as for the other, Amelia said almost unthinkingly, That's my mother.

It's always about dead mothers, thought Paul, who had a crude, forceful notion of what fiction was, and whose mother was dead. But he didn't take it personally, since, at some point, the statement would be true of all mothers. At some point all mothers were dead, and lived in the stories that young lovers told each other in rented rooms. But this wasn't the beginning that Amelia Dehr, being more cunning, creative or simply more wounded than him, had chosen for her story. It's always about misunderstandings, Amelia said later, sprawled on the bed, Paul around her – it was hard to say which of them was supporting the other. Maybe they had slipped into a pact, Paul thought, ready to welcome this prospect, a shared space of sorts, almost an extension of the bed they lived in. What a tragedy misunderstandings are, she said, while his fingers traced the hand-sewn blue embroidery on her tunic. Even he could sense its delicacy, its complexity, he tried to convert the stitched thread into hours of work, into fingers numbed by holding needles and dioptres lost by straining eye muscles – was this how people became near-sighted, he wondered, was this how they went blind, by toiling away for women like Amelia? But he lost track of those calculations. The threads' loop-de-loops along Amelia's collarbones and arms, radiating around her solar plexus, oddly enough avoiding the outlines of her breasts, which could be glimpsed beneath the white, almost transparent cloth, and needed no elaboration – these patterns transformed, in his mind, into strange scenes that accompanied her voice, violent yet beautiful scenes that he had no hope of escaping, not even by shutting his eyes, the blue embroidery now seeming to be inked on the underside of his eyelids.

Mountbatten pink was an invention of Admiral Mountbatten. A grey tint, verging on mauve, that was developed during World War II for strategic purposes – the admiral was interested in camouflage, in invisibility; he thought that the British Royal Navy fleet would be able to avoid being sighted by the Germans as a result, especially at those delicate hours of dawn and dusk; but in terms of disappearing its success was only relative. The ships actually seemed to be more vulnerable. Not to mention that they were, of course, pink. My mother and Albers decided to try their hand at the matter, but they had no luck. Or maybe they did. Or maybe one of them did and the other didn't. In any case they were friends, better than friends, Amelia said; Paul was slightly dismayed by that declaration, and right then he couldn't make sense of his feeling of having been let down. He moved even closer to the body he loved, but later on it dawned on him how profoundly it had hurt him. Amelia's outlandish ideas, the disappearances and monuments yet to come, notions he considered quite original – he understood the extent to which all that had also been inherited. He understood just how alone he was in this world where his father had nothing to pass on to him, no actual or intellectual wealth, not even a vague nostalgia for better days. The legacy he did have would only become clear to him much later. Amelia told him the rest that night, above the retouched Soviet photographs, beneath the bedspread sprayed, or not, with flame retardants; between the sheets, deep within the particular world she lived in and into which Paul, without really realising it, had followed her.

3

Some ten years earlier, at the end of the twentieth century, her mother had tried to stave off a war, and then to stop it, and it had been the death of her. Amelia could have left it at that and nearly did. That sentence said it all, it was grammatically and factually correct, but even though the sentence said it all, it also said nothing, it wasn't the language she spoke, the one she'd been taught, so she continued. Is it possible to be contaminated by a story, Paul wondered later. Are there tales that kill? But slowly, gnawing away, like those unusual martial-arts holds that appear to be nothing but a light touch, barely any pressure – but then, a year later, the heart suddenly stops. Could a story carry out such a perfect crime?

This woman, her mother, was a peace activist: that was her calling, maybe her vocation, and so we can grant her the kindness of glossing over the enormity of her personal failure amongst the hundreds of thousands who died or disappeared. A city shelled for nearly four years, snipers on the roofs, blood in the streets, and, ten years later, cemeteries everywhere, in the stadiums, in the parks; cemeteries and oddly healed wounds; children who would become adults unable to sleep with windows open, or with windows shut. And the children of those children, who would inherit strange rituals despite not having lived through the war, the siege, so many perilous street crossings; who would sometimes keep their shoulders pressed close to walls, would sometimes raise their eyes, unsure what they were looking for – their eyes flicking up, checking for snipers lying in wait whose salvos they wouldn't have actually endured. These ubiquitous realities: precision shots, mortar rounds, blackouts, tap handles turned only for no water to come – these sorts of experiences would be passed down in strange ways, from generation to generation. Some would go so far as to say that the fears in one era carry over to the next, or haunt the reptilian, most primal part of the brain, where *I* does not exist, or barely does, or only as a body in danger, gnawed at by hunger yet determined to survive; I believe, personally, that it's a matter of language. A matter of stories – inoculated, as with viruses, by what people say, and also by what they don't say. Paul, huddled against Amelia, had the distinct feeling that she was reading his thoughts, or rather that she anticipated them, and gave them a form that he could only blindly sense.

It was the start of the European Union and in an odd way it was already the end of it, revealing to those who wanted to see it – or who had no choice but to see it – an absurdist performance of orchestrated powerlessness, arguments, and rhetorical questions – was this, properly speaking, a civil war or not; had there, properly speaking, been a genocide? Who knew what? Who did what, let what happen? The British knew but didn't do anything. The French had acted, but hadn't known anything. Or the other way around. A long chain of responsibilities that were interchangeable, power and powerlessness both leading back to the same thing; words that signified nothing. The mere mention of Americans sent a shiver down everyone's spines that was either hope or dread, was a sickly gleam that flashed in everyone's eyes. At the time everyone who had – or felt they had – some stake in this war had to read the signs, learn the secret language, master an alphabet of symptoms, delusions, pathologies.

Amelia's mother was what some might call an adventurer, or an explorer, or at least a traveller. She'd left her hometown at the end of the sixties as easily as discarding a dress she'd outgrown. She'd cut short her hair and her name alike before going to discover the world. In fact, all she did was cross the border into Switzerland. She was a poet, which now seems ridiculous to say, almost obscene; but she very much was. (I barely remember anything of this: I was ten years old when she went off, she left me with Albers, Albers took me to my father, everything I know I've had to piece together.) She was a twenty-year-old hanging around Geneva, around Locarno, effortlessly witty, draping her long arms just so along the arm-rests; someone saw she was bored, handed her the keys to an apartment in Paris, one of those hideouts that no longer exist, not as far as I can tell. It was a place with huge rooms and barely anything in them, and nobody cared whose name was actually on the lease; it was already lost in the haze of the past. People were invited over or simply dropped by unannounced, they scrounged up what coins they had to get extra keys cut, and then they loaned them out, lost them, or just gave them away; people stayed there for nights or weeks or years; it was an ecosystem of artists and intellectuals and revolutionaries and, like any ecosystem, it was self-regulated. At some point someone changed the locks, or the police broke down the door, looking for someone nobody knew or had ever heard of; once the place was all but empty, the whole process began anew, quietly at first, then gaining momentum. Places like it could be found in every city – those sorts of places were where Albers wrote her thesis. Those sorts of places were where they met each other. Two women looking for figures in the haze – the haze of tear gas. And so my mother, with her ridiculous belief in words, took up or made up a particular form that she called documentary poetry and was meant to be, or was, or should have been, an alternative to the journalistic language that had ground down our way of thinking and living to the point that we'd been hollowed out, in the face of reality (that's what she wrote; personally I'm not even sure I understand what she means), to being starved outlines in a cave. That's your so-called objectivity, she lamented. It's in her first collection, you could read it if you wanted to, part of it was written in Mexico and something in the way it reads, the rhythm of the lines and the spaces between them, makes me think that she composed it not necessarily *with* Albers, but at the very least in her presence.

In a way it's a history book and in a way it's a book specifically on vision. They were in Mexico in 1969. They might have met that man, the one who installed mirrors in the land, buried them halfway, or hung them in trees, and they reflected the sky, the leaves, and called it art; Albers saw in those acts of displacement a strange attempt to mend the wrongs the Americans had committed in Yucatán. A sort of white magic that was meant to restore what had been stolen: temples, innocence, sight. It was in the jungle that my mother wrote her book, which was also a manifesto, and told of the Americans who were there in 1840 in order to dismantle the old Mayan cities and send them, piece by piece, back to the East Coast – the rising centre of power, the one that would swallow everything. There was also a doctor amongst them, a man who was considered a practitioner of the surgical arts although he had no sample of his skill with him, and who decided to operate on the Indians of Merida for their inward squint, the strabismus that he interpreted as the embodiment of their inability to distinguish between meum and tuum. The book read like a report, or an essay, everything in it was true, but unlike reports or essays it wasn't situated *outside* the surgical operation, on the contrary, it pulled you into it, you felt the knife in your hand and at the same time on your eye (there was no mention anywhere of anaesthesia) and gradually this became unbearable to read, physically unbearable because you could feel it from both viewpoints – that of the one operating and that of the one operated upon. It was drenched in blood, it was a nightmare, spoke to a primal fear. The theory of information, according to my mother.

Did she really believe she could revolutionise reportage? That's what Albers claimed, but I don't think so, or maybe she, my mother, was out of her mind. Stark raving mad. But I don't think she was. At least not at the beginning, and I hardly know anything about the end. Amongst the intelligentsia she remained something of a mystery. Even if Albers insisted that she was the point everyone strained towards but never touched. A vanishing point. I don't know.

When the war broke out in the former Yugoslavia, she took refuge in the Sarajevo Elisse (my god, Paul thought, who for the first time felt he was only just starting to understand and now mourned his ignorance). The hotel where, in short, the conflict had broken out. The roof on which two snipers had opened fire on a row of peaceful protesters. The hotel was made the headquarters of the international press and several intellectuals who, like Nadia Dehr, felt as though that was where they were meant to be, the exact location where the ideals of the twentieth century and its Realpolitik had culminated: in carnage. *Drawn-out* carnage. One of those places where violence was both extreme – bodies exploding in front of a water fountain, in a market – and sustained over time. The war drove my mother mad, Amelia said, because she was convinced she needed to find the right words to describe it and at that stage, there would be no option but to cease fire. She needed to find an artistic means to stop it, so that the scales would finally fall from the eyes of onlookers the world over. And she thought that was her task. The task of poetry. To find a way to transport this reality somewhere else. Beyond its limits, into the heart of the West, into the heart of those who read it and who, after reading and experiencing it, would no longer be able to ignore it. She wrote. Sometimes she ate with the others, the journalists, the intellectuals; sometimes they found Italian pasta and cooked and that, in their eyes, at that time, amounted to a banquet. Sometimes she'd call me on the phone. I'd cry; she wouldn't. She was just writing. She was convinced that the breakdown in the peace process was her own fault, a failure of her own poetry. Of all poetry. After three years, she finally faced up to the facts: everything she wanted to show the world, the world already knew. Had known from the start. And didn't care about. It wasn't the fault of words, or of those who used them; it was the fault of human nature, of those who refused to listen. I suppose it was at that moment that she lost her mind. She stopped writing, she stopped calling. I have no idea what she was doing. I suppose she was digging tunnels. Literally or figuratively. I suppose she started working in the black market, that she put all her energy into trafficking food, trafficking arms, so that the besieged city could keep on going. Nobody knows what happened to her. Nobody ever found her body. After the war, I inherited a box. A cardboard box, like for printer paper. It was full of her fragments, full of all her attempts at documentary poetry, all her failures. That's all I have of my mother, said Amelia. All I had, to be exact.

I've only opened this box once. I pulled out a poem at random, a poem about a man being tortured. They had set a pigeon in his mouth. A live pigeon. He didn't mean to, but he ended up grinding his teeth. His body itself played a part in the grinding. Someone laughed and one couldn't be sure if it was one person, or two, or the whole world. When I slid the paper back in the box, I realised that I was laughing, too.

Paul was at a loss for words. Then, in horror, after a minute, he started laughing. It was uncontrollable, sharp, like a cough: a bodily revolt. He couldn't stop. A nightmare.

Exactly, said Amelia.

She had sold the box to the highest bidder. Albers had helped arrange the sale. There were still people who remembered Nadia Dehr, who felt she had a particular position in a particular context, in a particular era, and it hadn't been hard to get rid of it, for a tidy sum, far tidier than she could have imagined. Not so much to make money, in any case, as to protect herself from what it contained, the naked truth. And to spite a mother who had abandoned her. She would never know what she had written during nearly four years of war but the very thought of it was unbearable. She herself could never have endured it. She was convinced that abstaining – her form of revenge – was the wise thing to do. She was convinced that would be how she'd save her own skin.

She was starting to doubt it.

*

And all that while, all those months, those years when her mother and others like Susan Sontag and Juan Goytisolo were digging themselves deeper into the hell of a besieged city, into the hell of words that nobody wanted to hear – during this time when her mother was slipping scribbled lines into her box, or tending to victims, or, on the airport runway, pulling white sheets over hunks of meat that hid contraband arms, flouting embargoes right under the noses of the blue helmets not seeing anything or pretending not to see anything, the blood slowly soaking the sheets, a universal code for wounded or dead, a fully formed language everyone shared – during those months, those years when her mother was slowly ceasing to write and beginning to act, or perhaps lying limbs akimbo, head blown apart, in a pit – where was she, little Amelia, with flyaway hair and wide-gapped front teeth? Sometimes she was with her father, but their relationship had always been strained. He was an impatient man. I loved him but he never seemed to care whether I loved him or not. He wasn't bringing me up to be his wife, Amelia said, a line that would lodge itself uncomfortably in Paul's memory until he got to meet the man many years later – a line he would finally feel like he understood, only to realise, later, after coming across a particular novel, that he was wrong. Those words, coming out of Amelia's mouth, didn't mean what he'd presumed. Rather, having nothing to say about her father, or not wanting to say anything about her father, she had simply relied on one of her tricks, one of her sleights of hand: a quotation.

Yes, where was she as a child? The simplicity of the question belied the difficulty of its answers. Paul knew exactly where he had been – always in the same place, waiting to be done, planning his way out, the most logical and realistic one being the one that scared him most (studying), but as usual with Amelia a few words were never enough, silence was never enough, images had to be invented to pull together something that had always been scattered. Everything and nothing. Amelia remembered her childhood as a story in which some parts, important ones, might have been told to her in a foreign language or in her sleep. Cause and effect erased – whispered into her ear while she was dozing in her bed or sitting in a guest room waiting for her father to come get her, or stretched out on a long velvet bench, in a pile of coats.

She remembered long nights when people forgot her and long afternoons spent staring at a piano, a chess problem, or worse, a puzzle: it was a lonely existence that drove her insane, drove her to stuff one or two jigsaw pieces into her mouth, to chew on them methodically before spitting the unrecognisable things into her hand just to avoid having to complete the picture; she remembered being so alone that when she went to school on Mondays her head felt in another place, she felt like an outcast, greeting her friends in a hushed voice and feeling almost surprised that they said hello back. I'm actually here, she realised. Now the week can start. She became most present on Fridays, she reached a sort of maximum density of being, but then dissolved so thoroughly over the weekend that she would start questioning her own existence. She had to start existing again two days later. She was an only child.

She was a child amongst adults, whose only reason for being was to see and remember things that otherwise would have been forgotten. The names of birds, of mammals, of trees; of stars and minerals and their properties; the sentences whispered over the phone so she wouldn't hear them; lines and stanzas and entire poems even if she didn't understand what they meant at all; the names of medicines and their side effects, the ingredients of lipstick tubes, the agglomerations of syllables that were not so much names as designators of the food dyes, preservatives, acidulants, and artificial flavourings of candies which deteriorated into doubtlessly poisonous numbers and letters. She got horribly bored, to the point of insanity, and all the same she never stopped taking in these memories. There was no worse loneliness than that of a child kept in a world of adults.

She was obsessed with children. Everywhere she went, she insisted on asking if there would be children – how many, who they were, what they were like. The moment she entered one of those huge apartments her family always visited, she started searching for them, hunting them down, greedy for contact – finally, a counterpart, someone like her. Held hostage in a world not meant for their size, where door handles were too high, countertops out of reach, books too heavy, glasses too large – finally, there would be someone she could look in the eye, with skin as soft and perfect as her own, skin that wasn't even ten years old – incredible, when she came to think of it now. We fought wars and suffered impossible loves. When we were together, everything shifted slightly and started to make sense. I was obsessed with other children, drawn to them. I got very upset when it was time to leave, like I was an animal that couldn't migrate with all the others.

When there were no children and she was alone, a horrible torpor came over her, and she fought against it by exploring these apartments of vast darkness and bursts of laughter, as she darted into unknown lands, forbidden rooms in which she discovered jewellery boxes, lingerie drawers, relics of every sort gleaming in the shadows. Everything was ethereal, everything was the scene of a past crime that had never been noticed, much less solved. She was naive enough, unthinking enough, that she started getting high. Sniffed acetone and stain removers and nail polish, permanent-marker ink and pens, and even some mineral spirits since she liked the name; she breathed it all in deep, until her head was spinning. Huffed paints in the artists' studios, especially the metallic tones, and turpentine as well, never mind that she had never been shown how to do so; being lonely forced her to learn. Sat down on the icy rims of bathtubs as the vapours of solvents and removers carved walkways and emergency exits within her brain, passageways by which she could escape the mortal boredom of a childhood without other children.

Sometimes she started small fires on the tiles, in the bathtub. She tried on fancy lipsticks and then attempted to melt down the lipstick bullet so she could erase all trace of her crime; she broke open thermometers so she could watch the mercury swirling in the sink, swirling, then escaping into the city. She set small puddles of antiseptic on fire, got high, glided though these wild laboratories, wallowed in this chilly voluptuousness, this supreme eroticism, these enamel surfaces and mirrors that ensnared her, as in some modernised myth where the divine lover would appear in the form, in the features of an impeccable bathroom, in smooth, hard, unchangeable beauty – in appearance. I still carry these neutral spaces within me – but as soon as I try to revisit them, that neutrality I'm reaching for turns into anguish, mute terror. Steel-jaw traps, love-children of what is human and what isn't, what is human and its opposite, a new stage of the species, dissipating in the impersonality this had forged out of nothing – and now there's nothing left but a faint whiff of medicine and smoke, a young girl asleep in a bathtub.

Where were they? Where? Some of these apartments, some of these houses had a child's bedroom. But the children were nowhere to be found, and she wandered through what, in their absence, had become just as forbidding as it was welcoming. The teddy bears watched her, the floral-pattern quilts watched her, the tiny slippers and the doll's houses watched her – as did the dolls, their eyes constantly fixed on hers, ravenous for her hide. The styrofoam solar systems trembled in a draft that she didn't feel, the spheres turning slowly until Jupiter's red spot, its one round eye, zeroed in on her forehead, her face. No children anywhere, and everything stared at her until she beat a hasty retreat. She backed out of these rooms without any idea of whether they were empty for the night or forever – where were the children? Mysteriously gone, but none of the grown-ups seemed to care, she heard their gales of laughter and their conversations about art, money, the ups and downs of the stock market which for some of them were the ups and downs of their own lives; then they lowered their voices and they talked about the non-aligned countries, about dissents and wars. She, having retreated to the bathroom, regained her composure. On her knees under a sink, her nose in a bottle of detergent, she took her revenge for the absence of children on herself.

The summer of the first conflicts, which would lead less than a year later to the longest siege of a major city in the modern world, her mother had taken her on vacation (*on vacation*, Amelia had repeated incredulously) to this land that was soon to break apart, a fracturing that her mother would soon internalise, a fracturing that would in turn engulf her. A few months later, Yugoslavia as it had been known no longer existed. They stayed on the Adriatic coast, in one of those chain hotels that was all the rage at the time, a hotel with hallways tiled in a green verging on black, where she was especially charmed to see how the lights made her cast at least three shadows. The room overlooked the swimming pool, which itself overlooked the sea. Everything was identical, endlessly reproduced empty cubes.

It was obvious her mother wasn't very happy. The reason wasn't entirely clear to Amelia, considering that the two of them had the entire hotel to themselves – it felt like her father had booked the whole place for them, as if to apologise for his absence. Around noon, that time of day when she was forbidden to go outside, she took the elevator to the top floor and tried all the door handles, from the first room to the last, a bit disappointed that all of them resisted her efforts. She didn't understand how they had the run of the hotel but, somehow, not the rooms themselves. She didn't understand how the hotel could be anything other than the sum of its spaces; as she floated all alone in the pool, she counted the balconies, every one identical, to figure out where she was sleeping, and she always lost track unless she saw her mother come out.

In the afternoons she loved watching the increasingly sharp, increasingly long angles of the railings' shadows along the walls. Her mother barely smiled. But she had promised Amelia that children would come, that children were on the way, and so she waited and did not protest, did not complain, out of fear that her mother might change her mind and tell them all to turn back.

That summer, Nadia Dehr had three dresses that were identical in every way except for their colour: pink, powder blue, pistachio green. She changed between them on a whim: sometimes she left the table between one course and the next, abandoning her daughter and her plate in the huge, deserted restaurant, only to come back in a different dress – different and yet the same – leaving her to wonder if this wasn't some sort of code, not unlike signal flags on naval ships. But a code for who, for what? The hotel was preternaturally empty. As I splashed about, the sun reflecting on the water created hypnotic shapes, rings, sideways figure-of-eights. I heard, Get out of that water, there's so much chlorine, you're going to poison yourself. I was heatsick and lonely, seized by sudden fits of terror and frustration, and my mother tried to calm me down by telling me, flatly, as though addressing the idea of her daughter rather than a real girl: Be patient, the children will come soon. The children did not come. She spent long hours on the front-desk phone, her brow furrowed; she didn't speak much, sometimes didn't speak at all, as if she was waiting for the person on the other end of the line to pick up a receiver hanging off its hook, forgotten, as the sun went down.

Amelia caught a fever, the balconies multiplied, their railings seemed to dissolve. Still no children anywhere. She sometimes glimpsed them here or there, hiding when she got close, disappearing up stairwells, through doorways. Her mother tried to say something with her pink or blue or green dresses, which sometimes seemed to be all three colours at once. That was how she communicated with the children, how she instructed them to avoid Amelia – and now I have to deal with this, too, Nadia Dehr complained as she poured aspirin packets into the tap water. Amelia was hallucinating. A secret was being kept from her – a secret she couldn't solve in the ever-changing number of balconies, in the sun's reflections on the water, in her mother's dress and the way her earrings sparkled, which had to be a sign, too, rather than mere chance. Was the deserted hotel really empty? The infinite sequence of vacant rooms, their beds, their pillows, their black screens of unplugged televisions. I heard or thought I could hear the pounding of music upstairs or the creaking of footsteps downstairs.

One night she woke up, terrified by voices. Was she scared that she had somehow managed to conjure them up? But I wasn't dreaming, there was no question it was my mother next door, laughing, for the first time that week or that summer or maybe both. Fevers have always dilated time, and blurred all points of reference for me – or was that simply an effect of childhood?

She was laughing with a young, brown-haired man, then she thanked him for the assistance he had offered (she declared it as if she were a nation unto herself). He replied with something Amelia didn't understand, and her mother said, The worst is yet to come. He seemed unconvinced, seemed to be waving away her words, and my mother kept going, Next time? There won't be a next time, you're coming with me to Paris. She was right, there wouldn't be a next time, but she was wrong, he didn't come with us to Paris. He woke me up at dawn, took me in his arms and carried me to the balcony. I'm trying to remember his face and I can't, at best I can see a version of my own, of my mother's, some sort of family resemblance. Don't say anything, don't scare them away – the children are here, I thought – the sun hadn't risen and the light was new and grey, for the first time that week or that summer. Down below, a doe and a fawn, both of them pinkish brown, about the same colour as the sandstone slabs, were drinking from the pool, their heads lowered, gently and earnestly. I didn't say a word, I didn't scare them off, but my heart did twinge at the thought that they were going to die from it, from this chlorine-poisoned water, this water poisoned just for my swims, since nobody else had been in the pool that summer.

That day, they began arriving. The refugees – women and children, displaced by something that was happening up north. The hotel had been requisitioned. War was what she thought she had glimpsed through doorways, in stairwells. And war was what had slept in the empty beds.

Her mother, on that last day, finally started playing. She checked every room, from the top floor down, dragging Amelia behind. Some doors opened, others didn't: the war was only just starting. The ones that did open revealed suit-cases packed in haste, their contents spilling out on the beds, and glassy-eyed women frozen mid-gesture as if they had been stricken by sudden amnesia and were now wondering what it was they were holding – in this case, a coat hanger – and why they were holding it. Sullen children who didn't look at Amelia or her mother gripping her arm as she looked for this man who had come, who had been so helpful, whom she had bought a plane ticket for on an airline that soon would no longer exist or perhaps had already stopped existing. Amelia didn't care, she wanted to meet the children who, all together, it seemed, had made their way down and were now jumping into the pool. A torrent of displaced children pelting down on the water's surface in underwear and shorts – nobody had actual swimsuits, there hadn't been time for that. Ten, twenty, fifty children cannonballing like small birds with a death wish, impelled by a herd instinct, then climbing back out only to dive in again with such violence that huge waves slopped over the pool's sides; children of different ages, boys and girls, who just hopped joylessly on top of each other, their bodily impacts muffled by the water, splatters across the pinkish slabs, a streak of blood on wet skin. Her mother hadn't been playing, after all; she barged into the rooms the same way the children hurtled into the water, looking for a man she would never see again. She filled her suitcase with those three dresses that had done their duty. Amelia didn't care. She was looking for her swim-suit as the children had finally come, and she absolutely had to go and play with them, right now, while there was still water in the pool, otherwise she would never be able to – but her mother, already in her travelling outfit, navy trousers and two-tone shoes, yanked away her swimsuit and towel.

The officer overseeing the hotel's requisition greeted her with a deep bow, his back ramrod-straight, and her mother rolled her eyes. Nothing annoyed her more than the refined elegance of war's beginnings, before everything came undone and one finally saw the world for what it was: a realm of reck-lessness and unremitting cruelty. He also thought (maybe rightly) that she was annoyed at the hubbub of those young bodies splashing in the water. I'm going to empty the pool tonight, he said. The sea isn't far off, after all. No, the sea isn't far off, she repeated, her mind on someone else. He must have left right after the deer, which was not the plan at all. She looked for him on the drive to the airport, she looked for him in the terminal, she never said his name but I could see quite clearly that all she now saw was his absence.

At the airport, all the phones were busy or maybe already disconnected. Amelia and Nadia were the only people on the flight back to France, and Amelia didn't dare to turn around and face all those unoccupied seats. Nadia never saw this man again. Amelia never saw the children again. I never talked to them, the whole time there had been a balcony between us, a window; she was sure she would never forgive her mother, yet before long she found herself burdened with yet more resent-ments, bitterer ones.

Upon their return, her father was so beside himself that he marshalled an army of lawyers, some formidable experts in their field and others doing their best to bend family law to their will, as if families could be handled like the entities her father's company sold abroad. He locked Amelia in a room and wouldn't even allow her pathetic mother to say goodbye. She had already decided to leave again; he assumed that she wanted to take me with her, and was taken aback that she didn't so much as suggest it. She didn't want anything from him, anything at all. That autumn, her mother plunged back into the war and Amelia was sent to a boarding school in the mountains, in Switzerland or thereabouts, amongst other young girls – one of those places where they played tennis, where they all sold their souls to the devil, but she was too young for the devil, for him to be interested in her or her in him. Later on, she decided that the photos of her at eleven, in a leotard, were compromising – so she destroyed them, unaware that she was, in her own way, helping to erase her biographical materials. It had never occurred to her that these might be finite, and she had acted like any organism unwittingly working towards its own disappearance. No other photos of herself as a child would ever come to light. She had taken part in this extinction; it would soon become difficult to convince others of her existence.

She had few memories of this boarding school; the ones she retained mostly blurred into scenes from a notorious horror flick, although one of the least frightening parts. Her father had decided to send her away, and she didn't think it was because he needed to get her out of his hair, but she wasn't any more convinced that it was out of any kind of love. She never saw her mother again, she only stayed with her father for short stretches. She came to feel, at moments, like she was nobody's daughter, even though she never stopped being their child. The very idea of family lost its solidity; it flickered off then on again, and at some point she stopped thinking about it at all. In any case – in Switzerland or thereabouts, at boarding school in a small school-uniform jacket – I came to understand that my father just couldn't resist the idea of trying to hide or camouflage me – and as always Paul found himself wondering about the money, how much there had been, where it had come from, and where it was now. As for the school, Amelia believed that she had entered it willingly – and left it willingly as well. She had been expelled for some reason no one quite understood, something about her having had unwarranted male visitors – but, for crying out loud, her father said, she's just eleven years old! By which he meant, of course, that she was too young to be interested in such devious activities. There was no use arguing, however; she had to say goodbye to her friends in the crisp mountain air and go home. She could still remember the excitement, verging on hysteria, she felt upon finding herself amongst other children, young girls like her. Other children at long last, other children every-where. She had been like aspirin in a glass of water: reacting and fizzing and dissolving.

She had made up a friend; that was why she had been expelled. An imaginary friend, nothing unusual there, who embodied everything she was homesick for. We can call him Paul, if you want, she said. Later, he wondered how many times she'd told this story, in bed, under the shower, how many times she had changed the name of this non-existent man to suit her or someone else's fancy. The other Paul (the first Paul, thought Paul, this is unreal) had appeared in the train station, a young man older than her. The moving trains and her rising anxiety had conjured into being, so she believed, exactly the kind of companion she needed as a little girl travelling alone. He was strong and considerate; with him, every danger turned into a game. She had invented him, she thought, out of nothing, an imaginary friend like so many others, but they had become so attached to each other that, even after she was settled in at the school, he stayed. She saw him once or twice a day, no more, and ended up telling her new friends about this brown-haired Paul. She told them about his doings, skiing, shooting, and how he'd saved a tiny animal. They clustered around her, clamoured for more stories of this mythical man, all these girls around her, awestruck, all dressed identically, with pleated skirts, white blouses, knee-high socks (if my father came, she thought, foolishly, he wouldn't know me from the others, he wouldn't know which one to take with him: I'm safe here, she thought). To meet their demands, and satisfy their ravenous appetites, she started telling her tales in the present tense, and the humdrum lives of these rootless little girls took on a new shine. Copy down this geometry problem, Paul's solved it. He was always right around the corner – he was there not a second ago, you've just missed him – he was a nice way to kill time; and then, one night, something odd happened. Milena walked into the dormitory wearing an oversized T-shirt, a souvenir of the Olympic Games that had taken place several winters earlier in the land where her mother had gone as a peace activist, a T-shirt that nearly came down to Milena's knees like a dress, and blithely said that Paul had given it to her.

For a long while, Amelia kissed Paul, the real one (or maybe, Paul thought, the substitute one), and then she continued: So they all started seeing him when I wasn't there, they started to meet up with him behind my back, this tall brown-haired boy was made into their idea, they all adapted him to their needs. Miranda, the precocious one (at twelve years old she already seemed to be fifteen), kissed him while going round and round in the huge revolving door. Carlotta (twelve years old but terrified of men and bras) reported all this to the head-mistress, who started investigating the rumours, discovering with horror that a young man had insinuated himself amongst her little girls, coming and going quite freely in spite of all the locks and bars and other safety precautions. Nonsense, said her father, glaring at her, you do know he's completely made-up. But the headmistress, who was wary of the devil's wiles and unnerved by the sway this Paul had over her charges, would brook no argument. Don't you see that only makes matters worse, she said. And so Amelia had to say goodbye to her friends and come back to Paris. All that remained of that time was a school notebook with a geometry problem in it that had been solved in a handwriting that wasn't hers – although the distance of all those years had made it clear, abundantly clear, that of course it was her own, its telling details knit deep within the less-awkward cursive that would be her handwriting as a grown-up, set down with an insistence, a speed she hadn't had then, and this final paragraph had been like a triangular self-portrait that, she felt, was worth just as much as a photograph.

After the fiasco in Switzerland or thereabouts, her father had sent her to the United States. She never did understand this drive to send her far away. She was welcomed to upstate New York by Albers, who drove a '70 Ford Thunderbird with no regard whatsoever for safety recommendations – Albers was the sort for whom grace was meaningless without risk – and took her to see Niagara Falls half-hidden in the snow. She no longer dressed like a man but her artfulness was still evident in her cuffs and lapels – there was a certain je-ne-sais-quoi in every outfit she wore. On the plane over, Amelia lied to the woman beside her about her last name, her first name, where she was headed and why. She would never see her mother again, her father had decided she was inconvenient, but of course she didn't touch on any of that. The woman spent a night in the air beside a complete fiction.

She missed her mother, she talked to her every so often on the phone, across great distances, or distances made all the greater by bad reception. The line broke up often – she didn't remember their conversations so much as the interruptions that made them lose each other, drove them apart – a metallic clinking sound would drown out their voices, reverberating in the earpiece, like Morse code. My mother would crack a joke – why, hello there, my dear eavesdroppers! – but her voice hollowed out more and more each week, as if she was being drained away. The noises were as harsh as cleavers; they came from our devices, from the network, they made what had been abstract all of a sudden concrete: distance, electricity, the fact that all progress carries its own dysfunction.

She had never believed that they were being listened to, any more than she had ever believed that her mother might have dabbled in espionage, but she often thought back to those noises that impeded their conversations, the darkness and abstraction creeping into their relationship, poltergeists summoned both by practically nothing and by everything across the miles upon miles of submarine cables that had been laid down.

It was while living with Albers in America that she learned English, that she became a teenager, although from then on she'd always feel much younger than she was, as if the bone-chilling winter of upstate New York, with its unrelenting snow and its unfamiliar language, had halted her growth. Far off, the war, no doubt, would end. Albers told me about the snow, the phone lines, meeting my mother in Paris, the tear-gas canisters. She talked to me about architecture: we were driving to Buffalo while dreaming about houses that grew like living organisms. Even though I didn't say it I was thinking about a place that might come into my life the way my imaginary friend did. To console me, Albers gave me science, art, the world – or, at least, its dominant language at the time, which was neutral and soothed me; and then a capacity not to be bound solely to here, to now, to oneself. Secret passageways in the depths, miles upon miles of submarine cables, forming the greater part of global communications – how could these immense distances, the crushing weight of the ocean, not be felt in some of our conversations? The cables could be damaged by earthquakes, by shark bites, we forget so easily what a mad adventure it is to communicate between one continent and another. They emerge on the coast or directly within secured buildings, all the humdrum backwash of our conversations, all these overlapping voices, and I think that above all Albers conjured these ideas to try to create or recreate relationships that didn't seem to exist, or at least not any more. I shut my eyes and, through these oceanic depths, I followed the cables to what had been my parents' living room, in what had been my home.

The rest of the time I looked for girls my age who would become my friends, my confidantes in this new country. But in this area along the Canadian border, that winter – perennially harsh and interminable – girls disappeared, teenagers sublimated. One night they had been asleep in bed; the next morning, they were gone. Sometimes there was an open window. Snow fell into pink-and-white bedrooms, soaking the carpets – that was the first thing their mothers noticed – this fatal yet beautiful blurring between inside and outside. It was as if the girls themselves had turned into snow. Snow covered everything. Curfews were instituted, with little effect on my life with Albers, while in Rochester, in Buffalo, in all of upstate New York, girls were disappearing – an epidemic of kidnappings – but more likely they were runaways. Rarely were their personal belongings missing. They left with nothing but their coats.

These were suburbs with borders lost in the snow, with streets that abruptly ended in a vast white expanse. No horizon, no depth; visibility stopped after thirty feet. Winter was a geographical region. The most ordinary landscapes sank into abstraction, entire towns ran the risk of being forgotten. The snow came up to their knees, then their thighs. Amelia wore legwarmers, fur boots; she'd never been so cold or friendless, but she'd never felt so safe as during those long, hazy months spent with Albers. The suburb's other houses were shaken by a rumour that weakened their foundations and fissured their walls: talk that a man or several men were watching the girls sleeping. But Amelia was protected from that gossip by her loneliness and Albers's common sense, even when she found herself thinking, My friend is here and he's looking for me. In the schools, it was all anyone talked about, frantically, to the point of near-hysteria. The blonde girls down the street mentioned it, yes, a man, sometimes outside, sometimes inside – how he gets in, nobody knows – he's there, he doesn't do anything, he just watches you sleeping until, if we're to believe it, you disappear.

She waited, and waited, but the few times someone did come, it turned out to be a dream.

They were found in the spring, all these girls who had fled. Often they turned up in Portland or Denver; those most afraid of the cold in California – teenagers now perfectly accustomed to perpetual sunshine, to living easy, to specific drugs. Others, however, hadn't gone far, they'd walked at night in the snow to the end of their street then the edge of the suburb, and into this strange expanse where they had ended up falling down or falling asleep. They were found in the spring as well, small blonde creatures curled up in balls, as if an inner force had driven them there, as if there had been an imperative to forget themselves, to cast themselves out. The human race seemed so cruel in its demands, in insisting that an entire category erase itself: that year, several young American girls, perhaps too quiet but seemingly of sound mind and body, were forced out of themselves, out of this world by all this white. Everyone knew that these wintry lands could drive people mad, that nature abhors a vacuum and that this vacuum where vision became blindness was sometimes full of unspoken, dangerous ideas. Or maybe, Amelia thought, *she* had been the one to trigger this instinct to flee. Maybe, because she had finally stopped moving, some act of transference had made her the cause of their own flight. Or maybe they, too, were victims of some distant war in a land they might never have heard of. As vast as the world is, there's still no escaping it.

4

Time passed. They loved each other. Paul wanted all of Amelia: her mind, her spirit, her body, its radiant warmth which he could feel inches away, and which, if he fixated on it, felt like immediate contact. Alone and together, apart and embracing became false binaries. She was always with him. He wanted to see what she saw, to know what she knew. At his insistence they went to museums, to those venues of a culture foreign to him and deeply familiar to her. As a guide, she was both wonderful and terrible; she knew the artworks on the walls like the back of her hand but she had no patience; she raced through the rooms without pausing to look, talking as she charged ahead. As they hurtled past so many masterpieces, Paul wondered what made them masterpieces – it wasn't obvious, he wasn't sure he saw or understood what gave them that particular quality – while Amelia was obsessed with talking about paintings that weren't there, missing images. He wanted to understand, to learn how to *look* at Cézanne's paintings, for example, and she talked to him about the *Mont Sainte-Victoire* done by an American who had decided to reproduce the master's paintings freehand, in charcoal, from memory, in thirty seconds, with his eyes shut tight. An act of regression, of sorts, a return to blindness, a way of showing how art could be inscribed in one's memory – always imperfectly, a child's fumbling, a barbarian's muddling. So that Paul, in front of this:

was supposed to see this:

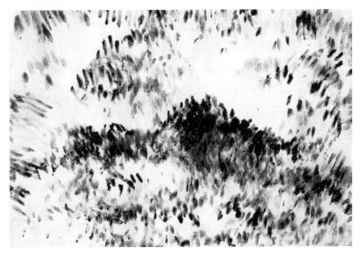

She walked with him, rolling her eyes – she was unconvinced and made a show of it. Why are you wasting your time with these relics? You're worth so much more than this, she told him, you've got a positively *feral* intelligence, you're the only panther I know – and I'm lucky enough to have you in my bed, she whispered right into his mouth, biting his lips gently, I'd give everything in the world to be like you, I'd give it all to *be* you. Paul, on the other hand, knew that unlearning something was nothing like never having been aware of it in the first place. His own ignorance bewildered him. Deep down, he was experiencing his first love as keen suffering; he mourned everything he had never known about, everything he could not have known was missing from his life – a nostalgia that Amelia would never comprehend. She kept going, the two of them still wholly unaware at twenty years old that the derailments defining her life were not merely a series of ruptures but, in fact, her fate; or rather that these fracturings themselves traced an inexorable, straight line that would be her ruin, her downfall; they would drive her, much later, to meet the ground five storeys beneath her.

＊

Paul never talked about where he came from. He wasn't aware, at that time, that people could be defined just as much by what they left behind as what they strove for. But what could he have said, anyway? He didn't have the words he needed. He came from a place defined just as much by its geographical location, its per capita income, its unemployment rate, as by its lack of a story. It did have its history, an accumulation of anecdotes such as the one about the sickly blue street lamps that kept junkies from finding their veins, or the one about how Paul's father first arrived and was wise enough to change his name as soon as he could to make it more French, calling Paul *Paul* – but maybe he had been more naive than he thought. After all, there were other ways to find out about someone's origins, as if they weren't implied in the dense, slightly bluish-black curls of his hair, in his long, thick eyelashes, in his sharply arched eyebrows and the intense, pleasing orderliness of the expressions that resulted; not to mention all the rest that was beyond sight: blood, genes, patterns and figures on a screen. An entire history of which Paul was mostly ignorant, that had not been relayed to him – and so what could he have shared of it, especially with Amelia, a woman like Amelia, who had crossed oceans more often than she'd crossed the motorway ringing Paris? He came from a place that he both was and wasn't surprised to hear regularly invoked as an example of an urban disaster; he wasn't surprised because he knew deep down just how ugly, how dangerous, how dysfunctional it was; but he was surprised because, even so, it was his home, his ground zero – it just *was*. He was more ashamed of the way this place lingered within him than of the actual place, which already felt distant, far away, almost off the map; and yet its essence seemed to have defined Paul inside and out – his way of moving, his way of reacting to any threat, real or imaginary, he might sense. And it took Paul, who had grown up within a certain degree of risk and fear, some time to see that fear was now something his own body aroused. It was only when he gestured in frustration, at the cafeteria between classes, and noticed everyone's reactions, that he saw it. He was astonished. Deeply ashamed of it, as if he had betrayed his new self. He had exposed himself and it was a breach of etiquette. And so, when the city that was no longer really *his* was plastered across every screen, he did not say anything. Numbly, he watched the news bulletin. A kid barely younger than him was dead. There had been a manhunt and he'd hidden in an electrical substation, because he was so scared of the police – it wasn't the first time, it wouldn't be the last – and he'd been electrocuted. In a single second, probably the moment he'd trespassed, the entire city had been plunged into darkness, a pause that was temporary for most people but not this boy or his family. Paul, sitting on the edge of the bed in room 313 as his mind was elsewhere, took in the images on the screen, Amelia behind him, her chin on his shoulder, her legs crossed around his waist, her arms wrapped around his torso – they didn't talk, but something passed between them, something circulated, not the image on the screen, which bore no connection to it – something internal, murky, secret. Paul's body retained some memory of the perimeter wall, of having scaled it, then of crouching down, holding his breath, feeling sheer terror at being betrayed by the inevitable breath of air escaping his lungs; and there was something else, maybe, not a memory but maybe a feeling that got harder and harder to shake; the speed of electricity running through a teenage body, the smell of flesh burning, jaws clenching to the point

79

of teeth shattering, a nightmare that, Paul told himself, might well have been drawn from Nadia Dehr's box – a nightmare that amounted to documentary poetry. Maybe Amelia was thinking the same thing as she stroked the tensed muscles that she still loved, or believed she did. Maybe it was then that her greatest fear took shape: since she hadn't opened her mother's box, everything seemed to be coming out of it; every horror, every injustice. It was the origin of the modern world – the world according to Amelia Dehr. She thought she had rid herself of that box, but instead it had engulfed all she knew.

She wanted to take part in the protests that ensued; that teenage boy shouldn't have been hunted down like an animal. It drove him crazy that she – who claimed to know everything about the world – should suddenly be so naive; it awoke the worst in him. He told her not to go. He said out loud, I forbid you, furious that he should have to say it. She didn't stoop so low as to break the silence; instead she looked at him with an unreadable smile – it wasn't quite disdainful, but amused. Of course, she went, she was arrested, she came back with ugly bruises on her face that terrified Paul, who couldn't stand the idea of anyone raising a hand against her, much less of her body being marked by what he had been determined to escape – the sickly blue public lights of those ugly, inhospitable nights. Now, those origins he had detested and fled were imprinted upon her face, the holiest thing in his world. He was sick with rage and (although he wouldn't have admitted it) fear.

So they didn't always see eye to eye. Of course they didn't, despite it all – but only at moments. Paul only realised it later, in the stark hindsight that made a bleak landscape of the past. They kept to themselves at the hotel, or at Albers's, as Amelia had left the university's lecture halls for good. What was she doing while on her own? Nothing, clearly. Paul lived for the two of them. The light bulb in front of room 313 kept burning out, and he kept changing it. Once, he met her father, who had come to pick her up. The man was nothing like his own father: he had green eyes, a cashmere overcoat, he looked around the place worriedly and nearly didn't shake the hand Paul proffered as he introduced himself. Another time he met Amelia's old friends (or old acquaintances, rather, she said). They were all that remained of her disjointed childhood: between Swiss boarding school and upper-tier prep schools, between long American winters and tennis courts, swimming pools she could have floated across for months and played at drowning in. It was a life Paul couldn't picture, having never seen anything like it, not in books, not even on screens, as that particular echelon of society prided itself on its discretion, its aloofness, and hardly needed to be seen to feel that it existed: the world was its oyster. Huge apartments, glass doors, polished wood floors, long hallways that twisted and turned, a certain way of carrying oneself: Paul was more curious than impressed; he seemed to be there incognito, disguised by wearing the right shirt and holding the right cigarettes; but someone outside the kitchens (because in these immense apartments everything was multiple, multiplied: the kitchens, the stairs, the doors, the windows) distinctly referred to him as the handyman, which resulted in amused laughter, and Paul felt attacked, he felt both seen and dismissed. Unmasked, he thought, and an icy panic came over him because for the life of him he couldn't figure out what had given him away.

Towards the end (though he had no way of knowing it would be the end), Amelia insisted that they go stay at a particularly fancy hotel, nothing like the Elisse chain. The impish look on her face was one he'd seen once or twice before, and he loved it. The place had survived successive eras; its name alone commanded respect. After many delays, the decision had finally been made to revamp its legendary interior completely. And, just as the months-long closure was about to begin, some PR pro had had a genius idea: before the renovations crew arrived, a group of carefully hand-picked guests – young, rich, photogenic, overwhelmingly white – would be let loose on all the hotel's floors, with endless magnums of champagne and full licence to blow off some steam, to unwind, to demolish the royal bedrooms and the presidential suites, knock down wall after wall, yank out draperies and tapestries, rip open mattresses upon which a number of them had actually been conceived. That would be the first time he saw Amelia's fury, her rage – finally she was finishing what she started, following through on her lazy gestures that barely got nine-tenths of the way, because the final tenth, the missing tenth, was outright destruction. Amelia ripping out beaded crystal chandeliers. Amelia throwing bottles, empty and full, at the tall mirrors that seemed to contort at first, then actually caved in. The expanding rings of cracks reflected a fractured, multiplied image of Paul and Amelia. He had never seen her like that

– nothing, not even sex, aroused such passion, such radiance. She was in her element there, seemingly at home; and for the first time he felt slightly afraid of her.

In the memory he would have of that evening and the demolition party, Paul was nothing more than an onlooker, watching this orgy of annihilation in a daze. But there were other memories apart from his own, and one in particular is collective, unmoored from any one single mind, in the form of a short, slightly shaky video. It shows young brutes, their eyes set blazing by drugs, alcohol, and their own unbridled strength, amongst them a tall, hulking, dark-haired, almost wolf-like man, and if he ever saw the clip Paul wouldn't have recognised himself, not immediately, even though it's him all right, kicking down a door and dragging a willowy redhead in before kissing her against a wall. He slips his hand under her skirt, pushes it up. It's impossible to make out their faces which seem to be welded, fused together – if they pulled apart at that moment or someone pulled them apart, their features might well have been scrambled, jumbled together forever. She holds a hammer, her stiletto digging into the wall, and then the scions and socialites break into the penthouse and run amok. The guy isn't just kissing her any more, and her leg is wrapped around his hip. He absentmindedly slides his hand up the wall, as if putting his weight on it – and instinctively, without even looking, yanks a sconce light out, a blunt gesture inherited from a long lineage of neckbreakers. And then there's nothing in the room, nothing but shadows.

*

And then came the end. It was calm: Paul was studying for his finals, Amelia seemed to have given up all pretence of wanting to learn anything, and was watching (Paul thought) porn while eating crisps, staring straight ahead, her mind somewhere else, although Paul couldn't really be sure where; he hardly had time to think about it. After finals, he told himself, I'll talk to her. His ambition or his fear of failure, which amounted to the same thing, had shifted his mental focus back on himself for the moment. A few days during which the world wouldn't be revolving around Amelia, who was perfectly capable (Paul thought) of accommodating this revolution.

He was back at his job, at the front desk, and sometimes everything blurred together; he looked at the monitor screen like a textbook and at the textbook like a monitor screen. But he was getting better. Albers had told him that she wasn't worried about him, using those exact words, and he was flattered but also saddened, as if she were abandoning him – deep down, he wanted his beloved professor to care. His work at the Elisse hotel exhausted and desensitised him in a particular way. There were moments when he wasn't sure whether he was asleep or awake, and everything became muddled: theory and practice, classroom abstractions and first-hand experiences, here, now, the present coming away, floating a little.

*

Architecture from another, bygone century, which was never meant to last. Despite the emphasis on cleanliness and hygiene, the very proliferation of hotels made their growth parasitic. And just as any single termite or flea has no more distinct an identity than any other termite or flea, so was any single Elisse hotel just as good as another. Species could have a history, but individuals – if it was even really possible to talk about individuality in this case – couldn't. Apart from the encroaching, all-encompassing history of how they spread from one continent to another, of air conditioning or electronic locks – using white cards that Paul, with a casual swipe, keyed and rekeyed for each newcomer, and which opened the rooms and the elevators, for renewable yet always finite lengths of time. All the Elisse hotels were built on the same model; only the scale changed. The front desk always facing the elevators, always to the left upon entering, past the revolving door that a motion detector set spinning, the door's glass panes sweeping across the floor with a soft, pneumatic sigh; identical marble floors, each one weathered an almost otherworldly greenish-black.

The number of rooms varied from location to location, of course; each one bore the Elisse trademark – a double bed topped by a sideways figure-of-eight, shrewdly alluding to the helices behind the hotel's name; a sideways figure-of-eight, a small chain of minuscule stars akin to asterisks, as if each one corresponded to a footnote, a contractual stipulation in such fine print that no eye could even see it – no way to know what, exactly, one might be agreeing to here, and the motto *We won't sleep You'll sleep better* imprinted on every tenth door. In this way each location, no matter its size, was a cell within the Elisse Collection, a network growing as exponentially as a mathematical sequence or a viral outbreak. If Paul had perfected one skill, however, it was that of filtering out his immediate environment; and all this, he thought, ought to have practically no effect upon him.

In purely statistical terms, night drivers will fall asleep without realising it for several minutes per hour – a fact corroborated by the data for car accidents. What goes for these drivers ought to go for Paul in front of his screen. By definition, he has no way of knowing, in the moment, that he's fallen asleep – one of the advantages of his job being that he's hardly risking losing control of his vehicle. Unless the vehicle in question is his own head, which might grow heavy, might shift this way or that, might sag on his shoulders. And maybe that's what's happening, he thinks he's awake but he isn't, he thinks he's awake but he's dreaming and his dream is an exact replica of what he's seeing, of what he's paid to see and what has been broken up over the night, has crumbled apart without his noticing it to become another world; maybe that's why Mariam is suddenly there and calling his name, touching him, tapping his shoulder, but as soon as he comes to, she's a couple of feet away, her arms flat against her torso, as if to underscore that everything is as it should be again, Paul awake and Mariam not touching him. Nobody ever touches Paul, unless he falls asleep, and he always, at least the overwhelming majority of the time, sleeps with Amelia.

For a while, at the very beginning, it would have been quite possible, quite easy, for him to sleep with Mariam, but they didn't work the same shifts: she did housekeeping very early in the morning, right when he was clocking out. He admired her long, toned arms, her striking skin, her face with its singular features – her cheekbones, her Cupid's bow lips, the hollows of her eyes on either side of her nose – all gleaming, as if polished by an expert hand. They had *had a moment*, as people say (as Paul said); they had flirted a little, barely, but no one had done anything untoward, and so they could act as if nothing had happened. Ever since he'd taken up with Amelia, Mariam had looked at him every time they saw each other as if she were trying to hold back an uncontrollable laugh. But not today. Today she seemed concerned. Paul, there's a problem in 313, she said. Mariam never called Amelia by her name, maybe she didn't even know it, she said 313 the way everyone else did; but in her voice he could actually hear the capital Ts of *Three-Thirteen*, the only trace of irony she allowed herself, as she otherwise considered such derision beneath her.

What do you mean, a problem? Paul was visibly disoriented. Mariam usually looked him over as though holding back a contemptuous laugh, a wild laugh, which if released would never have stopped, but this time was different. She was wearing a white uniform that was stretched tight, as well as small white tennis shoes perfectly suited to her bounding footsteps. Paul wiped his face, met her gaze; Mariam was always wearing some crazy new get-up, and this time it was coloured contact lenses, lifeless green things that slid around her deep black pupils, shifting slightly with every blink of her eye, and the next time he saw her again, an hour or two later, she had thrown them away. It had to be four o'clock, five o'clock in the morning. What do you mean, a problem, Paul repeated. Mariam shrugged pointedly, and he got up.

Strange how something so banal, so common as a hotel room can suddenly become troubling. All it takes is for a door to be ajar in the middle of the night, for the light in the hallway to be slightly dimmer around it – Paul cursed the bulb that always went out in front of 313, plunging the doorway into shadow. All it takes is for the cracked-open door to reveal total darkness, perfect blackness; this slight variation, a one-inch strip of night – it doesn't take anything more than that for Paul, hovering on the threshold of the room where, for weeks, for months, he'd fucked, showered, eaten, read – to be seized by a sort of anguish not unlike the sort Mariam was feeling, the two of them thinking of things they had never come across: bodies hanging in a closet, bathtubs full of blood, gruesome deaths, equal parts unreal and plain as day, in other rooms identical to these ones, in other Elisse locations. These second-hand memories flow from one place to another in the minds of those who clean hotel rooms, wipe down windows and change sheets, impersonal memories whirling through the vents, seeping into the carpet and its synthetic fibres, into the paintings on the walls, waiting to inhabit a body or two again. Paul and Mariam looked at each other and neither of them was entirely sure where this sinister premonition had come from, if not from the space itself.

What are you going to do, Mariam whispered, a sentence that left him standing alone in front of the ajar door to 313. No, she didn't want to laugh any more, she actually seemed to feel sorry for him, the front-desk guy who was utterly com-promised, who had gone to the dark side and now had to pay the price, was already paying it without his realising it. Mariam had seen him ransack a palace, kick down a door violently, she had seen him screw an heiress against a wall, pull out a crystal wall sconce, she had seen him act like he was one of *them*, like he was part of their world. He had gorged on this dream like a wild animal might on blood. From these shaky images she had deduced what he wanted to be and never would, and that made her laugh as only a woman scorned could. It now gave her pleasure to see him asleep, unshaven, without even realis-ing he was asleep, in an uncomfortable chair, under fluorescent lights that accentuated the dark circles under his eyes and made him look even more tired. She saw the love he had for a rich girl, a mad love; she also saw that this rich girl, like all rich girls, believed that being loved was the natural state of things but was incapable of returning the sentiment, and she had other problems besides. Amelia was insane, and Mariam knew it. She laughed at Paul's failure. At all his present and forthcoming fail-ures. She laughed, but tonight was different, it was different as she stood at four or five in the morning in front of Paul whose heart was only a minute or two away from breaking.

Amelia? he called out softly. He pushed the door with his fingertips. It's like a gruesome horror flick, Mariam thought, although one of the least gory parts. Paul was afraid, and it was because of the tension created by the fact that he already knew and at the same time still didn't know.

Amelia? He reached out to turn on the light.

The room was empty. Completely empty. No clothes on the chairs, no piles on the desk, no books under the bed, nothing. Nothing at all. Paul stood helplessly in the place where he had experienced the most intense moments of his life so far. The place was stripped of the slightest trace of anyone's presence, as if nobody had ever lived there, as if nobody had fallen onto the bed, had jumped under the shower or into the bathtub alongside him, had fogged over the sealed window with her breath while he'd held her from behind, while they'd had sex looking out on the city. Nothing. Or rather, worse than nothing. He finally found something – almost an outright subtraction. The bathroom waste bin was full of red. Long, silky hair – one year, two years, five years of red hair; a mass that slipped through his fingers like water, that seemed to be still alive, but likely no longer was.

it's complicated

I

He was distraught. He did what anyone would do; he did it, then he talked about it. He recounted everything without holding back, picked at his memory like a scab, never found a foreign body there, let alone extracted one. He tore up photographs, gave away books, foisted off clothes. He slept around. A guy who kept rattling off his sob story in bars, filthy dive bars with sticky floors that were all named after women, beautiful foreigners who had died of heartache: Carmen's, Aida's. A bleary-eyed guy who talked to strangers, who spilled his guts to them, and who, one day, at dawn, pulled out a hammer and set it in front of him, amid the empty glasses, then stared at it, unable to say what the tool was for or how long he had been lugging it around, and whoever had been listening was, of course, even less help there, and silence closed in around them. An unshaven guy who stumbled down the streets in the wee hours, hammer in hand. Its heft was reassuring. He slipped it under his pillow to protect him from dreams in which she lingered. Dreams in which she whispered everything he should have said and done to make her stay, and in his dreams he understood – he understood everything, he was overcome with gratitude and love and that joy jolted him awake, sheer relief shook him awake, but when he tried to remember what she had told him, he was faced with a void, a blank that stretched out and out.

One night he drank too much, got into a brawl, pulled out his hammer, and between his heart's mad beats the strange idea crept in that she was the one who, as she left, had slipped this tool – a head mated to a shaft – into his bag, as a way of saying goodbye, knowing that one day it would come in handy. And after having used the hammer he went back home in a dark red haze, threw up all night, then all morning, a bout he had never thought was possible, as if his body were revolting against itself. He ended up falling asleep on the bathroom tiles. When he awoke he was freezing and, as if he had managed, with great pain, to expel the poison and the source of his sickness, he had forgotten Amelia's face.

After that, things slowly got easier. He threw the hammer into the Seine and, when his father asked, claimed not to know what he was talking about. His father bought a new hammer and that was that.

Paul focused on his studies. Success was his ultimate method of camouflage, the best or only way he knew to blend in. In his free time, he did what everyone else did, he spent hours in front of increasing numbers of increasingly small screens and before long they fit in his hand and his pocket. A few years later, when Paul started to make a good (very good) living, he went to find his father and asked him where he wanted to go. I'm taking you on a trip, he said. They had never gone anywhere together. To the best of his knowledge, his father had only ever known two countries: the one he'd left, and the one he'd had Paul in. He'd spent more time in the latter than the former. His father didn't say anything; he just reached for a piece of bread and some sharp cheese, but Paul could see in his measured, efficient movements that he was thinking. His father thought with his muscles. His father thought with his joints, with his limbs, with his whole body, and now his whole body, small and keen and light as a boxer's, and lean as a boxer's, despite being a labourer's – his whole body was considering what answer to give, amongst all the answers possible, to this question his son had asked. And as his father thought, Paul realised that he didn't have the least idea what he was going to say. He chewed his bread and cheese in silence and Paul realised that all the destinations he was expecting were destinations that he, Paul, would have liked to go to. The sixty-year-old man in front of him seemed strong and steady and in full possession of his faculties; his age showed only in the deep crease of his forehead that almost seemed to cut through the skin into the depths of his skull. His frowning motion was a tremor, a tectonic shudder of his bones – not just his bones, a revolt of the gelatinous mass within, his grey matter exerting itself. Paul looked at the crease, which reminded him, although he wasn't entirely sure why, of his mother's death – and then at the sixty-year-old man chewing across the table from him, and, realising that he in fact had no idea where his father might have wanted, would have wanted to go (nowhere, maybe?), he felt ridiculous, ashamed at his offer. I've come all the way out here just to lord it over my father, he thought, and, after a second mouthful, and a long stretch of silence, he realised: the truth is, I don't know this man at all.

His father finished his second mouthful and carefully prepared a third and Paul was convinced he wouldn't answer. Yet he looked up with an expression he hadn't seen before – shy, almost coy – and asked: Anywhere I'd like? Really? Paul, suddenly touched, oddly touched, said: Yes, Dad, wherever you want. His father finished his bread and cheese impassively, but his son had the impression that he felt like a great weight had been unburdened from his shoulders. He stood up, a thin but vigorous man, took his plate, washed it, dried it, cleared the sink. Maybe back to the homeland, Paul thought, maybe he'll want to go back to the homeland, or to New York – or maybe he'd like to go to Rome, or Naples, or Greece. My father's slaved away all his life; where would he possibly dream of going? He hadn't dared to say the word *vacation*, he had said *trip*, he had thought about the way of suggesting it that would offend him the least. He remembered having seen his father watching wildlife documentaries thoughtfully; the cycle of life, the savannah at sunset, big monkeys screeching in the jungle; strange, pale creatures of the ocean deep that were all jaw and weak light. He knew that his father barely had any hobbies – though he played cards and dice a bit; he made bets on cockfights and dog races, though never on boxing matches, nothing involving *human persons*. Paul had always wondered who these *inhuman persons* might be that the phrase seemed to imply existed. The last few years had been straightforward, he thought; he was working on a site that, oddly, seemed to have no end in sight. There was always something to do, and by the looks of it, things did progress, but actual progress was so slow as to seem non-existent. It had become a running joke between Paul and him, this construction site with no end in sight, the infinite, dusty building work. For some obscure reason it reminded Paul of Amelia Dehr, whom he tried not to think of, like someone trying to walk straight in total darkness. It had become a running joke, and his father accepted it, but over the last few years Paul had noticed wounds, bruises, long scratches on his father's torso and on his father's back which looked like they had been made by a wild animal, that in their own way also reminded Paul of Amelia Dehr. But he knew this time that it had nothing to do with her and everything to do with old age, which was swooping down on his father. Clearly he could not go on working interminably, forever. That was what Paul wanted to talk to him about on the trip.

Maybe a safari, or maybe Alaska, or, no, more likely the countryside. More realistically one of those places where the older folk pulled their chairs out in the sun every morning and put them away every evening and chuckled amongst themselves as they declared it a day well spent. Or maybe nowhere, Paul thought again. The more he thought about it, the less he was able to picture his father anywhere other than his exceedingly tidy, exceedingly bright little apartment. Paul had trouble imagining any place in the world smaller, tidier or brighter than his father's apartment.

After mulling it over a long while, as if all the way to the tips of his fingers, Paul's father said: I've always wanted to go to Hawaii.

Paul was now working at a reputable agency, on very expensive, very competitive projects, where he was in charge of windows. Whatever the request for proposals might be for, a museum or a hotel, a shopping centre, an investment property, one of those new cities somewhere in a deserted region unfit for urbanisation but about to be urbanised all the same – he was the windows guy. It was good work, and yet he knew he wouldn't keep doing it forever. He knew it because, more and more often, when he thought of particular places or he found himself in particular places and his attention turned, quite naturally, to the windows, he imagined, with great pleasure, how the place might look with all its windows shattered. He imagined the cracks in the glass, the points of impact, and the radiating fractures; their effect on the light, on the way that light entered the space, and the shadows reminiscent of sunshine shattered across a swimming pool's surface and forming patterns on its bottom. This, too, reminded Paul of Amelia Dehr. Ever since their relationship, he found, he had been quite fortunate in love, precisely because he had never truly loved again.

He took care of everything and filled out his father's pale-green questionnaire, *Have you ever been or are you now involved in espionage or sabotage; or in terrorist activities; or genocide.* He gently took it out of the elder man's hands, at an altitude of thirty thousand feet above an ocean that his

father had never crossed, because he was carefully and dili-
gently reading each question and, at each question, *Have
you ever detained, retained or withheld custody of a child from
a US citizen granted custody of the child?* was absorbed in a
long meditation, maybe even racking his brain to figure out
whether or not he had ever been judged guilty of these acts.
Paul quickly checked the No column for each scenario, and
his father watched him proudly, as if surprised that his son
knew him so well. Paul spoke English on the plane, ordering
Bloody Marys for them both although his father only drank
the tomato juice, quickly slipping the miniature bottle of vodka
into his sleeve with a wiliness that Paul hadn't known he'd had
in him. He hadn't expected his father to be so light-fingered.
Paul spoke English at the Los Angeles airport, his father waiting, like a well-behaved child, to be told to step forward; I'm
taking my father to Hawaii, he told the immigration agent,
and the other man nodded – Paul and he were about the same
age, and, as two sons, they understood each other. You were
talking about me, Paul's father later said to him. It seemed to
have made him happy.

   At Oahu he struck up a conversation with some seasoned,
grizzled sailors who took him to see a trimaran, and once
they'd worked out a deal they made fun of Paul's suit, which
he was wearing without a tie, and teased him about his dress
shoes. They wore shorts and those Hawaiian shirts that Paul
was astonished to see weren't a myth, and the old sailors tried
to recall the last time they had put on suits. One wearing an
eye patch stamped with a golden anchor, who hadn't put on

a blazer since the day he'd set foot on the island – before Paul had even been born – told him not to trouble himself on their account, and after some bargaining he agreed to take Paul's father and him on a decently sized sailing boat to see the other islands. They spent eight days at sea; every so often Paul's seasickness caught up with him but his father was fine. Eight days of being real men, the sailor and the labourer – as sinewy as each other, unable to talk to each other, and yet able to get along perfectly well.

They knew their way around knives, both of them. Paul didn't dare to ask his father how he had smuggled in his pocketknife. It vaguely reminded him of his childhood, and also, for some reason, of his mother and her death. He suddenly recalled that when she had died his father had peeled an orange for him with this very knife – he could still smell the juice and the metal. He didn't think he'd seen it since, but he had always known it was there – wherever his father was, so was the knife. They talked about his mother. In terms that surprised his son, Paul's father described a dress she had worn. Flared, buttoned up the front, polka-dotted. The dress and these buttons also reminded him of the knife, even though he didn't know why and didn't dare to ask. Paul talked a bit about Amelia Dehr. He said that they didn't come from the same background. He said that in her arms he had been sure that his heart was beating under her skin. His father seemed to understand. Then they were quiet for a long while. They saw turtles, and dolphins, but what his father liked best were the whales, swimming peacefully, amiably, assured of their strength, wholly unaware that men might be a danger – or perhaps aware but uninterested in keeping their distance.

When they came back to Honolulu, his father surprised him again by expressing his wish, a bit like a child who knows or thinks he knows he's asking for too much, to spend a few days by Waikiki Beach. It was the most expensive and touristy part of the island, and the tackiest, but his father was absolutely besotted by it. Paul booked a room for them at the ritziest hotel on the beachfront, a huge colonial-style establishment directly overlooking the sand, which occasionally spilled over onto the floor of the restaurant and all the way to the lobby, like in a ghost town. At this point in the trip his father was tanned and wearing a University of Hawaii T-shirt, and he watched – more out of curiosity than lust – the young blonde girls walking barefoot down the streets with huge drinks in their hands and climbing into massive SUVs before slamming the doors, leaving Paul's father's face reflected in the tinted windows. Most days he went to watch the surfers. He never stepped into the water, and Paul found himself wondering whether his own father actually could swim, but he sat on the beach and watched the waves and the surfboards and the teenagers doing their best to stay upright on them. Then he pantomimed the riskiest-looking positions for Paul. That was the one thing Paul's father always had his attention on, no matter what else he was doing: the danger at hand.

Most nights he turned in early and Paul went back out. He walked up and down Waikiki, which apparently never slept. A sensation of strangeness welled up within him, as if he were alone in the world. Everything struck him as fake. The streets made him feel curiously claustrophobic, as if they were unreal, as if it weren't already unreal that this island should be lost deep in the middle of the water, in the middle of the Pacific Ocean. He tried to imagine all this blackness from above. From a plane. Some nights he drove a long way west, where ruined neighbourhoods teemed with guns and meth, and he listened to the sound of waves in the dark, waiting for his uneasiness to subside. One night, he was smoking on the beach in front of the hotel and saw a woman walking out of the water – a woman he was sure, absolutely certain, was Amelia. He watched her stumble, giggling, towards a man whom she kissed right on the lips, as if she'd won a bet. The man was wearing a wrinkled shirt and light-coloured shorts and Paul almost felt her wet body against his own wrinkled shirt, his own shorts. Then he saw a second man close by. He noticed him because he was staring at her as she pulled away from the first man to run into the darkness. She kissed him, too, the same way, passionately. It was a nightmare for him. The next day he ordered a stiff drink at breakfast, and by the light of day everything seemed better, but when he walked by the front desk, they told him that someone had left a message for him, and he was transported right back to where he had been the night before. He ran a hand over his face. But it was just the Agency.

If his father noticed anything wrong, he didn't let on.

*

After Hawaii, which had been an attempt, even if neither of them would admit it, for his father and him to say goodbye, Paul set on an obstacle course for the Agency; the obstacles facing him, however, were neither physical nor material. On the contrary, nothing stood in his way, all doors automatically opened, all stairs were easy escalators, attentive young women seemed to anticipate everything he might need. Even in restaurants, dishes were presented ready to wolf down, underneath transparent plastic covers, on narrow conveyor belts. His routine was to see what looked appetising on the first circuit and, on the next, to reach for what he wanted or thought he wanted – which sometimes weren't the same, sometimes didn't correspond, and that would leave him feeling oddly dissociated, like a body without a head, or a head without a heart. For weeks, months, he didn't touch any cash, any bills, any coins, anything his father, with his third-world common sense (to use Paul's words), considered real; anything that would give him the particular pleasure that an older man, a widower, might take in finding, deep in his pockets, bills worn soft. A pocketknife. Cash. My father has found this way to feel the power he has. He may not have a lot, but it's his, he can touch it, hold it in his hand, close his fist on something tangible that gives him strength. Impact. As for me, Paul thought, doors open wherever I go. My body is outside time zones, rhythms, biology, I don't know whether that's good or bad, a strength or a weakness, but I don't dwell on it, I just keep going. That's the power I have. It isn't nothing.

It wasn't nothing, but he sometimes trembled for no reason. It really wasn't nothing, but one day, in the middle of a desert, a land where glassed-in parks were being built, glass-domed ski runs – Paul, the windows guy, sometimes assisted on these projects; this time, though, he was dealing with a tower: a vertical kingdom, an empire without an emperor. It had been a long time, he thought, since he had proposed or thought of proposing anything other than tempered glass, bulletproof panes being the latest fashion, the latest standard – if your work or your identity didn't result in someone trying to (to use his father's words) pump you full of lead, then your life was a sham – and that day on the thirtieth or fortieth or fiftieth floor of a tower under construction in the middle of a desert, he was standing behind the window, observing the city that several decades earlier had been just a camp, the heart of the space back then being easy to make out, beating as the wind filled the tents' canvas. But these days that beating heart was lost, or hidden, or buried, or stopped – he was blinded by the light playing on the skyscrapers' panes, short and long flashes of light dancing on the glass walls – a detail that nobody had noticed apart from Paul, the windows guy, and a little girl sitting cross-legged on the sixty-fourth floor of a building out of his view. I must be losing it, he thought; he knew better than anyone else that these panes of glass were sealed, immovable, and that there was no way they could be flashing. He considered the possibility that these flashes – some short, others long – were an otherworldly language of sorts. He thought about the workers, tens of thousands of workers coming from other countries and continents to build this city, an underpaid army that sometimes suffered horrific accidents, dying without anyone really knowing or caring. I'm losing it, he decided. A few days later there was an emergency evacuation of all the Westerners. Something had happened and now he was in the back of an armoured car, wedged in amongst strangers, and for once nobody was yapping about air conditioning.

He ended up back home, watching a disaster on screen that hadn't been clear when he was in the middle of it all. It had come into focus through the bumps along the road, through gunshots in front of the airport, but never so clearly as now in the aerial footage of blazing flames and summary executions. At what moment does one become the enemy, the windows guy, now on leave, wondered. He slept for forty-eight hours, waking up only to let melatonin pills meant to reduce symptoms of jet lag dissolve under his tongue. He woke up to wonder about how subjective that word, *symptoms*, seemed to be, as his head for the moment felt too heavy to raise.

Once he had got enough sleep, he showered, put on a clean shirt and ventured out for some coffee, to enjoy the simple pleasures of being at home. Then he did what he had long held himself back from doing: he went to see Albers.

2

Simply walking into the university's buildings was now, for Paul, an extraordinarily complex matter. He remembered it as an intermediary space, both indoor and out, with no barrier to entering or exiting. Arcade after arcade, rows of picture windows, emergency stairwells leading up to terraces where everyone smoked and hung out, as close to the sky as anyone had any chance to be while in the middle of a city. So Paul was surprised to see security guards, vestibules, protocols. He had to exchange his ID card for a temporary access card; the security personnel – ex-cons or young people of modest means – walked him to the building entrance; and yet, he told himself, this all somehow made him feel less safe. The place was stuck in a state of suspended deterioration due to neglect as well as intent. His memories came back, memories of how it had felt to walk down these grungy corridors that he had once considered cosy. When he pushed open the heavy door, the lecture hall was dark; images were gliding, for lack of a screen, right across the whiteboard, slipping along the wall, and the whiteboard's edges cut through the video, giving it a jagged physicality. Paul leaned against the back wall, whispering an apology – for there were kids everywhere, on the steps, or sitting three to a seat, one on the cushion, the second on the armrest, the last perched on the back. They were so young; expressions flickered across their faces and left no trace, as if over the surface of flat water. Was it possible that they had never, in their whole life, felt anything long-lasting? And, at the bottom of this arena, almost at the students' mercy (he'd never realised just how vulnerable that position was), stood Albers, whose features he couldn't make out, drowned out so thoroughly by the projector's lights that she seemed to be an emanation of the film, a series of moving images suddenly given flesh. It took his brain some time to make sense of them, to assemble them into something coherent: they were too strange, too shocking, too disjointed in these different layers. Anton's face, her small hands fluttering around, the desk behind her, the whiteboard, the wall, so much visual complication that made the process of deciphering all the more difficult. (Paul wondered, were those unfortunate, optically disorienting conditions part of the class, *were* they the class?) Finally he had to accept what he saw: a lab, a monkey, and a rabbit. He had to force himself to look, because scientists had removed these animals' skulls, the part that was perhaps called – he wasn't sure – the skullcap. And there they were, their brains exposed to the air, and lab assistants had stuck needles into these skulls, expertly discharging light (or maybe not so light) electrical stimuli, and, given the circumstances, due to scientific experimentation, the physiognomies of these otherwise placid animals revealed pure terror. Although it was easily seen in the features of a capuchin monkey, so closely related to our ancestors, Paul was surprised to see that the rabbit, too, with its rabbit's head and its downy ears dangling around its bared meninges (such a small, pinkish, almost translucent brain – it could have fit in a baby's hand) – that the rabbit, too, expressed fear, which Paul's own brain, well protected in the darkness of the thickest bone of the human body, immediately recognised, and if I see its fear and understand it, that has to mean, he thought, his heart pounding, that this rabbit has a face, the same way I do. He ran his hands over his face; he was more exhausted than he thought.

Fear has a spatial component, said Albers: if there is no space, there is no fear. Fear is primarily located in an area of the brain that can be activated, as these images show. Whether or not these images should exist at all is up to you. Fear is also located, at least for mankind, in darkness. In the night. The absence of perceptible boundaries, a formless space – and night, in reality, is the opposite of a definite place; it's an area, a vagueness. Incidentally, it seems that intense, unrelenting fear makes one more receptive to abstraction – and I will leave it to you to establish a *fearful* history of modern art, the explosion of abstractions after World War II and the Holocaust, for example. And it is also the case that fear is located, as we will now be considering, in cities. Lights, please.

A slim young blonde sitting near Paul, who smelled faintly like mint, flicked the switch; the fluorescent lights hummed on. Albers was illuminated in the deeply intimate gesture of adjusting her lapel; she looked up at these kids who were simultaneously her subjects and her judges – and she saw Paul, and smiled at him. It was a sweet, playful smile that was at once childlike and motherly, one that softened her face and her eyes, and Paul felt at home. By the end of this class, Albers, as was her habit, the title of the class notwithstanding, still hadn't developed her point about cities, still hadn't touched on the theme of tomorrow, and he made his way, against the current of students leaving, down the rows of seats; the last ones who lingered, both the shy ones and the ambitious ones who wanted to say something quickly, one-to-one, were surprised to see their beloved professor throwing her arms around the neck of a tall dark-haired man whose face she, standing on tiptoe, held in her hands as she exclaimed: My little Paul! What a surprise! It's been years!

They went down to the car park where Paul had sometimes worked while a student. Albers had put her arm through his and he felt like an adult at last, as if he had gone on growing all this time, even though he had of course already reached his full height by the time he had hidden, terrified, in the sentry box with its Plexiglas covered in the whorls, the small greasy galaxies that were the fingerprints of those who had worked there. He had to curb the impulse to stop and rub them away with the hem of his sleeve. Albers was nattering away beside him. This time, it was he who drove the German car, still the same one, still parked in the same spot, as if nothing had changed, although he noticed an uneven scratch along its gleaming side, as if someone had scraped it with a long talon – or, more likely, a key. He raised an eyebrow, feeling protective. Albers waved off his concern.

As they entered her building his heart began to pound; he was afraid the place might have somehow become smaller, afraid of being disappointed as one is when revisiting the places one has grown up in; but no, nothing had changed, and he padded around Albers's spacious apartment – it could have housed a family but she was living there alone – where every facet of her personality, every one of her moods had its own corner, its own privacy, as if she were, in her own eyes, an entire tribe, several generations coexisting peacefully. What a perfect life. Books everywhere; chairs and lights that Paul now knew the designers and prices of; and even a pinball machine that sparked a pang of melancholy because Amelia and he had given it to her. An old thing from the eighties, with a scantily clad heroine emblazoned on it, a cascade of blonde hair, roses and brambles around her: kitsch martyr-dom, black romanticism and Japanese manga fetishism, an eighteenth-century Frenchwoman who had dressed as a man, and lived through the Revolution, and whose name no one would ever forget. Paul was amused to find class hand-outs and half-finished articles covering the glass top. Albers let out a soft laugh and handed him a glass of wine. What do you know, it's become my second desk – they say that sitting is the new smoking, and sometimes, every so often, playing it helps me think a little. (Albers didn't say *pinball*; instead she referred to it, quite formally, as *electrical billiards*.) She was every bit as devoted to her work (the end of the world) as she always had been, and she couldn't resist telling him about her research, there, in front of the old arcade game, before even offering him a seat – everything about her warmed the very core of his heart. Albers had been writing not long ago about exile and flight as principles of spatial organisation.

She had aged a bit; her hair was grey – she took, as she told Paul, a certain pride in it; she had chosen the sheen carefully, gone to the hairstylist; her eyes, equally grey, stood out even more. Moved by a feeling that was rather unlike him, Paul put his arm around her, making sure not to knock over their glasses. Albers laughed. My little Paul! Come here, tell me everything. Of course she already knew everything – the Agency, the windows, the uprisings in the desert; she knew that he was making a good living; a very good one; if she was disappointed by the career he had chosen, she didn't let on; not everyone could devote themselves to research, to teaching. That wasn't the path meant for Paul; he had struggled too much with his own background of poverty, and the deep-rooted rage he felt towards the leisure class that he had infiltrated, that had adopted him – a rage he himself wasn't aware of, not really. Sometimes this fury became, briefly, something perceptible, but more often it was ghostly, a rift in the space–time continuum, a breach of the allegedly universal laws regulating the world. His rage was practically foreign to him; when he felt it he was literally beside himself, as if possessed; even though it was the most genuine, or truthful, expression of who he really was: Paul, the windows guy. Of who he really was when windows were taken out of the equation, along with tailored shirts, and refined gestures, and all the nights spent meandering around world capitals with colleagues he considered friends. In these last ten years he had learned not only how and when to talk, but also how and when to be quiet; he had learned how to play office politics, how to detect the political underpinnings of personal relationships, the betrayals; these days, he seemed to be no different from any of them, he smiled (and, on the inside, blushed) at everything he'd been oblivious to when he was younger, when he thought belonging was a matter of the right brand of shoes or cigarettes, whereas it was in fact a well-timed shrug of the shoulders, a wry aside, a silence. Yes, even silence was a different thing here. It wasn't at all like his father's silence: not only had Paul come up several social classes, but he had come into a more self-assured stance that lay in knowing how and when and especially why to be quiet. Few people had any suspicions that this placid man was in fact blazing with fury, had in fact an unquenchable thirst for justice; few people had any idea that his well-kept hands could wield a hammer on the fly, could land a blow to the face, and feel jaws and molars shattering on impact, thinking all the while about his own grief and the rising dawn. Some nights, when he was with a handful of businessmen – all in high-flying careers, thirty-somethings in search of a thrill, all dressed in identical suits and ties – sometimes he was singled out from the pack. A bouncer or some other minor authority figure covered in hair or tattoos or piercings or scars would recognise something in him that the others didn't have and let him in, just him, and nobody else in the group, and he would always give them a small, apologetic smile before going in, breathing more easily once alone, and the night was his oyster: the disused factories where the thumping bass became his heartbeat, the fancy townhouses where someone would stick a circular, triangular, star or virus-shaped sticker over the camera lens of every guest's phone, and in this guaranteed anonymity, they would only be able to see with their own eyes, and they would see all sorts of things: dominatrices and orgies both human and animal, faceless men and crotches everywhere, and all their worldly accessories – heels, riding crops, toys of all sorts, baroque get-ups. Paul would stay for an hour or ten or fifteen, and by the time he emerged, and found his colleagues, his acquaintances again, it had become a joke, a mystery, nobody could understand what shady quality he had that made him someone to reckon with, someone so unexpectedly desirable. And Paul would simply smile, and say nothing.

Standing next to Albers, however, after so many years and hotel rooms and time zones, he felt a peace that he hadn't experienced in a long while, and he felt innocent and new again. They caught up, she ordered some takeaway – Albers didn't cook: rather, she had to admit, she put stuff in bowls, sometimes on plates. When the delivery man buzzed, Paul insisted on getting the door and paying for the order; for a few days afterwards, he could remember the exact amount but barely anything about the man who had shown up at the door. That was the thing in those days, nobody ever looked at anyone else's face – here, a delivery man just like any other, in the bustling gig economy, young guys on bikes with sinewy muscles and uncertain futures. Later on, once everything had changed – fallen apart – a man like that would show up at Albers's door, she would open it, and she would take a bullet straight to the heart, another to the head, and nobody, of course, would be able to remember the man, while the better world she'd had in her heart and her mind was bleeding away from the only place it had ever truly existed, pooling on the floor in red puddles, the future of utopias congealing on the ground.

Hours went by. Albers turned on lamps here and there, their circles of soft pink or yellow light falling gently across every surface, and as he caught his reflection in the living-room window, he saw one of the panes was cracked: a fine web of radiating fractures that would inevitably catch a visitor's eye at one moment or another. A projectile thrown from down below, from the courtyard, he presumed; a pebble or a coin, now gone, its impact a visible trace in Albers's living room, marring it – wasn't this, after all, the one place in the world where Paul felt safest? It reminded him of the long scratch on the silver car, and a children's story, and a proverb in a foreign language; it reminded him of a desire deep within him that was now reawakening. He lingered in front of the cracked glass a long while, he – the windows guy – perched on the couch like a child, on his knees, turning his back on his hostess, touching his fingers to the pane. Finally he went and sat by Albers again, and she must have seen the question on his face before he was even able to put it into words. Oh, she said, when Amelia came back, she didn't have the keys with her. Actually, I wonder where they are, she must have lost them, in a forest somewhere; I've found myself wondering if, with rainfall, the keys have somehow imbued the dirt all around with their molecules and now the plants and trees growing there retain some memory in their foliage, their leaves, of the door locks, the apartment, maybe even my sleep, my work, my solitude. But Paul wasn't listening, not really. He was floored, as if he was the one being hit, now, by the hammer he had swung ten years earlier at dawn. Albers broke off her train of thought: But didn't you know, Paul? I assumed that was why you'd come.

3

Amelia had looked like shit. Paul wanted to retort, what a surprise – but no words came. She had shown up in the courtyard without even a handbag, just the clothes on her back, all skin and bones. She'd thrown things at Albers's window until the professor was irritated enough to leave her desk and go see who or what was making all this ruckus. When I opened the window and I saw Amelia down there, Albers said, I didn't even recognise her. At first I thought I was looking at her mother! I felt a jolt of happiness; my body was convinced my youth was coming back to me. Nadia had spent her life coming and going and I'd hoped for so long that she might reappear – but no, Nadia had pulled off this final trick of disappearing without a trace. Or maybe she did come back, if only in Amelia's features. I can't say if it's a good thing for a daughter to be haunted by her own mother. I don't think it is. But unlike other people, unlike myself when I was a mother – fourteen months may be short, but once you've given birth, there's no changing that; I may be childless now, but I'll always be a mother (all that was maternal in Albers manifested itself otherwise, elsewhere: in her lectures, between the lines of her books, in the gaze she now fixed upon the dumbfounded man in front of her) – when Nadia had her daughter, she decided that she had earned the right to slip away, that she had passed along something essential – nothing personal, nothing genetic, Nadia wasn't self-absorbed like that – no, she saw her child as something abstract. It's hard to explain to someone who's never met her; there was some life, she had given some of it, it's really in those terms that she was thinking; she had paid her dues and could now focus on whatever her heart truly, secretly wanted. That's how, I think, she understood motherhood: some life had passed through her, and was going to persist, with or without her, there or elsewhere. You don't know Gilles, do you? Amelia's father? No? Well, of course Gilles thought that was no way to raise a child. In this sense he was more maternal than Nadia – in other words, he had an almost brutish tendency towards convention. If there's one thing that Nadia and I have both always agreed on, it's that there are many ways to be a mother, just as there are many ways to be a woman, from not being one any more to never even having been one. Nadia and I were trying to determine our times; it never occurred to us that the times, in turn, could end up determining us. I suppose I'm trying to explain why I didn't do anything myself to hold on to her: because I thought, then just as much as now, that there's no getting in between a woman and her choices, and that there's nothing that can get in between a person and her freedom. Not her purported responsibilities, not her children. Freedom is like skin; it has many layers, and can only be removed at great cost.

Paul listened, silent, and his emotions recast the space around him, a place that had been familiar and safe and no longer was – he had discovered another side of it. The stakes had suddenly shifted. He was afraid. Nothing had

117

changed but everything had changed; fear slipped into his heart, through the sentences Albers enunciated – not only the words but the silence around them, silence that was no longer neutral nor necessary but terrifying. He finally asked: Where is she? She's sleeping, Albers replied. He considered getting up and leaving. He couldn't bear the idea – which should have been bearable, maybe even desirable, since he had just landed on that possibility himself – that she might be somewhere there, hidden, behind a door, a wall. Such moments in a life (instants of animal instinct; pure panic) were not to be underestimated. Albers herself described having become who she was – a woman who looked for ways out – after noticing the space around her, one day, in her child-hood: on a narrow landing, facing a wild animal. Paul had forgotten what kind, or rather the story had been told so many times that it was now like a myth, told in numerous variations that, rather than cancelling each other out, rein-forced one another, deepened the story. A snarling dog, or a fox, or a wolf. And, facing its jaws, she intuited the exact proportions of the space she was in; she keenly, instinctively knew where the exits were. Or should have been.

Ten years earlier, when he had opened the door of 313 only to find nothing there – nothing aside from that auburn mass of hair in the bathroom waste bin; a lifetime's worth, he guessed – he had called the police. Not for a second did he imagine that it might be anything other than a sordid crime, an act reported in two lines in a tabloid newspaper, the kind that he and Amelia had read aloud to each other every morning, secure in their belief that none of that whole circus of human misery had anything to do with their own lives. Everything about them felt so wonderfully ordinary: a short night, a black coffee, a bag of books resting on one knee and a lover's hand on the other. He had called the police and waited on the sidewalk, in the night, for the car to come, sirens blaring, blue revolving lights flashing at regular intervals – light from another world, every four seconds. Every four seconds, the scene was commonplace – a picture window, a hotel, a small crowd; every four seconds, it was submerged in a parallel, underground, almost nightmarish dimension. The blue tended to saturate everything, to erase the difference between people and things, to flatten walls, fabrics and faces to a uniform surface; to drown dark circles under eyes just as wholly as the whites of those eyes, just like the veins that disappeared from Paul's hands, from his furrowed brow. Yes, nightmarish, he thought, unable to answer the most basic questions, four seconds of life, four alien seconds.

Paul didn't know it but for a few minutes he had been the first (and sole) suspect in Amelia Dehr's disappearance. He maintained that he had not left his desk that night, hadn't seen her leave. In his terror he could already see the fragmented, choppy sentences in the trashy headlines, REDHEAD PACKED UP and LIMBS & LUGGAGE ON WHEELS. He could already see the security footage showing some guy leaving with a heavy suitcase, filmed from above, and Paul wishing him a pleasant evening without any suspicion that the woman he loved was folded up in that small space. But in fact, the suspect was him, he who had been with the missing woman, he who had returned to the crime scene, he who had, quite simply, looked the part. And then the security footage was reviewed, and after having been taken for the perp, Paul now seemed to be the fool, because everyone saw, clearly, undeniably, a buzz-cut Amelia stepping out of the elevator in white tennis shoes and a bulky, light-coloured coat (the jeans she wore were – had been – Paul's), glancing at the front desk, at the receptionist's head, tilted almost comically to the side, and her own face bore an enigmatic, inscrutable expression. She sat for a moment beside the useless fountain and ran her fingers over her head, exploring her skull like an unknown country, a lunar surface. Retied a shoelace that hadn't come undone, looked down the hall and at the sleeping man for a while. And then, finally, Amelia Dehr stood up and left the hotel, did not turn around, never turned back.

Now he was being scolded for having called for no reason, for crying wolf, and wasting the time of the city's finest. This was how things were – the reality of Paul's station in society – in this country: no matter what had happened, something was always his fault. But Paul was far too devastated right then, and too enraged, to think about that. Injustice was interchangeable with the fact of Amelia Dehr. Amelia Dehr who hadn't been kidnapped, or murdered, but had very simply left, in the only way she knew, left definitively, and he (the animal in him) believed he would die of it. He had ended up on the landing of Albers's apartment; he didn't even have the strength to ring, he'd just curled up on the doormat, and in the morning when she'd opened her door he'd tumbled in like a dog nearly frozen dead.

He'd looked for signs, some sort of explanation: maybe she'd never loved him; maybe, from the beginning, she'd taken him for a fool. But his pride told him he couldn't have been that blind, couldn't have deluded himself that much. He looked at the photo of Albers and Nadia Dehr above the fireplace, saw at last how Amelia Dehr mirrored her mother – it took an act of extreme cruelty for the family resemblance between them to become clear. At Albers's, he had read Nadia Dehr's first collection, the cradle of documentary poetry – a thin volume titled *Life L* that left him unsure whether the L was a Roman numeral or a Latin letter – a book written on multiple continents, in cars and in garrets and under trees. Who knew what remained, in the lines, between the lines, of the movements, of the lost landscapes of the sixties and the seventies – whatever there was, it wasn't what he had been looking for. He was looking for the smoking gun, and he ended up finding it. Amid a welter of horrors, several lines of verse (*was* this even poetry?) that, to him, in the state he was in, seemed more horrific than anything:

> *this boy is charming, he could be*
> *perfect*
> *he could be perfect for us – if only someone,*
> *before us, had been kind enough,*
> *willing enough*
> *to break his heart – he would have been perfect*

for us if only
if only someone had done him the favour done us
but at this moment, at moment M, in this life, in life L
we can break his heart
we and nobody else
and thereby
make him perfect
perfect for us
of course that means
(everything comes at a price)
forsaking him
forever

And whether *we* included Nadia Dehr and her ego, or Nadia Dehr and her madness, or Nadia Dehr and Anton Albers who at that time shared everything equally, the world and the people they met; or even, who knows, Nadia Dehr and the daughter she didn't have yet, who would be born years later, remained an open question for Paul, an emptiness he sometimes ventured into when he needed a respite, in hopes that intellectual work might distract him; which, of course, it always failed to do.

Some time after she left, Amelia tried to call him. Only the hope of receiving some sign from her had kept him going; but it was too little, too late. When he picked up and heard, after a pause, after an exhalation he immediately recognised as hers, his name in her voice, *Paul* – hesitantly, ashamedly, sadly – all the love he still had for her, or thought he still had for her, had immediately turned into hatred. He had hung up. After that, she had written him emails every so often that he deleted without opening, and one or two letters had arrived at Albers's that he had contemplated in dread, like something altogether disgusting, a bloody organ. He hadn't touched them, and he didn't even want to know whether Amelia had stopped writing to him, or Anton had stopped informing him of the letters. He kept his distance. Avoided Albers's apartment, politely turned down her invitations, kept going to her lectures but sat elsewhere in the lecture hall, and while he set his mind even more determinedly to his studies, his focus was now on practicalities: materials, costs, the complex question of cost-effectiveness underlying site development and profitability. He set aside philosophy, ideals, and even ideas themselves. Abandoned museums. Never returned to the hotel, took on security stints elsewhere. Nothing else to do now, he sometimes thought, just surveillance. Monitoring things, people, places. Sometimes in a uniform, sometimes with a dog or a baton, in warehouses containing valuable goods, in huge underground garages, in empty offices that by day produced some intangible, barely comprehensible value; solitary, nocturnal jobs meant for healthy young men, and assigned based on their physical strength but also on the colour of their skin, in spaces that were somewhat dark and dangerous, places they patrolled as their footsteps echoed, as their watchdogs panted, reduced to a strange expression of their usefulness: a man in an empty place. He went home more frequently to see his father, who did not talk about the present or the past, who did not talk, pure and simple. Sometimes he went with him to construction sites, knocked down walls, his hair and eyebrows caked in white dust; but as soon as he started doing better (as soon as he started hating Amelia Dehr, whose name he would only utter in front of his father many years later, on a boat drifting in the Pacific), the man he owed his life to refused his company, and Paul understood that he didn't like working with him nearby, had only tolerated his presence owing to the unacknowledged, extenuating circumstances. Fundamentally, he was modest, and he disliked doing what he did in front of his son. He didn't need a witness, an audience to be who he was. Paul went back to university. He had sex (he would never say *fuck*; her use of that word had banned it from his lips forever) as much as he could – mechanically, maliciously, for his ego and for his health, to put as many bodies as he could between himself and her, between himself and the man he'd been with her. He finished his classes, he grew detached, mercenary, he became who he would be known as – the windows guy – he earned money, more and more. Time passed, more and more – but this stretch, and his defences, and his own reservations, all immediately went up in smoke when he heard Albers say that Amelia was back. And that she was asleep.

Of course, they saw each other again. He was hoping he would find her ugly. And yet he was relieved to recognise her – to recognise what he had loved of her, even if she had changed, undeniably so; they were now at the age when a man is still young and a woman young *but still*. She no longer stood quite so straight, her neck and her hips now tilted at slightly altered angles, more sinuous, almost interrogatory; even her nose wasn't as straight as he remembered, its slope a little imperfect. She was wearing men's jeans, cut right above the ankle; a white tank top; no jewellery except, just above her elbow, a thin gold armlet; several loops coiled around her biceps ended in a serpent's head with two white stones for eyes. Flat sandals, three pale leather straps that by some magic stayed on her foot. Hair that was neither long nor short, or rather both long and short; silky, soft, almost weightless strands, which seemed to cling by the same sort of magic to her head, a cut that was both masculine and feminine, or rather masculine first and, upon reflection, wildly feminine, fiery. No make-up. No bra. At her neck – where age really could be seen, where the future really could be read in the lines of a life making and unmaking itself – were two new grooves, one deeper than the other, which she did nothing to hide. Too thin, probably. She had that particular pallid glow that results from malnutrition, anxiety was gnawing at her bones and making itself visible despite her attempts to mask it. She had gained in photogenic quality what she had lost in iron, in vitamins, her feet were trembling, her hands were trembling, and she didn't realise it. Her knuckles were reddish, as if she had been too cold for too long. Her smile was sincere, but sincerely sad, and Paul understood that sincerity and sadness were now one and the same for her. It seemed she no longer had anything of the twenty-year-old firebrand he had had kissed too many times to count, none of which he could recall. She had forgotten the city, she hesitated at intersections, he had to guide her now. Nothing remained of her old toughness, her old self-assurance. It was the other way around for Paul. It was new for him, he had been ready for everything but the fragility, the precarity evident in every aspect of her, as if the least footstep, the least word demanded infinite energy from her. He didn't want to add to her suffering. He knew he was capable of it but couldn't make himself do so. It seemed to him that something in her was wavering, was on the verge of breaking down. He found himself slowing his pace down to hers, aligning his silences with hers, with a care and concern that he had never felt before. She's paying with her body for the way she walked out on me, he thought, which comforted him, even if deep down he knew he was granting himself too much importance, that it had nothing to do with that – nothing at all, really – and he didn't want to acknowledge this, he didn't want to be let down, for a second time, by Amelia.

She had left. That was a fact. Without telling him – that was another. She hadn't known how to do so, words had failed her. If she had told him, she said, her plan would have fallen apart, her willpower would have slipped away. She who played with words, whose thoughts came so easily to her lips, hadn't found any way to explain her decision. I thought that you would understand, she said. Then: I thought it wouldn't be that painful. Then: I couldn't grow attached, I didn't want to grow attached, it seemed beneath me. I had better things to do than fall in love. Falling in love is no way to live.

Paul kept silent. Ten years on, he wasn't suffering any more, he had established causes, consequences, entire hypothetical landscapes as expansive as the world he would go on to explore, and they had ended up being reduced to a single line. She left because she left. A tautology that cancelled out everything, revealed how absurd the very notion of a relationship was, this occasional dream of knowing another person perfectly, of fusing, of achieving transparency. It's been a long while since I stopped trying to understand, he said, and you don't owe me anything. If you owed me something that would mean there was still something between us and as far as I can tell there isn't anything. Anything at all, Amelia. I'm no longer who I used to be and I can't do anything for you. I don't want to do anything for you. Oddly enough, that made her laugh. I tried to apologise, she added, don't you remember? He remembered everything but said no. It seemed easier that way.

This lie – of having forgotten, of reaching some closure – laid the groundwork for them to meet anew. In a way it was true, there wasn't anything between them, but in another way it was false – long after all that had happened did happen, something immovable still remained, something impersonal that moved between them, outside them – he dreamed about shattered windows while she actually shattered windows. It could mean something; then again, perhaps it didn't. Paul tried not to see anything in it. One night he took her to an exclusive party at a hotel that had just opened, a former brothel with obscene patterns on the carpet, red-lit or blue-lit or half-lit rooms; young people showering in the open, alone, in groups, endless shameless showers for which they were, had to be, paid; young singers, young actresses staggering, glass in hand; bathtubs full of champagne bottles, except for the one with two eels swimming in it, two long muscular eels, and Amelia sat on the rim and watched them, let three fingers touch the water's surface. Those fish are obscene, and so is their fate, to be caught barehanded by a chef or his assistant, their heads chopped off with a single blow in front of onlookers, and carved up to be sautéed, flambéed, on a makeshift stove by an up-and-coming cook. How strange it is to consume a being that you've seen alive, that might even still be somewhat alive within, in other ways, thinking its wordless, mutinous thoughts, unwilling to surrender, to give in, to understand – in this way victorious even in death. I'm tired, Paul, said Amelia, and he held out his hand, which she considered blankly, as if information had trouble moving from her optical nerve to her brain, to her heart, to her red, chapped fingers – she looked at it the way, ten minutes earlier, she had looked at the eel that was now continuing its indeterminate existence in Paul's stomach, in the stomachs of strangers already making their way elsewhere, disseminating the dead creature throughout the rooms, the building, the city; and whether that added to its inchoate strength or diluted it he wasn't entirely sure. Finally, she took his hand.

*

He mishandled the situation, waited three days to call her back, following the unspoken rules. Respected the laws of desirability, performed to a T the mating rituals of all the great primates of his era. She couldn't have cared less, seemed oblivious to how much time had gone by, to conventions; she could spend an hour on the phone with him describing what she saw outside her bedroom window just as she could leave his calls unanswered for a week or call him up him several times in a row to ask him how to order a car, a meal, some plants; she said yes to everything in a gentle, distracted way that he found far more upsetting than if she had said no to everything. He wanted to grab her shoulders, shake her; she never seemed to be properly awake and it was a dream he seemed unable to escape. In short: she had gone, she'd left. She had wanted to find her mother. She had been bored. She had hated love, had hated what love did to her, a twenty-year-old eating crisps while watching porn, waiting for a man who had his life together. Are you fucking kidding me, Paul thought, it lasted a week, two at the most. You had it all and I – I had *fuck*-all. But he didn't say that aloud. She wasn't who she had been any more either, after all. In the wake of the war in the former Yugoslavia, as in the wake of all other genocides or attempted genocides, the search for the missing had become an entire industry, both a sector of the white economy and a part of the black market, and Amelia had decided to try her own luck in this new Wild West that the post-war Balkans had become.

4

She'd had to take two planes to get to what had been the besieged city. From cover to cover, Amelia read the special issue of a popular science magazine – the sort that Paul liked. She read it attentively, page by page, as if performing a ritual of sorts. The magazine's theme was memory. It transpired that our memories are not stable. That, contrary to what had long been believed, they evolve. We reconstruct them every time they are recalled and each recollection – rather than consolidating them – fragments them. Meanwhile, a memory is never as fragile as when it's being recalled. Recollection, in fact, is the best moment to modify or erase the memory in question. With electricity, for example. With electric shocks. But if an unexpected disruption occurs – say, an explosion, an attack, or maybe simply a power failure, an inopportunely timed phone call – a memory can be spontaneously weakened. The next time we recollect it, we don't realise that it's altered. Forgetting, in fact, is the brain's lifelong operation. Forgetting is not a defeat but an enzyme. Each remembrance is a counter-effort.

In conclusion: our lives are invented. The more time passes, the more our lives are invented.

Which doesn't bode well for my investigation, Amelia realised. She thought about her mother. And about the search she was now undertaking, that she had imagined might be an adventure but which doubtless would only be a particularly elaborate mourning ritual, a barbaric exercise she would re-enact without realising it. She shut the magazine. Then her eyes. This wouldn't be in vain, because once these sorts of rites were completed, if they went well, it wouldn't be unlikely for the initiate to find some sort of presence. Some sort of peace or presence. Maybe those were the same thing. It wouldn't be any more unlikely for the initiate to die during these rites, she told herself, her eyes still shut, given how incomprehensible, how frequently violent these ceremonies are.

I won't draw any shapes on the ground with chalk, Amelia thought next. I won't drink any foul concoctions, I won't light any candles, I certainly won't sacrifice any small animals.

She contemplated leaving her magazine on the plane, since of course there would be other readers on the flight back, but ended up throwing it out, because its science struck her as malevolent. She didn't want this shtick about invented memories to contaminate anyone else; it offended her sense of justice and fairness. People couldn't go verifying everything all the time, they couldn't go and change the rules of the game once it was underway, otherwise they'd be bound to lose.

Well, we're bound to lose, Amelia thought quite clearly. Her entire brain was determined to drown this thought in the more than seventy per cent of its composition that was water, and she forgot it before she had even managed to put it into words – nothing remained of it, except for a vague twinge that she attributed to the plane's tilting as it landed.

She looked at the sky a bit. And then she was in what had been the besieged city.

Of course, she stayed at the Elisse. It was night when she arrived, she waited at the front desk a minute, imagined that the man soon to appear would be the one she had left – in which case either all would be forgiven or she would have proof, absolute proof, that she was living in hell. But it wasn't him, it wasn't Paul.

She didn't sleep well.

*

When the Elisse hotel chain was established in Sarajevo on the occasion of the 1984 Winter Olympics, the hotel immediately emblematised the country's openness, its prosperity; if not already present then at least soon to come: the national prospects were sunny and the gold-tinted glass cube gleamed in the dawn of a new era. Ten years later, during the city's siege, under the international embargo that hit what had been, but no longer could or would be, a single, unified country, the yellow bunker served as general headquarters for the international press, which to a small – very small – degree protected the building from gunfire. Even so, the upper levels were mostly destroyed. The few photos that bore testament to it – often the photos were indeed taken from there – showed something that resembled a futuristic ruin, a pyramid of sorts with glass and steel levels, sometimes smoking since small fires kept breaking out in the rubble of the upper floors. After the war, the cube was restored from top to bottom. Rebuilt, just like the rest of the city, exactly as it was. But *exactly as it was* meant little; the Elisse hotel might not have changed, but the same could hardly be said of the times and the mores. What had been cutting-edge in the eighties, a promise of the future, was now both outdated and self-obsessed, that is, rather ridiculous, a cumbersome specimen of former visions of the future, like so many places and, even more so, objects (Walkmans, fax machines) which were met with some bemused looks. The Elisse chain belonged to the realm of science-fiction films from the turn of the millennium: a vision of a potential yet abandoned direction. A temporal impasse, an evolutionary dead end, an avant-garde that had become kitsch. Olympic palace, ostentatious bunker, high-class memorial – all these eras were layered atop one another and enclosed within the huge tinted windows that (to all appearances) nothing could mar: huge, perfectly square windows seemingly dipped in gold. What a sight it had to be to behold the end of a world filtered through those panes. Here as elsewhere they blazed at sunset, turning, for a few minutes, this apparently soulless place into a gleaming cube of gold, its edges disappearing in a halo of light. During the war it was the entire city's favourite sight. And, as Amelia would come to discover, sunset had been the only moment to get some fresh air: the air conditioning had stopped working after the second week of the siege, and so they took advantage of those reflections, which blocked out their silhouettes in the snipers' sights. The irony was not lost on the experts; for the sake of democratised luxury, all the rooms of the Elisse hotel had a view: as such, all of them were almost equally open to enemy fire. Often people slept in the hallways. Over the course of the siege nearly all the windows were cracked, shattered, or smashed. Only bits remained of the upper floor, but even so at sunset the glass cube still stood as an undeniable reminder of its own existence, its sturdy form reminiscent of certain Aztec step pyramids: filigreed, worn down, but still standing.

*

A day or two later, ashamed of her own fear, Amelia ventured out. Solid, reliable information was hard to find, and what she did notice would go on tormenting her thereafter – all the while corresponding, in a vague way, to an unclear, hazy vision of things that had haunted her for a long time, since child-hood, in which her contemporaries were swift to see symptoms of mental illness rather than an especially keen knowledge of the world. What she noticed: Nadia Dehr multiplying, Nadia Dehr vaporised, Nadia Dehr apparently existing in several states at the same moment. And she wasn't the only one; this was something that the war seemed to do to people, to who they were. Nadia Dehr wasn't the only one, it bore mention-ing; she hadn't done anything special. On the contrary, she had more or less adopted the habits and customs of the wartime city, had more or less blended in, so perfectly that the wartime city had ended up swallowing her up, and she had disappeared without leaving any trace – or, rather, by leaving contradictory traces that were swept away like stick drawings in the sand. And so the facts would have to be re-established – later; when there were no longer lives to save. But who would report on the confusion, on what seemed to be confusion but was in fact order, however temporary yet real – who would recall the chaos that made possible these shifting states, these new skies of artillery shells and cluster bombs? In this way the petty criminals, the thugs who became war heroes, took part in the same infernal regime: they were everywhere at once. Normal laws no longer applied; *here* and *now* changed their meaning and could be both decisively *here* and *now* (the moment a bullet entered one's leg while running errands, for example; even when hiding behind a makeshift shield – a metal trash-can lid, for example, or a passenger door from a burned-out car) and not at all *here* and *now*, the opposite of *here* and *now* that would therefore be something like *everywhere, all the time*, and as such one could be in many places at once, play-ing many roles at once, a poet and a smuggler, and even in many states at once: wounded and unscathed, clear-headed and insane, and in the most extreme cases, simultaneously alive and dead. The besieged city was an experience at a 1:1 scale. Getting involved was just that; one couldn't simply be a witness. Everybody had a part to play. Everybody was waging war. Seeing images on television, hundreds or thousands of miles away in another time zone, while chopping vegetables, or decorating a Christmas tree, or talking on the phone: that too, Amelia said, was waging war.

And speaking of parts to play, Sarajevo became a stage of sorts. Cameras from all over the globe were trained on the city, journalists rushed there, activist intellectuals came for a stint there; they were framed in the cross hairs of cameras rather than snipers' rifles. It was one of the paradoxes of the besieged city: everybody rushed there and yet everybody also wanted to flee. For those who had suitable travel documents, the porous borders verged on the dramatic and the obscene; the obscene and the sinister; and more than once Amelia, in her search, heard about those Westerners who came for a bit of war tourism, some who would even pay whatever it took to go into the mountains or perch on the roofs to live the sniper experience, take part in manhunts, gun down civilians in their own streets or even through their own windows – and Paul, shuddering, saw symptoms of mental illness there, but whether the mental illness was Amelia's or the world's he was in no position to decide; it all seemed to him like a myth, as dark and cruel as any legend, but maybe his mind and his body, his physical self, just refused to accept such depravity. He simply blocked out such an unsettling prospect, while Amelia had no way or wish to resist it.

And speaking of theatre: Amelia's future husband told her about a part he had played, as a child, during the war, in a performance directed by someone he thought had to be Nadia Dehr, even if she no longer used that name – or even *any* name – at the time. A play that had left behind no trace, no relic, apart from the memories of the children who had become arguably troubled adults and vaguely recalled having played trees, trees descending upon us, that was one of the lines he (the husband) remembered, not entirely sure whether, in the play that Nadia had directed with the children, it had been a threat or a promise. In any case, he had been this camou-flaged child walking amongst the others towards the stage, towards the centre of the stage (which wasn't a stage but the basement meeting room of the Elisse hotel, and he remembered the football games he'd played there far better than those rehearsals, chaotic scenes that, going by his memory, only happened during power cuts – which might simply have been a way to endure those outages; in the darkness they had candles, he was sure he remembered that; but not always). But maybe he remembered wrong; as that, specifically, was what he was always doing, as a child, during the war: looking at the mountains around him and wondering whether they might descend upon the city. Whether the cabins, the trees, the flurries of snow would descend upon the city, whether the enemy army, or the guns of the enemy army, would. This is what he – we can call him Paul – remembered as an adult; is more or less what he remembered of Nadia Dehr. Before trying to find my mother and failing, Amelia said, I didn't realise just how relative everything is. Just how easily anyone can be both alive and dead.

So: the Serbian army was shelling the city, which was resisting. How? With what? The epicentre of international impotence, the world capital of the black market. Like a huge stage, and in this way everyone was guilty: those who conspired, of conspiring; those who survived, of surviving; those who looked on, of looking on; those who knew, of knowing; those who did not know, of not knowing. The most gruesome mass crimes were carried out without any witnesses, outside the city. Ethnic cleansing, torture, those things that Nadia Dehr had written about, with which she had filled a box. Had she seen them? There were ways to get in and out of the besieged city, unwritten laws decided how porous the borders were or weren't. Planes that didn't show up on screens. A tunnel in the mountain. Then she disappeared, we lost all trace of her, said Amelia, the way we lost all trace of the war profiteer who people say – and I have no reason to doubt them – held court at the Elisse hotel, at the bar of the Elisse hotel, and speculated on cigarettes and medicines and then vanished one day; and who people say (or maybe my mother just wrote it) woke up, his mouth dry, his head pounding, outside the city, in the forest, on the front lines; who people say woke up amongst the foot soldiers, the cannon fodder, the sixteen- or eighteen-year-old boys sent out to defend the city and who fell dead, and he barely had the time to realise what had happened to him before he was hit by a bullet. The besieged city might be the world capital of the black market but there was no question that a fundamental sense of justice held sway there – a wartime justice.

Science progresses, Amelia said. There are thousands of ways to raze a city, thousands of ways to wage war, and they change. They progress; some even claim that they *are* science, its most direct expression. Whereas the ways to resist – that is, to live in a besieged city – are always the same. You hide. You pray. You seal down windows, keep the rooms poorly lit or not at all, or with candles, with makeshift lamps. You wear several pairs of socks, or all your clothes. You burn books to stay warm, from the least-liked ones to the most beloved ones, from the least important ones to the most necessary ones (a book's use in wartime bears no relation, of course, to its charm in peacetime). You look (in the eyewitness accounts, it comes back over and over) at the gleaming tails of airborne project-iles. You wonder who could decipher the birth chart of this new life you're leading, in which all futures are impermanent, shuffled again, negotiated anew each day, each night. You slip into the darkness like cats; you celebrate for no reason; you set up music bands; rock keeps your soul going, that's the long and short of it – there had never been so many rock musicians or bands in Sarajevo as during the war. You say or think or sing or nod while walking down the road: kill me, kill me if you want, I won't exist any less, maybe it'll make me exist even more. A regime, a heretofore unknown intensity of existence, wholly unfamiliar in peacetime. You perform in theatrical produc-tions staged by idealistic, half-insane foreigners; a childhood amongst trees, a childhood as a tree – and afterwards, people forgot everything, pretended to forget everything, what mat-tered was what came back, what remained and what people refused to talk about ever again; or only did so with great difficulty.

I'm rediscovering words, Amelia added after some time. It isn't just a question of language. With you I can say things that I never say. I gave blood. For DNA identification, databases – for the mass graves which are still being uncovered nowadays, because someone reported one or a heavy rain, a mudslide uncovered one. Because nothing visible could distinguish

Nadia Dehr's femur or humerus from another woman's femur or humerus. And that, too, is a black market – a racket – if only you knew. Bribes. False hopes. False hopes were an entire industry during the post-war years I spent in this city. False hopes were a national economy. But if my mother's there, in one of those anonymous mass graves, it would be the acme of documentary poetry, its greatest triumph: proof not only that one can suffer from someone else's suffering, but also that one can die from someone else's death.

*

Reconstruction was bewilderingly swift, practically overnight, so to speak. Shrapnel vanished from the walls, bullet holes were plastered over and repainted, and the entire city – from the centre, the historical areas that were also commercial areas, to the periphery – smelled like fresh paint, hot tar, a huge film set. Looking for her mother, Amelia realised that she had come too late, that life's relentless forward march had erased not only the traces of the siege but also the memories of it inscribed in bullet-riddled, gouged-out surfaces that no longer existed. The more the city became what it had formerly been – and more – the less the people she met seemed to remember Nadia Dehr, who grew less believable, less consistent, who vanished into thin air. Became a myth, a ghost, a hazy memory not of a person, of a flesh-and-blood being, but of a legend, recalled with more or less certainty. Amelia found herself fleeing the reconstruction, taking refuge in the outskirts, in the neighbourhoods where the city still bore the scars of the conflict; but her endeavour was,

like fleeing a massive wave or even time itself, doomed to failure. She wasn't alone, however. Others also had their reasons
for not wanting the war to disappear from the city. They had
lived through it, grown up within it. The city was their mother.
The war was their mother. And this was how she met him.
We can call him Paul, if you want, she said to Paul who didn't
want to, not at all, but didn't say anything. He was young, but
not younger than her. He had grown up in the besieged city,
he knew how absurdly, impossibly constructed the stories, the
rumours, were; at the beginning she relied on him, he was a
guide, an interpreter, a machine for going back in time; then she
learned to understand him, his obsessions – he wondered if the
snipers' bullets were still buried in the walls, under the layers of
primer and plaster and paint, if they were still there like foreign
bodies, like pearls, fossils; and which hearts, which heads these
projectiles were aimed at even though people presumed they
were frozen, because their timescales were no longer human
but geological – geologically speaking, nevertheless, it was
clear that they were still on their fatal trajectory. Imperceptible
but fatal. At night he filled the scars left by mortar shells on
the sidewalks and roads with resin, with a red, vivid material
that solidified like pools of blood, which always looked freshly
poured but was as hard as ice or amber to the touch. This was
another idea of memory. Another idea of art. He felt personally
insulted, dispossessed, by this intentional, desired-for return to
something that they called normality but which remained reso-
lutely foreign to him. Which no longer existed for him, which
had been lost in mornings without water, afternoons of mortar

rounds, nights in blackouts. He felt as if he had been expelled or immured, like one of those bullets stuck in the walls. *His* city was the wartime city.

She mishandled the situation. All the love she had thought she could rid herself of by leaving Paul was transferred onto him; she thought she could see within him, within his apparently healthy body (and what a body, what eyes), a kindred soul, all her own obsessions reanimated in someone else – they spoke a common language that she had learned by staying with Albers, and he by watching television, and each time they thought they understood each other, she said, in reality they didn't. But she dreamed of an agreement, she dreamed of the understanding that she had denied Paul. Amelia was burrowing deep into the warrens of her words, and Paul at first didn't understand that *he* was the Paul she was talking about here. She mishandled the situation: she tried to save him from himself, she didn't see that she was the one who was drowning. He was getting drunk, he was getting violent towards her, she was already so lost that she believed those were the proofs of love everyone kept talking about. He yanked her shoulder out of its socket, he broke her nose. She stayed. Paul's stomach sank; the fact was that such violence was the one thing he couldn't have given her. He would never have raised a hand against her. The husband told her about the days, the years of fighting, and guilt gnawed at her, she wanted to shrivel up in light of his own experience. He made this woman, who had enjoyed peace in other parts of the world, pay. He made this woman, who had had the sorts of thoughts that Western children who bore no connection to the war thought, pay. She was both happy and unhappy. She got pregnant once, twice, it didn't take either time, the life she so wanted to feel within her failed to stir; it stayed there, however, a small leaden bullet, a foreign body. Fucking hell, Paul said. I felt at home, Amelia said, it's hard to explain. The more my body betrayed me, the more I felt at home.

She's gone mad, Paul thought.

She stayed with him a long time, several years. They lived together for as long as the war had lasted. Her husband (yes, Amelia confirmed) wove her narrative around these actions that he undertook at night, in secret – the resin, the plaster removal. This man, this body that had lived through the war, became the puppet through which she could express what she otherwise, she presumed, would have had no standing to express. Reconstruction as obscenity, erasure as crime, as continuation of war by other means. Or, maybe, the melancholy rage of a mind seeking, somewhere in the world, a landscape commensurate with its own devastation. She wanted a world in ashes out of which to revive the still-flickering embers of her heart. She made an artist out of him. He became famous. He dyed the fountains of the old world and the new world alike a vivid red. He fired machine-gun bullets into the ceilings of famous buildings and called it art. She was both nothing and everything; she was the wife. That suited me, Amelia said, and Paul knew before she did that she was lying. He travelled. He crossed the world and spread his message, an appeal for memory to becomes an arena and an experience, freed from the limited spaces to which it had been confined. Even the biggest plaques, the biggest monuments, were a stream of false memories, an artificial synthesis meant to free us from what they were designed to commemorate: instruments of forgetting. He travelled in this way, lived off this polemic against cities turned into museums and wars turned into museums and reigns of peace turned into museums; if it keeps going like this, he said (and it was she speaking through his mouth), soon, in the West, there will be only survivors and tourists. People listened to him, rapt, as an exception, an anomaly. Time passed. Amelia never accompanied him. She stayed there, at home, in *their* home, she said, even though those words rang hollow. She didn't find her mother, she didn't have any children. The city was rebuilt, then expanded. One day she came back to the house and she found him sitting at the kitchen table. They looked at each other for a minute, then he aimed the barrel of a pistol at his head and blew out his brains.

See? You had a close call! she said to Paul before letting out a low, mirthless laugh that sounded more like a cough, and quickly devolved into one. They went back to the museum. Do you remember what Albers used to say? About a *fearful* history of art? I was sceptical about it at the time but not so much now: Albers is always right. It just takes time. I assure you, she said, slipping her arm through Paul's in front of a huge picture by an American painter (an abstract expressionist whose worth was divine, exorbitant, preposterous, and who had painted a piece that several of Paul's colleagues, none of

whom knew each other, insisted they had seen unceremoni-
ously sitting in the bathtub of Amelia Dehr's father, whose
worth was equally divine, exorbitant, preposterous); an artist
whose works had derived their form and their function from
paint flung aimlessly across an unprimed canvas – I assure you
that you can't look at things the same way once you've seen a
wall splattered with brain matter.

She had odd hobbies. She walked down streets and counted
steps. She walked down streets and counted park benches, or
surveillance cameras, or worn mattresses on the ground, or
shattered bottles, or shards of glass. They saw each other more
often. They wanted to talk about art; crimes kept getting in
the way. They saw images of chaos, scenes of violence in which
they didn't recognise their city or country. They could count
mass killings or attempts at mass killings on the fingers of
one hand, and yet came to filter all urban experience through
them. The first time, he called her to see where she was. The
second time she was the one to call him. The third, they were
together and had to think about who to call. Can a city die of
fear? Paul wondered. It reminded him of something from his
younger days although he didn't recall what. What is it that
dies in a city that dies of fear? He nearly asked Amelia, but
held back. One day she said to him, Imagine there's an attack.
Right here, right now. She had pointed at the nearly deserted
halls of the museum. Imagine. What would you save? Paul
reflected. It would have to be something precious, of course,
but also light, he told himself. Or maybe something that
could stop a bullet. Imagine, said Amelia, smoke, explosions,

gunfire. The ground shaking. Screams. What would you save of the twentieth century?

Paul ended up shrugging. My skin, he said. She had laughed, that hollow laugh she now had. You're the best, she'd said, I always knew it. You'll bury us all.

The darker the hour, the more Amelia was herself again, was lively again. If only I'd known . . . I could simply have waited here for what I'd gone to find down there, she declared one night, in one of those extravagant restaurants that Paul took her to, more to prove something to himself than to her, for whom everything seemed equal, except maybe for danger.

She tried to live. She really tried, he knew her and watched her do it. She drew up lists on pale yellow sheets, chosen for the light that seemed to radiate from them, a wintry sun that must have been missing from her days. Shopping lists. Things she desired, things to desire, just writing down their names was enough for her. One day he saw at the top of a page, in small caps, like a title, THE BEST OF ALL POSSIBLE WORLDS, and nothing below. She bought lipsticks and organised them by shade, then by texture. They made love. The first time was hesitant, awkward, sublime. They were out of sync, clumsy, moved. The second time, already they were in harmony, efficient, a mechanical ballet that nothing, not even the heart, could disrupt. Paul felt sad and used. Amelia felt used and sad.

Get an apartment, Paul told her. You can't live like that, in your suitcase. (He travelled so much that he mixed up languages, or rather translated everything out of the nationless English that was now a black hole sucking in everything it touched.) She half-followed his advice, no longer living in the hotel but in other people's homes; for weeks or months she inserted herself into domestic fictions, in show apartments for a life not her own. She organised her lipsticks in the bathroom, pretended to be at ease. Paul worried a bit; he couldn't help it. She bought a pale coat, an off-white one with big wide sleeves, a big wide collar, and a belt – a garment that let the wind in in all the worst spots; the wrists, the neck – a snowy coat that she roamed the streets in, that she brushed every night, examining it as intently as a crime scene, plucking out imperceptible specks of dust, brightly coloured fibres, sometimes strands of hair that weren't hers: proof that she had been in the city, in the world, that her encounter with them had indeed happened. She wore trousers that bared her ankles, billowed elegantly, always in-between lengths; her wardrobe called to mind her unfinished gestures, which invariably fell short of their goal – before hitting their target, Paul knew, who understood her, who knew that any action Amelia completed wasn't so much an action as a blow. She tried to live but everything was complicated. Sometimes, she whispered to him, I look in the mirror and I don't recognise myself. One day she called him to ask where she was. I don't know, Amelia, Paul said, taken aback. He thought at first that she was lost. What do you see? The Eiffel Tower, Amelia said after a while. Take a cab, Paul said. Take an Uber. No response. Paul, Amelia finally said, if I see the Eiffel Tower, does that mean I'm standing in it? A chill came over him, and it had nothing to do with the weather. No, Amelia, if you see the Eiffel Tower that means you aren't in it.

147

She drew maps freehand, maps of abandoned cardboard boxes and the men who lay in these boxes, abandoned mattresses and the families who lived on these mattresses. Every day, every two days, the maps had to be redone. The city that had once seemed immutable became mobile, floating, even its smallest markers ended up disappearing. She gave away money. She gave away her coat, her watch, her address. Slept on Paul's couch. Then she didn't sleep any more. I don't know, she said, I'm afraid. Afraid of what, Paul asked.

She was afraid of disappearing, or of some essential part of herself disappearing (let's say: my feeling of being myself), or of a crime happening, with her or some essential part of herself (let's say: my sanity) the victim and another (let's say: this part of myself that I don't recognise) the perpetrator. Do you need to see a doctor? Paul asked, and Amelia rolled her eyes. He went to see her after work. He would watch her as she fell asleep. She wasn't self-sufficient any more, she needed to feel that she existed in his eyes. It might well, Paul thought, have been someone else's eyes, but as it was, he was the one who was there, in the apartment of a stranger greedy, perverse, or poor enough to open his personal space up to other strangers – something that would never have occurred to Paul. As Amelia was neither poor nor greedy, he worried about her lifestyle choice which was, Paul thought, not at all a lifestyle choice. More than once he ended up sleeping on the bed beside her, or on the floor, or in the armchair he was sitting in. One morning, in a kitchen, where they drank a coffee in silence, caught in a beam of light – the composition of the scene recalled both a Hopper painting and various advertisements – he, poorly shaven, still improbably attractive in his clothes from the night before, she in a pale-pink kimono that almost revived the glow of her twenty-year-old self – she said, in a joyful voice that was like the abrupt return of the previous Amelia, the long-gone Amelia: wouldn't it be funny to hide things in these apartments? Under a floorboard? In a wall? Nobody would know. And, one day, six weeks, six months later, when we're not even in the city any more, or this country, or (she didn't finish the thought) – boom. In the act of bringing his cup to his lips, Paul was stunned into stillness – there was a shift in the ordinariness, the banality of the moment. What had changed was the impression that this morning could have been lived and acted out by other people; the serenity of knowing that it could have been experienced by anyone else their age. And Amelia had forced them to view themselves as only them-selves – not others – by invoking this catastrophe. She broke out laughing. Deprived of the comfort of not having to be himself, Paul wasn't sure how to react. They had sex standing up in the sunlight, but decided not to talk about it, not to think about it, and soon it was as if it had never happened.

*

Of course, he had done some research. No sooner had she turned her back than he'd pulled up all his screens to gather the necessary information about art, war, revolvers; he put all the pieces together in a matter of seconds, down to the model of the gun he'd used to kill himself. We can call him Paul, if you want; that wasn't his name, of course, but that didn't slow him down, or barely did. Everyone's identity was reduced to a net of words that wrenched an absent body, wrested it, wrung out the opposite of words: an image. The photograph of a hulking, sad man with a beard, his arms crossed, thick gold and silver bands on his ring finger and his little finger. Bands, but no wedding ring. Index, thumb, and middle fingers that he used for everything, including pulling a trigger, all sensibly unadorned. We can call him Paul, if you want – but why should he? Paul didn't want to. He pieced together all the facts but never knew what it was like, to step into a room that he had called home, and to see a firearm, a mouth (a chin? a temple? so many particulars escaped him); he never knew what the light was like, what that strange dissociation was like – that thing that had settled between she who saw everything without feeling anything and she who felt everything without doing anything, without being able to do anything – between one and the same person. Amelia, with perhaps a shopping bag dangling from her hand, maybe heavy enough for her bluish veins to stand out on her wrists and the back of her hands, it's possible to figure out a woman's age that way, too, her hands clenched and relaxed. So many things one never fully knows, Paul thought; and if art means the contagion of an experience, the inoculation of an experience that wasn't lived yet was still felt, then all that remains is to find the form through which it can all be internalised: the light, the strange sentiment of being nailed there without any sentiment, the gunshot, the smell, the smells, a whiff of bone, powder, seared brain and hot blood. Of course, if this form existed there would be no way to distinguish it from life, and in that way it would amount to torture.

As for art, the husband's career had been brief and not as notable as Amelia had made it sound. Less notable, but, perhaps, more interesting. One day, he had released a wolf into a downtown park in Berlin – the only European capital that supports art to this degree, or *this* kind of art to this degree – a wolf who had terrorised the population, a wolf seen by people and photographed in the bushes, *there*, a wolf that might have been two animals, or a whole pack. Wolves are intelligent, social animals; they have a code that doesn't allow them to abandon a member, even if old, even if wounded – yet wolves carry a sad reputation. It was a wolf people protested against all day and all night, in front of the park, on the sidewalk, protected by railings. It was a hunted wolf which revived ancient, deep-rooted, seemingly long-forgotten fears; it resurrected the nearly obsolete art of battue hunting, the principle of which had remained and would remain unchanged – which itself revived a continuity, a tenuous thread through human experience: armed men padding through the grass at dawn. It was a wolf that they forced into the open and took down one day, and another – but they were just dogs, and the lupine madness reached a point of no return until it became clear that there was no wolf; there had never been one. No matter how many officials insisted otherwise, the wolf kept on being sighted, it went on haunting particular dips in the land near the lake.

Amelia, oh, Amelia, thought Paul.

*

The video of a conference in a museum auditorium. The man starts talking in shaky, heavily accented English – he seems drunk, or quite simply ill-suited, yes, wholly unsuited to this context – and it's mortifying, but also thrilling; the schadenfreude of seeing a man drowning in his incompetence, and not feeling obligated to help him out. Not feeling obligated to ask if he *should* be helped out, in fact, because the incompetence had begun elsewhere, before, and would continue on forever, whether or not there were any witnesses. (This was one way of looking at it.) He tries to explain about the wolf, the park, he thrashes around in his words; he digs himself in deeper, like sinking into quicksand and finally, in exhaustion, he gives up the fight. The silence builds up; just when it becomes unbearable, he smiles, as if an idea had suddenly occurred to him, and he bends down for a second, the camera too slow, lagging behind his movements. There's a box by his foot, a cardboard box that he opens before the camera lens finds him again. Out of it comes or has come or is still coming something or several somethings that can't be seen, something or several somethings slipping under the tables, into the audience. The expressions captured by that tragically slow camera evince disgust, pure terror. But the camera never manages to show what has emerged from the box, a dark shadow going this way and that; it's clearly alive. A woman climbs up on her chair, another on the table. Very slowly, stumbling backwards, the ones in the back row attempt to escape. The others don't dare to move a thing apart from their faces, which coalesce into a collective mask that Paul didn't believe he had ever worn himself, but which even so he immediately recognised. This was the sort of art that Amelia created by proxy. The continuation of documentary poetry by other means.

In several photos of the artist, there seemed to be a presence in the background, someone who could have been Amelia but wasn't. Amelia's lodged within his skull, Paul thought as he studied the portraits of that unlucky rival, Amelia's the wild gleam in his eyes. Was it Amelia he was trying to chase out of his head with his gunshot?

5

Well, if she wants a child, Paul thought, I'll give her one. Why not? At no point did he ever doubt his, or their, ability to reproduce. A man knows these things, rightly or wrongly. But she did not seem to want one any more, or at least not one by him. She complained about having been shunted back and forth her entire life, this way then that, and if that had been the case when she was a child, was it still so today for her, an adult woman apparently unable to do something as simple as renting an apartment, putting her name on the door, establishing boundaries of some sort between inside and outside, between public and private. It's up to you, said Paul, whose sole mission right then was to get her to eat, to watch her sleep. He was discovering a groundswell of words within himself, words he had never used: *replenishing, revitalising*. He thought them without saying them but it was enough to put a scowl on his face. At the heart of his love for her – a love that was less and less a matter of flesh and blood and sex – at the heart of the compassion he felt in watching her struggle like this against herself, there had been a bedrock of anger, of rage: as if she had been above it all, too good for him, for them, for the game they were all playing. The homes and lives that everybody, Paul included, struggled to build were undone by her. Whether by choice or fate – a compulsion she had to obey – no matter which, her refusal of work and family cast a pall over everyone else's existence. Sometimes Paul hated her, especially early in the mornings, when he left for the Agency. He hated her because she alone could grant herself that insanity, he thought, that slow disruption of her health, of her mind; could grant herself that freedom not to be professional, not to make a living. But he would rather ignore those unfair, unrefined emotions. All Paul had (he believed) was what he had earned himself. He was taking such care to avoid all judgement, all unkind thought towards this woman, and yet he didn't realise just how much this proved he was his father's son. He set aside these feelings and tried. He really tried. He changed apartments. He had never liked furniture, furnishings, but he did love space, yes, a particular ceiling height, a particular brightness on the walls, of course not all whites were alike, he picked a dusty tone with the same care that others did their household appliances, their mattresses; what mattered to him was light. For this city, for Paul who had no inheritance to claim, it was an impressive place. He imagined Amelia crossing it barefoot, in one of his shirts. When she crossed it barefoot, a Wednesday, late afternoon, the light warm and slanting, his shirt pale, her hair red, short, ablaze, he got a glimpse of what would be a dream become reality, a fantasy that could have been his alone just as easily as it could have been emblematic of the city, the era: comfort, a sense of entitlement and belonging, security. Or what passed for such. He had rarely felt so proud, so satisfied, to have been able to give this to Amelia, an instant in space. Of course it was really for his own gratification, this trajectory of a few seconds that had cost him so much time, so much money, so many sacrifices, a loan, not only the decades gone past but also those yet to come, years devoted to repaying the interest that would accrue after the moment that had just taken place. She did not notice anything – for her, this moment in this place was all banal, ordinary, not worth any attention. He wasn't upset with her. He was never upset with her for not wanting what could be wanted. All that, the apartment, the shirts, he did for himself, not for her. He was afraid of what she aspired to; at heart he knew that he didn't have much time, that he would have to rush to experience, with her, a pale shadow of what they could have had, which did not interest her at all, not at all. He feared regret.

He took her to restaurants. He took her to London, to Cabourg, to all the natural history museums he could find, to the homes of imaginary detectives where they could none-theless admire the lounges, the bookshelves, and try on the detective's hat; it looked better on Amelia. In bed they had their routines, as they did on trains – straightforward, plain gestures, which made them seem like an old couple, although that was how they had already been acting when they were eighteen, at university. She taught him particular things, which cropped up again every so often and which she described, pensively, as if she were wondering why she knew what she knew – for example that people like to sleep with another person because the body is lulled by the heart of the other, by its beat, even when it can't be heard. I've never met anyone whose heart beats as loudly as yours, she told him, anyone at all. It's a strong heart, a swimmer's heart. Powerful and at the same time just strong enough that I never forget that it's just a muscle. At heart, your heart is just a muscle.

Of course, Paul said.

That decade he seemed to be a distant man, a cold man.

He introduced her to his father. They took the regional train, he had nothing left to lose. He wanted to experience, with her, these moments that had, in his youth, been unthinkable; now he wanted to test her, to make the world he had come from collide with the world she was from, to show her what she had never known (but it was worse than that: she knew about it, she just didn't care to think about it). Poverty, austerity, at best unsentimental pride – a pride that was a dead end, that came to nothing, and had no alternative, no possible way out. His heart was pounding when they entered his father's place. His swimmer's heart, that organ that allowed him to sense injustice, between these walls that despite repeated offers the man had never wanted to leave, these walls that unsettled Paul, spooked him. The smallest and tidiest place in the world (even now, it seemed to him, smaller and tidier than ever), he had no idea how it could hold all three of them, Amelia, his father, and him. Or all four of them: Amelia, his father, him, and the photograph of his dead mother on the wall, which his father introduced as though she were alive, there in flesh and bone, *my wife, Majda*, and genuine confusion passed across Amelia's face because that day she had forgotten everything the two of them, Paul and her, had in common: loss, longing, the memories they couldn't be sure were real or invented, pieced together from stories, from photographs, from secret wishes. Loneliness. But his past was different from hers. Where were the family legends, the grand stories, the political convictions? Where was the old money? Can one dead mother be equal to another, when one was an adventurer and the other a simple housewife – one who enjoyed being simple out of self-esteem, out of self-discipline, who was determined to love what she had, not to conquer what she didn't. Ruthlessly cutting off dreams of elsewhere which others might fervently pursue. A feeling of calm responsibility and dignity; an open heart – and when that heart stops beating, who would be so cold as to call it just a muscle? A mere muscle?

If his father was surprised, of course he didn't let on. He made some tea, and on the wall, Paul saw the traces from the sponge that it had been scrubbed with. Paul saw the grille on the window and beyond that the faded lawn and beyond even that a disassembled motorcycle, and secretly, he was happy to hear his father say to Amelia, I believe my son mentioned you, one time, a long while ago, at which he turned towards Paul, questioning and almost worried at having said too much, and for a moment he and she both looked at him, through the steam rising from the tea, in the tiny living room. He couldn't tell what his father thought but he knew, without a shadow of a doubt, what Amelia was thinking: that she had never before wondered whether Paul spoke of her or not. She assumed he did. She now realised she had been wrong.

A long while ago, yes, my father has an excellent memory, said Paul.

*

They travelled. It was in Paul's nature to worry, so he tended to overdo things, whereas Amelia, who wasn't easily swayed, teased him a bit for what she called his urges. His nouveau-riche impulses. She turned down India and the palaces. She turned down Malaysia and the beaches. He picked up his coat and walked out the door. In the end, they simply went to Italy: she rented a practically bare room for them in Ischia, that island of gardens and springs. He had to concede she had been right.

During that stretch, time felt strange for them, an interminable present that seemed to include the past, their youth, but which the future was pushing, pressing into already. Ischia was a verdant island off Naples, famed for its thermal parks where soldiers and civilians had come to recuperate. Even today afflicted bodies could be seen – and Paul had already noticed them – convalescing: bodies that the modern era generally shunned, considered distasteful, timidly revealed themselves at Ischia. It was both a shock and a kind of relief. The pink of burn wounds. Eczema. Stumps. Evidence that the world damages each of us. And, amongst scars, shaky gaits, prostheses: Amelia. Radiant. Her forehead slightly red, her shoulders even more so. Seemingly intact.

They meandered between thermal pools, scalding water and icy water, and ended up, illicitly, on a private beach, slipping under the nose of a lifeguard probably fixated on something more pressing. They weren't going to pay up just to bathe. The transgression made the moment all the more delicious; the mere premise that they weren't supposed to be there made the surroundings all the more breathtaking. Of course, I never feel like I'm supposed to be wherever I am, Paul thought, and so the world never stops astonishing me. Amelia walked towards the sea with a self-assurance that could have been feigned or could have been real, he couldn't be sure which, the self-assurance of someone who very much was supposed to be in the right. I swam, thinking that this green, clear water, this fine sandy beach, like the sun and the sky – that all this was due to subterfuge, and was, I confess, all the better for it.

When I came out of the water, she continued, when I'd got back to the beach chair and that silly straw umbrella – all those umbrellas arrayed in a line that, from the water, looked so pleasing – I stood a while in the sun. I was look-ing at Paul and thinking that he hadn't changed in all these years, of course time and fatigue had lined his features, had accentuated his jaw a bit more as with some kinds of men, but ultimately it was still him; still Paul. Unchanged in appearance. As if time had no hold on him. That was when a drone flew over the beach. I remember it made almost no noise, which was astonishing given its size. The drone slowed down, turned around, it descended to the height of an aver-age man or woman. Then the drone stopped in front of me, at eye level, and we looked at one another, the drone and I. At first, I folded my arms over my chest. I felt naked, which

I actually was, more or less, but I felt far more naked in front of the machine than in front of, say, Paul. She isn't lying, Paul thought as he toyed with a crumb from the loaf Albers had asked him to pick up before dinner. It was raining outside, and Albers had started a fire in the fireplace. He could remember that day clearly. Amelia kept going. I smiled, embarrassed, I shrugged, as if the drone was someone, and someone able to be appeased or just affected by a slightly ashamed look. Then I felt ashamed of myself. I wondered what this drone could be thinking. I took a step to my left and the drone followed. It didn't seem to think it was ridiculous to pay up just to bathe in the sea.

The next day I came back and I waited, but it didn't come again.

At the beginning, when they saw a drone, Paul and Amelia immediately thought of war. It was the first thing that came to mind and that day, on the beach, her body had reacted as if it were staring down a weapon. The machine had felt obscene to them, and they, Amelia especially, needed to sweep it away from their perception; it threatened them in a present that they still mistook for the future. Yes, this still felt like the future, Paul thought, but it was very much the present. Maybe he was getting old. After that the machines began to slip here and there into their daily life, all the way into their bedroom. On Amelia's computer, they looked at an interactive planisphere where they could see images taken by other people's drones. It was oddly addictive, even though they never saw anything especially interesting. It reminds me of the Elisse hotel, Paul said, except instead of the hallways and elevators in black and white they were looking at aerial views of fields, industrial zones, in-between spaces, neither public nor private, of uncertain status. And in colour.

*

Things happened that didn't seem like much. They carefully picked out furniture they never bought. He properly met the father, this immense, hovering presence, about whom Amelia had always been reluctant to speak and whom Albers never mentioned, but it was obvious he had played an essential, pivotal role in the fortunes of the Dehr women. A relative presence, and an unnerving one: the textbook definition of a twentieth-century man. A white, rich, powerful twentieth-century man. So many people were determined to think like him. He didn't think about them at all. The effort it inevitably took them to live with and beside him gave him the illusion of being universal. His relationship to the world was an over-powering one.

Paul remembered the one time he had met him; the man hadn't bothered to shake his hand; he had looked at him as if he belonged to the Elisse hotel or to the globalisation that had allowed Elisse hotels to spring up like mushrooms everywhere. Your father looked at me like I was scum, he said to Amelia, like some kind of mongrel – something I could never call myself. You're wrong, Amelia shot back, and I don't remember my father ever coming to the Elisse, so he can't have met you. Now, put on a tie. No, Paul said. Amelia laughed.

He was nothing like Paul had expected; the man he'd imagined was immensely lonely; coffined, almost. Amelia, moreover, had never mentioned her father remarrying, having other children or a wife barely older than her. Amelia had never mentioned that the woman he'd always believed was the most desirable one in the world had been an unwanted child, that his heroic love for Nadia Dehr had just been a lark, a fling, that at the time he was already married, just not to this woman who had scrubbed all trace of identity, all genealogical detail from her features, in favour of a narrow nose, prominent cheekbones, just in order to fit in. She had created for herself a face that seemed objectively, universally successful, and which in a few years would prove to be yet another relative code; by then, her features would already be sagging and slipping away.

So her father had turned into a patriarch, with sons likely conceived out of vanity, Paul thought. Lifeless, wordless teens as pale as if they hadn't seen the sun in years. What a chilling family, what a horrid man. But when the man in question, having been made aware of Paul's existence, pulled him close, into personal space generally reserved for those he knew well, for friends – he felt the heat of his ruddy neck – he was flattered. He couldn't help but feel strangely seduced.

He ruled an empire, claimed to have pulled himself up by his own bootstraps, which was neither true nor false. His own father had given him a few thousand francs half a century earlier; he had bought a truck; then thirty; then these trucks had transported goods, merchandise, but the real money had been in sand – that, Paul hadn't known. For buildings, for housing estates and hotels; but that's nothing new, of course. The sand was used to make concrete. Amelia went oddly quiet and Paul wondered whether Nadia, too, had gone quiet in the same way, for how long, for what reason. When her head turned to her half-brothers, she appeared not to see them, and they seemed to avoid glancing up at her; any time she entered their field of vision, they lowered their heads, as if it was important not to believe they were seeing a ghost. A vague, undefined terror seemed to rule their lives, and they almost seemed relieved to be able to fear Amelia. To be able to put a name to it.

And the father was still talking. The father who was a patriarch, a universal man, universally envied, and, undoubtedly, universally hated – his success, the story of his success, seduced Paul who hadn't expected to be seduced, who hadn't wanted to be seduced, and who had come without a tie, ready to stand defiantly in solidarity with Amelia. He felt drawn, despite himself, into the orbit of this man. He couldn't help but be spellbound, he felt himself turning momentarily away from the woman he loved, because he felt something in his blood, a desire to succeed, a form of individualism that, in other circumstances, could even have been healthy. Something was wrong in his relationship with Amelia, he knew it, in the way the limits between them blurred, but he refused to admit it. After the meal, he followed the man, as in a dream, into what he called his lair, his office, he wanted to hear about this project Paul was working on, about his desire to start up a business of his own and the reasons for this drive, he wanted to see if this guy had what it took, he was always interested in good deals, genuinely keen to hear other people's ideas; for all his egocentrism he could still accept that other people – younger ones, maybe, or educated differently – might have more of a finger on the pulse. This sincere, if self-interested, curiosity must have been what drew him to Nadia Dehr forty years earlier; but the pulse Nadia Dehr had had her finger on couldn't really be monetised, and as such couldn't interest him for long.

Paul followed him and Amelia let them go. She played with the stem of her wine glass, tipping it so that the candlelight caught in the crystal and light refracted onto Paul like signals in a language he was unable to read. He saw her so alone all of a sudden, as he stood a few feet away – he wasn't used to seeing her at this distance; she seemed strange, estranged from him, weighed down by a sadness that could break stone – just a few minutes, he told himself, a few minutes, being friendly with Amelia's father is, after all, a way of being friendly with Amelia herself. Of course he was lying to himself. He stammered out a few ideas, he sounded like he was talking in his sleep, convinced that the man was only listening to him out of forced politeness. Amelia's father asked him about his education, his career, which caught him off guard because he had braced himself to account for his background, had rehearsed retorts for every blow of condescension – but the oligarch simply didn't care. He didn't see a person in front of him so much as, maybe, an opportunity. As he talked, Paul could see Amelia through the door, twisting the base of her glass between two fingers, twirling a lock of her hair between two fingers. It had been a few weeks since she'd gone to the hair salon and maybe she'd decided to grow it out; the longer strands softened the angular face of the woman who'd grown up too fast. The man followed Paul's gaze and, misunderstanding, said, Her mother had beautiful legs, too – long toned legs, she almost knocked me out, it's unbelievable how much there is of her in her daughter, it's criminal, he declared. Paul started and furrowed his brow. Well, she owes a great deal to you too, he said. The patriarch smiled at Paul's reply since, fundamentally, what he would have liked were perfect clones of himself formed by spontaneous generation, but the stubborn Nadia Dehr had saddled him with a wild child. His second attempt had been with the next wife, who was gentler and calmer and more obliging, and that too had been a failure, his sons were quite spineless. What in this world would it take to have heirs worthy of their inheritance? And Paul laughed and said, We all get the heirs we deserve, and, sure enough, those words met with the patriarch's approval. He did seem to have what it took, this strange young man who seemed comfortable everywhere because he wasn't at home anywhere. He had known men like him, he thought, and always in times and in places on the brink of collapse. I'll be in the office on Monday, he said, call my secretary and she'll see if she can arrange a time for you to come in and talk about your idea, and Paul thought: so this is how he's fobbing me off. He couldn't bear being talked down to. And, of course, he had completely misunderstood.

*

She moved in with him. He convinced her the way he might have coaxed a frightened, wounded animal that had wedged itself in the tiniest recess possible, under a step, between two walls, and which he was trying to lure out without getting attacked. They told nobody except Albers, who came to dinner in the immense apartment Paul had had painted dusty white. She came laden with presents: books so heavy that their art, Amelia quipped, had to be in the scoliosis they induced. Massive bottles of champagne, fancy candles, each one guaranteed to burn for forty hours – forty immaterial, extraordinary hours (carcinogenic, too, Amelia insisted once they were alone), silk scarves that she unfurled from her handbag like those failed magicians who sometimes, although increasingly rarely, performed on the street. This is just too much, Albers, you really didn't have to, Paul finally said, but there seemed to be no end to all this genuine happiness, and even so all these objects seemed to be trying to hide something feigned, something false, that they ended up exposing all the same. Flowers would have been present enough, he said. Albers smiled, as if he were joking. She brandished a huge box that seemed to be even bigger than the bag it had come out of, and wrapped in shiny paper. Paul's breath caught. It's Nadia Dehr's box, he thought, those are Nadia Dehr's fragments, she can't do that to me, not now. The blood drained from his face as he remembered the man who had had a pigeon set in his mouth, a live pigeon, and who didn't mean to, but had ground his teeth during the torture. He felt like he was on the brink of spitting out feathers himself. I can't have that in my place, he thought. This place would always be his, not theirs, never *our place*. They already knew that their cohabitation would be short-lived, a kind of mourning ritual. But Amelia was already ripping off the metallic blue paper in which she saw, or didn't, her own faded, deformed reflection. They were genuinely surprised, for the first time, and Albers burst out laughing. It was a small drone. She remembered, she said, from their last vacation.

They could be found in stores everywhere but for them it was still the future; they gawked at the machine like country bump-kins. Later on, Sylvia, who was younger, would make fun of him for it; for now, however, Amelia sent it flying, and the future hummed in the immense living room. Sheesh, Sylvia would say years later, what's wrong with you? This place is way too big, it's way too empty. I mean, listen: it's *echoing*. You bought a cave! It's like a canyon, the sound's bouncing all over, it's ridiculous. What's the point, even? The little machine nearly crashed into the wall or the ceiling once, maybe twice, before Amelia learned how to control it properly. Albers must be offering us a bit of time, Paul suddenly realised. Albers must be offering us a future, and he wanted to hug her. The drone still represented the future, even as it had become the present for the conflicts just now brewing. They weren't unaware of its uses and had grown inured to them; these new weapons had, at that point, become little more than words, ideas, an abstraction, and they found the gift less shocking than they would have if Albers had offered them, say, a toy gun. Paul's father came the following week, walked through the apartment without noticing the high ceilings or the original floorboards, so fixated was he on other concerns: were there enough power sockets and radiators; where were the meters and the fuse box; was it all electric or were the stove and water heater still gas. He wanted to be sure his son hadn't been taken for a ride. Having finally agreed to sit down, he played at launching and landing the toy, nothing more. Making it take off, making it land, watching it just as inscrutably as he had, years earlier, watched surfers falling off their boards in the waves. Paul drove him back to his house in a comfortable silence that lasted until the minute his father stepped out of the car, buttoned up his fleece jacket, and said, casually (although Paul knew it had been very carefully thought through): I'm not worried. He said it as if he had been weighing up the decision, still considering the prospect that he might be wrong.

*

She wouldn't go along. She wouldn't let herself be loved. Not the way Paul would have liked. There were arguments, drawn-out ones, where he insisted on knowing where she was, and with whom; one or two early mornings spent calling everyone he could think of – he didn't know any of her new friends, assuming she had any; to assuage his fear and fury, he ended up calling hospital after hospital, because he had to do something, anything, and he lost his head at some point, heard himself yelling into the handset at people who didn't care, if there was even anyone listening. Here was a man whose wife wasn't really his wife, whose wife hadn't come back home that night. He shut his eyes and described her, first her hair, then her complexion, her lashes which were neither light nor dark; he shut his eyes and recounted how they met, and his hopes, which she had systematically set to destroying. Then he recounted things he saw, the wounds she must have sustained or (he understood later) *should* have sustained, as punishment for the nights and mornings she inflicted upon him. On the other end of the phone there hadn't been anyone listening for a long while, such a long while that there wasn't even a dial tone, and Paul described the horrible accidents he feared – he saw her with shards of bone jutting out of her skin, or trapped in a car on fire, or her side sliced open – and eventually he ended up understanding that what he now feared might in fact be what he, deep down, longed for. He stayed there, mourning not only her but also an idea of himself. She disappeared until Paul was forced, briefly, to face up to himself, wild with anger and fear. To see who he really was. To take the full measure of his buried desires, the ones he made a point of ignoring. Oh Amelia, he finally thought, just go ahead and fucking die, so we're done with this, and there he was forced to concede: I'm such a bastard, and he stayed there, worn out in the immense apartment that she didn't care about. Then, and only then, would she return. He would hear her setting her keys on a table, taking off her shoes; he would know at last that she was safe; he would feel relieved, disappointed, furious. He would pretend to still be sleeping. Another man, at another moment in his life, might have followed her, or have hired a professional, a private eye, who could have provided him with a detailed report on the secret life of Amelia Dehr; but not Paul. Yet another man, or maybe the same one, would have started drinking heavily, no doubt would have hit her; but not Paul. The one thing that did hold him back, he knew, had nothing to do with the empty, false idea he had of himself as a good man, and everything to do with his pride, with his self-love, which was, he thought increasingly often, the only kind of love that reigned in this home he had wanted to build and where, in the face of Amelia's absence, or of her secretive, slippery presence, there was too much of Paul, too many degraded versions of himself: Paul was confronted by all his potential selves, alcoholic Paul, violent Paul, self-conceited Paul, cruel Paul. Staying himself, someone he could live with, became quite the ordeal.

What a bastard I am, he thought. He was driven to despicable behaviour. Nobody would have said that, of course; on the contrary, they praised something they struggled to define and which was – although they had no clue – his survival instinct. Paul, however, knew that it was more complicated than that. In one way they were right, but in another, surviving Amelia was exactly what he was trying to do, exactly what made him an asshole: making a resolution to outlive her. The great betrayal he was preparing himself to commit.

When it did happen, it did so, in fact, quite naturally. One day, something within him gave way and he stopped resisting. He saw Amelia's father again. He went all out, swore fealty; they drank amber-tinted alcohol, smoked cigars, traded a few lewd jokes and not a few bad puns. In the twenty-first century, everybody will be in safety, he said as a foregone conclusion of sorts, with a handshake. The line struck him as ironic; he remembered, much later, that it was a misinterpreted sentence that Albers had once uttered. And then he thought: whatever. He took the money. Left the Agency. Started up the business he had talked about. The more self-assured, the more detached he became, the less arrogant Amelia now was – in a way, she was less herself. As if she were dwindling away, he thought. He seemed to be watching all this from a long way off; his distance tormented her. Her gestures lost their precision, she stumbled, she looked up to meet his eyes, uncertainty crept into her words. She regressed into the unloved, unwanted child she had been; one who made up imaginary friends. She couldn't make sense of what was happening. There she was, in front of him, raw and hurting, and he closed his heart off to her, refused to sympathise with her, because at this stage, Paul thought, only one of them would make it. Everybody believed that he was kind to her, more than kind, that he'd tried to give her everything, but she didn't want it. Even his father, whose insight and judgement he feared, was fooled. The truth, Paul knew, was that he was an utter shit. The truth was that she needed help, needed love, that she was sick and that refusing love was, in her mind, a way of accepting it, of asking for more, but he couldn't go on. He'd had enough. We can't go on like this, Paul said, You know this, Amelia, I'm exhausted, I can't do this any more, I deserve better than this. She looked down. At some point she lifted her legs slightly to slip her hands under her thighs, like a little girl. She cried pitifully, quietly. But you love me, she said, you do. It's too late, Amelia, it's not working. It never worked.

It was true in a way that she couldn't deny, but it was false as well. She didn't have the words to say it. It had been working quite well between them. And if Paul didn't like what had worked between them, that was his problem. Why did he have to go and shame her? It's tearing me apart, Amelia said, it's like my left hand is breaking my right.

Their gazes met for a moment and then, right there and then, Paul became one of those men who have power and wield it, at the expense of the women who made them. I'll call you a car, he said. Wait, Amelia said, but he wasn't having it any more. He was businesslike all of a sudden, determined to reject feelings and bankruptcies; feelings that became bankruptcies. There was no overt violence in how Paul dealt with Amelia's protestations; it would take some time to see that. In another century he would have been the sort to lock women up in asylums for hysteria, or have them walled them up in an attic or a cellar or some other dark cranny. Should something manage to break through the heavy stones – a plaintive moan, say – they wouldn't hear anything or would pretend not to hear anything or would say, It's the wind, whistling across the moors.

Wait, Amelia said. I'm pregnant.

night as it falls

I

And what do *you* do for your security? A reinforced door, maybe? An alarm system? Or just one of those solid, trustworthy, multipoint locking systems? A few simple rules: be careful in the dark, be wary of strangers; a so-called smart home that knows whether you're there or not; and that knows or will know soon whether your heart, tonight, is beating too quickly, beating the way a heart in safety never would.

The more money you have, the more paranoid you get. Paul knew this, of course, but didn't admit it. What he did say was: fear doesn't protect you from danger. He said: the average time for help to arrive, in case of a break-in, is X minutes in your neighbourhood. What you need, at least, is to be able to delay for that long. It's probably around half an hour: he updated these statistics regularly, painstakingly, neighbourhood by neighbourhood, case by case. All the numbers he had were reliable; more reliable than their sum, which was the picture he painted for them, the fiction he created – the hellish fiction his potential clients were all too eager, were being encouraged, to embrace. One cubic metre of oxygen per person was enough for five hours of total self-sufficiency, in case of a biological attack or a nuclear accident. Think it through, because the answer to this question will save your life: what do you need? Call me in three days. And they called. And their answer was never the right one. This Paul knew, but of course never said.

On the one hand were certain dangers that were real; on the other were fears that were irrational, even outright fabrications. The force field created by that tension allowed Paul to establish himself in a certain space, to grow and prosper. In the twenty-first century, he was in security. He created elaborate surveillance systems, alarms that just a breath could trigger – or maybe even a thought. He sold armour-plated doors and windows and walls, sensors that detected intruders deep inside buildings. Ironically, he also sold vault rooms that, hidden within an apartment, within a house, made it possible to live in absolute secrecy, wholly autonomous, and evade all the aforementioned devices. He himself had one, at his place, a clandestine monument or tomb of sorts, that he never stepped into.

*

She loved him even when he no longer loved her, obstinately, because she had denied her own feelings once and what good had come of that? None at all. Art. Crimes. Lost time. She loved him for nine months, loved the baby she was carrying since it was his, and she who had been so articulate and eloquent never found the words to tell him so, to convince him that she was there for him, now, that she was ready. But there was no point; all the while something in her was conspiring to pull away, yearning to drift away into oblivion.

He cared for her during the pregnancy. He was irreproach-
able, which, to her, was perhaps the worst reproach. Their
relationship had become purely transactional. She wasn't doing
well enough, didn't trust herself enough, to know what she
would end up understanding later, much later: Paul had loved
her and he'd only ever loved her, and even when he said he
didn't, when he didn't want to, he still did. She was the heart
beating in his chest, the powerful swimmer's heart that never
seemed to tire no matter how tired she, Amelia, was. The birth
was difficult; she nearly died, the baby too. There was a C-
section and, under anaesthesia, she thought she remembered
things she had endured rather than experienced, thought she
remembered the infant extracted from her belly as being blue,
a bloody eel of umbilical cord knotted tightly around its neck,
as if nothing that came out of her was or could ever be viable.
Barely born and already blue. Of course, she knew these things
only because Paul told her, later on, about the complications.
Had it always already been too late for them? When she opened
her eyes, she was in a hospital bed, a handsome man was sitting beside her, a tiny baby in his arms, and she didn't recognise
them. In her morphine-induced torpor she had turned towards
the nurse, worried, and, as if the two women were in front of a
scene, rather than within it, in Life L, she asked her in a whisper: Are you sure this is my family? Paul would never forgive
her for that either. She would never be able to tell him just
how intensely she'd hoped, right then, seeing them there – so
handsome, so alive – that they might be her family. She didn't
deserve them. She couldn't deserve them, not her, not Amelia

Dehr, daughter of Nadia Dehr and a man who had never loved her. Daughter of Nadia Dehr and an emperor of sand. It was something she would never find the words to explain.

There was a language of gestures, of reflexes that she didn't have, that didn't flow from her heart to her brain, much less from her brain to her hands. When the baby cried it was Paul who got up, Paul who slept on the floor, beside the cradle, who set the small body on his, who deep within his sleep protected it. He tried, even so. He tried in every way possible to make her a mother; he left her with the baby one day, without any warning, to force her to care, to love. Came back a few hours later to find Amelia and the little one in an armchair, under a lamp, the baby half-asleep, bobbing, its head heavy with heavy thoughts, with wordless images or no images at all. Its eyes were shut, almost shut, a thin white crescent appeared between its lashes; the pupils tucked under the lids; and Paul knew that his daughter sometimes slept like this, her eyes not entirely closed, but he still felt a pang in his heart, a small shock, because she looked like she had fainted. Amelia, holding the child in her lap, studied her face, her head, as though it were an object. Her fingers, her delicate hands which Paul knew well and which knew Paul well, were, Paul suddenly thought, probing the tiny forehead, the tiny skull like a stone. He inched forward like an animal, the way one might draw close to a potentially dangerous rival, made more noise than he would have liked, and asked in a low voice if all was well.

Amelia looked up at him – she seemed absent, or annoyed. Look, she said, in an equally low voice, so as not to wake up the child, or something else, or both; I think it's all fine but come look anyway. Paul leaned over the small sleeping head, its bluish temples, the blood present underneath. He sometimes swore he could hear it as if it were his own blood, his own pulse. I'm sure it's nothing, said Amelia, but she couldn't disguise a tension or a worry in her throat, a purely physical phenomenon. Well, I don't know, look – I thought, for a second, I thought she was a little – that she was red-haired.

Paul gave up after that. He took care of his daughter, and otherwise lived a solitary life, contained within a few stolen minutes here and there. One day Amelia saw him on the street with a woman who she thought at first was her. But if I'm over there, in Paul's arms, under Paul's kisses – if I'm over there, then where am *I*? The question defeated her. She agreed to everything. She took medicines that made her face and her wrists swell up, that numbed her, dulled her hair. She went to the hospital. The electricity that illuminated the city, that warmed homes and the baby's milk, fuelled the night light that bathed her bedroom in pastel tones of green, blue, pink – this same electricity ran through Amelia's temples to instil the light and warmth she lacked. That was what she told herself, even though she knew, deep down, that it was torture. Nothing more. Nothing less. That the night in her head was the only place where she could still be safe, and that it was being cleared away by force. She ground her teeth. She didn't mean to, but she did.

She got better, and when that happened, Amelia sat Paul down and told him that he was right. That it wasn't working.

Some life had passed through her. She had done her best, it was the best she could do, and now she was going to leave, because she couldn't be a cuckolded woman and the cold-hearted mother that she was, a woman who watched the man she loved with other women, who watched the face of her only daughter like a river pebble that would only reveal something in its grain if she looked hard enough, searching for a vague resemblance to something she'd once known and loved. It's better if I leave now – because I know what it's like to have known and lost one's mother.

Paul looked at her. He's looking at me like he's going to kill me, Amelia thought. Like he's going to pull a knife out of his pocket and kill me. A knife that wasn't there until I said my piece, a blade that my words brought into being, resting against the heat of his body. Is that how his mother died? He's never told me. I wonder if he even knows, Amelia thought. Did the evil she saw everywhere exist in the world, or only in her eyes? This question was at the heart of her insanity. Paul looked at her, and didn't say anything. He's going to grab my hair and drag me into that secret room he had built, Amelia thought, that sound-proofed vault impervious to everything, maybe even the end of the world. Maybe even the end of us. He's going to throw me in there and never open it again. Yes, it's like I'm already in there, she thought. That's where I'm going to spend the rest of my life. Banging. Screaming. And nobody will hear me. My daughter will grow up without knowing her mother is there, a few feet away. In the darkness. Forever.

Paul just looked at her.

2

What was left of Amelia? Nothing, apparently. Nothing, or very little. Paul ground his teeth. He didn't mean to, but he ground his teeth. He would have to talk about her to his daughter, he thought; what he would, or what he could say, he turned over and over in his mind – but what about the rest? What really mattered? His own art, his own crimes – his memories? What should I do, he wondered, with everything I don't have the words to say? And so he kept silent. At the beginning, as if unintentionally. And he took what Amelia herself had warned him about many times – the lesson of the expunged Soviet astronauts, the lesson of the effaced traces of Sarajevan conflicts, and he applied it. He applied it to Amelia herself, to the woman he had loved and still did, whose daughter he was raising. *That in death as in life thy body may be*, and during sleepless nights he completed the line of poetry she had recited, the only one that wasn't Nadia Dehr's. *That in death as in life thy body may be roses*, be roses and streets and neighbourhoods, be the city I live in, that oppresses and poisons me. Be all the cities, all the poisons. Be all the nights. Try not to think about it, he said to himself. But the past wouldn't let itself be forgotten, war wouldn't let itself be forgotten. The two crept in – how is that possible? You shut your eyes for just a second, or so you think, and she's already there. Her scent. Her pulse. There.

He wouldn't believe in ghosts. He had decided that from the beginning. They had decided together. They wouldn't believe in ghosts. They would believe in love, in words, in numbness, and in silence, but in nothing else. In nothing that could whisper in their ears. In nothing that could walk through walls. He put everything that remained in a box and sealed it shut. This visible absence, with its clear-cut lines, its evident volume, was the shape he intended to give the future.

Of course, you can't shape the future.

∗

He tried to be a good father and, the world being the way it was – in spite of what it was – he must have been one. Louise's first encounter with death was that of her parakeet, a yellow and green thing that had hopped in place for several months, stoically, with an indifferent, glazed, perhaps afflicted eye, in a cage shaped like a Japanese pavilion; the bird saved from its decorative role by the unalloyed, childlike love Louise bore for it as a pet. A living being smaller than her, and yellow, and green – Louise loved it. She wasn't afraid of anything, not its beak, not its claws, not even of the dark, nor of big dogs she clung to excitedly, with Paul, paralysed, shutting his eyes, sure of the worst. But nothing happened, Louise always ran back to him, he squeezed her small hand, swore to himself that he would never let it happen again. At first the cage seemed empty to her – she was too small to see what was inside, it seemed like a delightful mystery to her: shut cage – no bird. It had the promise of a riddle. But the small, lifeless body hadn't escaped Paul's notice, and he felt an urge to come up with something, a pretext, to explain away its disappearance, so that they would never have to talk about it. Louise wasn't old enough for that, he thought, which was absurd: is a fish ever not old enough for the water it swims in? Is one ever not old enough for the reality one lives in? So he didn't do anything; he let her approach it, stand on her tiptoes, look at the little bird lying there, What's wrong with it, Daddy, and he waited for her to take it in her hand, to feel with her fingertips the lack of life in the feathers, the body that she could now squeeze in her hand, feeling the air leaving not the inside, the organs, but the space between each feather, discovering that in fact there was an animal there much smaller and much more fragile than she could have thought – more nothing than anything. And yet, a life that no longer was.

Louise had seemed somewhat sad, but only, oddly enough, because her father seemed to expect her to be. She had whispered into the dead bird, as if she were trying, with her own breath, to fill the feathers again.

He had to ask, a bit insistently, very gently, for her to open her hands.

*

He tried to be a good father and suspected he wasn't. He didn't know what to do, he learned everything on the fly; he was overwhelmed, out of his depth, at his wits' end. Like every other young parent. He went to great pains. Lived haunted by his own betrayals. He tried to buck his usual assumptions when he might perhaps have done better to buck all prevailing trends. But nothing doing. He couldn't. Not him. Paul was, he thought, as he watched his daughter sleep, utterly compromised. He'd climbed up and up the social ladder; his ambition had driven him to reinvent himself again and again. He'd been unaware; he'd erased his identity; he'd erased his very origins. The one thing about himself he could feel certain of, now that he was as inconstant and changeable and fluid as water, was his love for Louise. He wanted to protect her, protect her from everything, from the world now ending and the one now beginning. But it wasn't enough to protect her; he would have to prepare her. Prepare her – but for what?

He missed Amelia.

*

He taught her how to swim. How to run. She had the same taste for effort that he did, the same seemingly indefatigable heart. They were good friends. They explored Paris through its swimming pools. On Sunday nights the father and his little girl slept in hotels. Never the same one. Louise loved the velvet benches, the strange lamps, the paintings or murals, the stairways they got lost in, the elevators that stopped at various floors, the room-service menus with which she learned how to read. On Mondays he dropped her off at school, her head still filled with their adventures. He was charmed by his daughter and his daughter was charmed by him. I'm not bringing her up to be my wife, he thought one day, and the strangeness, the obscenity of that line made him ashamed – where did it come from, this idea he'd immediately pushed away. It's not enough to entertain her, though, he thought. No. It's necessary to prepare her. But for what? He could have confided in Amelia, but not in anyone else. He would have liked for his daughter, his only daughter, who was growing taller and getting older, his daughter with a strong heart and a stubborn spirit – he would have liked, deep down, for his daughter to be able to kill a man with her bare hands. Only then would he feel like he'd come up to scratch, not before. When she no longer needed him. For now, she was four, eight, ten years old. Long lashes, dark curls. She resembled him. He was proud of it, and worried, because he thought first and foremost about Louise's safety and would have been more reassured if she looked nothing like him. He increasingly came to understand his own father, his determination to erase everything. His name, his language, his very self. He'd chosen to call his son Paul, chosen to live so that he could go unnoticed. All that, to feel safe. To blend into the background. Camouflage, really, Paul thought. Which meant committing unimaginable, private violence against himself.

Like his left hand was breaking his right.

*

In his later years, the grandfather turned to birds. He set a birdcage up by a small window and it was the prettiest and saddest thing to see, those darlings in captivity. Yellow ones, green ones. Blue ones. We'll set them free one day, won't we,

Louise, said the grandfather, and Louise in her little dress nodded, wisely and patiently. Her feet in her little slippers didn't reach the floor but swung in agreement. We'll set them free when they're ready, Louise said, looking lovingly at those sweeties, those treasures with distraught hearts that fit in her hand, and Paul knew that the birdcage was meant to console the child about something she had perhaps forgotten, that she didn't talk about any more, the First Death. And also, simply, to lure the wealthy son and the beloved granddaughter here, to this small apartment, the smallest and tidiest and saddest apartment that ever was, that the grandfather, who she called Gramps, refused to leave. Insisted that he never wanted to leave. Dad, that's stupid, you spend days on end at our place, leave this apartment, Paul said. But his father pretended not to understand, not to hear, a comical look of confusion on his face. Louise laughed. There was nothing more delightful or fleeting than Louise's laugh. Paul said it again, Come on, Dad, it's stupid, come live with us, there's all the space you could need – *us* being Paul and Louise, and, he soon learned, the neighbours' cat, whose real name they didn't know and whom they called, because of its beautiful feathery tail, Plume-Cat. Whenever the neighbours opened their window to let Plume-Cat out – to wander and live its secret, nocturnal, feline life on the roofs and terraces and gardens out of sight and reach – the cat simply went next door, to Louise, who cuddled it until her eyes were red and puffy. The catnapping was re-enacted each night, and the allergic child, whose Plume-loving lungs wheezed, couldn't handle her passion any more, and more than once Paul was struck by the thin red veins on the oh-so-white white of her eye before setting the animal outside as ashamedly as if he had been caught in flagrante. Louise cried, begging for Plume-Cat in between sneezes, and Paul, trying to console her about the reality of things, about cats and the night, lay on the floor beside the small bed, and both father and daughter shut their eyes as he told her about how the animal roamed over the roofs and terraces and gardens out of sight and reach, and how the cat's paws padded almost inaudibly on the zinc roofs; shadows – shadows that flowed where nobody imagined they could fit; the city that was immense and asleep or the city that Louise imagined was sprawled and stretched out in sleep, like a cat itself.

This is how I should talk to her about her mother, Paul thought, but the moment he thought that, they were both asleep, she deeply, he half so.

The birds are just a ruse, Paul thought. My father is well aware that she's a little rich girl, a little girl who's nothing like him. But he was wrong. About his father and about his daughter. The two stubbornly refused to be who he thought they were or who he wanted them to be. In this mystery was their identity. In this resistance.

*

He wondered what to say, and how to do so, and time passed. He didn't imagine, couldn't imagine, that what he kept silent about had a life of its own. He didn't imagine, and by not doing so gave rise to something unintended nonetheless.

189

Amelia had told him, though: you can be contaminated by what you know, but also by what you don't know. Silence is an organism. It's alive and it seeps in. But Paul didn't appreciate it, not yet, he would have to step back in order to see it fully; and he, with his own story, his own ignorance, was unnerved first and foremost by language.

One day he heard an incomprehensible babble coming from his daughter's bedroom. He barely paid attention to it – she was only five, and at the age of making up imaginary words and imaginary friends. He did as he usually did – a single father and a business owner – and opened a bottle of beer and the mail, and noticed, smiling, that Louise seemed to be chattering endlessly in her secret language, when she normally expressed herself with less volubility, weighing up her words with some degree of hesitancy, as one might count foreign coins. He kept on doing as he was doing, lulled by his daughter's chirping, until the moment when his paternal, animalistic brain, the one that only thought about danger, the one that was buried within his skull like a strongroom in a wall, heard an answer. An answer just as incomprehensible and long, but an answer in a deep, low voice that he didn't recognise and that made his hair stand on end. He rushed into Louise's bedroom, his heart pounding – and found the little girl in conversation with his father, his own father, in a very clean, frayed, impeccably ironed shirt, in very clean, frayed, impeccably ironed trousers, and they broke off and looked at him, with round eyes, polite, innocent eyes, waiting patiently for him to explain his sudden interruption. What are you doing? Paul asked, and Louise shrugged and said, in the humorously learned tone she sometimes took, Daddy, we're talking, as if he didn't understand a single thing, as if he were the child and she, at five years old, the adult. And they smiled at him, but they didn't say anything further, and he backed out apologetically. Soon he heard them again. This time they were whispering.

The language of birds, he thought idiotically, they're talking in the language of birds. But that wasn't it. They were talking in the father's language, from the land the father had left and spoken of so rarely to Paul, whom he had given that name and who had grown up feeling as if he had been set there, in an urban disaster, in an urban jungle, as unsteady as though he were on water.

Does it bother you, the father had cautiously asked him later, once Louise was asleep, her mouth open, her sights set inward, towards a world that belonged to her alone, the same way the roofs belonged to Plume-Cat, and the nights to Amelia.

Not at all, said Paul, not at all.

A pause.

But you never spoke to me. Never taught me anything.

The father finished emptying the dishwasher. He was pensive, measured, and the dishes clinking against each other barely made any noise.

It's different, now. Louise is safe, he said, with an unthinking gesture (but did his father gesture unthinkingly? Paul didn't think so) towards the walls, the floorboards, the high ceilings, the view of the sky and the Seine, the unsuspected strongroom between the walls, and maybe all the strongrooms of the city, unsuspected between walls.

*

Paul, on the other hand, felt that danger was everywhere. Everywhere. He talked about it sometimes with his mistresses, even met with them to talk about it, and once he'd run through all his worries or once they were turned on enough, they stopped talking and got into bed. If not for his father and Albers, he wouldn't have made it, he said. He had found an apartment for Albers not far away, a carbon copy of his own, not out of generosity or an overfull heart but because it assuaged something dark and fearful within him to be able to imagine Louise in the same exact setting on the nights when she wasn't with him. He knew, down to the nearest second, the time she had dinner, the time she took her apple-scented bubble bath; and being able to envision her so precisely freed him and allowed him to go about his business, whatever it might be, as a bachelor and as a predator of sorts.

There were daily, daytime fears; fears of falls and germs, fears of madmen and the future, fears of new weapons. Fears of robots and pollution. Fears of attacks, explosives. Knives, hammers. Fears of driverless cars but also fears of cars with human drivers, of reckless drivers. Fears of epidemics that spread from birds to men or from birds to cats or from cats to children; fears of illness, fears of mental illness, fears of academic failure; fears, no matter what he said, of difference; and some of those fears were ones that Albers, in her carbon-copy apartment, shared. The decisions, however, were his own; this was why the paediatrician, holding a gun of sorts that shot compressed air, got ready to inject a small chip beneath Louise's tender skin that would allow Paul to follow her position remotely. More and more parents were doing it; others weren't, others said that their child wasn't a cat. Paul said it as well, and yet this defence was futile against his fatherly anxieties about the world as it was. If something happened, he would never forgive himself for it. He had quickly weighed up the pros and the cons. The pros were the world and Amelia. As there was this inherent, inchoate danger that Louise might be, would end up being, her mother's daughter. A risk Paul couldn't fathom. Or maybe (and this made him shudder) it was to be expected. The cons were a lack of decency or respect for Louise – for who she was and who she would become, but in these new times that seemed short-sighted, a luxury that he was not allowed to indulge in, despite having access to everything. Yet it also seemed gentle; something that provoked nostalgia, and he didn't want that. The pros and the cons. Everything could now be broken down into columns, into statistics, have I gone the wrong way? Have I gone completely off the rails? Paul stifled this worry in order to reassure Louise, who barely needed to be reassured. It won't hurt, kitten, it'll just be a little pinch.

She had a bruise for several days, a bruise in that shamefully beautiful blue shade of other people's pain; but when he logged in for the first time to check where his daughter was, he saw the map that confirmed that she – this luminous dot, glowing blue – was at Albers's, exactly where he expected her to be, in the dining room which was a perfect copy of his own. A peacefulness that he hadn't felt in a long, long time came over him. Like every parent of his time and class, he tried to prepare her against all the dangers he could think of. But the problem, a sympathetic yet mocking voice within Paul said, is the dangers you don't think of, the ones you *can't* think of. The unforeseeable is the apex of danger, and to predict it you need something other than your ever-younger, ever-prettier girlfriends – who couldn't imagine anything for the life of them, except perhaps new ways of coming – something other than your paediatricians and your screens and your pitiful, domesticated fears.

When she turns sixteen, I'll tell her everything. I'll tell her everything she should know, he decided. Whether that was a threat or a promise, he wasn't sure.

*

Once a month Louise slept at her grandfather's in that unpleasant, unsafe little town. It meant that for Paul or for Albers, it would be a bad night. But the ritual was important; the child clung to it. It was the night when they bathed the birds, she explained to her mystified father. The night when they took them, one by one, from the cage, so carefully that it was as though their hands themselves had a mind of their own. Very tenderly and gently, they put the quivering creature in the bowl of warm water, a metal bowl with an enamelled flower – a trembling image – at the bottom. They washed the little things, let them flutter around, shake themselves dry in the fountain they had made, and into which Gramps sometimes poured a little bit of water from the kettle. That was what Louise liked best in the world. A fragile, living ceremony in a language that was secret.

It's all fine, Paul told himself, but he still slept badly. He sometimes woke up for no clear reason, his throat clenched, his heart pounding. He heard his daughter crying when she wasn't; he heard windows opening when they didn't. His exhaustion took strange forms; lights alarmed him even in the middle of the night, even in the darkness. He shut his eyes, buried his face in the pillow, but the light was relentless and it left him no rest. Leave me alone, he sometimes said in his sleep. When he woke up, he didn't remember anything.

He still didn't believe in ghosts.

Yes, it's all fine, Paul told himself, which didn't keep things – the world – from getting worse. There was, apparently, too much of everything. But not enough peace. And water was getting scarce. Louise pensively watched it come out of the tap. She turned the water on, turned it off. Watched the small helices it made as it flowed into the basin. Of course, the innocent girl had no idea the desert was spreading across the globe and into hearts. The love we have for our children is a Trojan horse, Albers declared on a talk show. Louise watched her, slack-jawed, she who usually walked indifferently past those newsflash images following each other endlessly: murder and investigations, ruins and war, immense cities that weren't cities but tents, arrays of tents in the desert, where those who no longer had a city now lived. Louise touched the surface of the screen – it was, and wasn't, Albers.

A Trojan horse. The love we have for our children is how an indefensible world can seem defensible and ultimately is defended, is welcomed. Lies. Global surveillance. Insidious militarisation. Who wouldn't want to know that their children were safe? Who wouldn't be willing to pay a high price for that? It's out of love that we reinforce our cities, our streets, our houses. But evil is what gets in. Evil, and all our errors will haunt us. They'll come and gnaw away at our sleep, our bones. We live in a world that has given in completely to brutality and injustice. Every man for himself. Every man for himself and his own children. His own genetic material. And in the meantime the driving force of the world has become expulsion. Families on the street. Cities razed, entire populations forced to flee. Everywhere I turn, I see unreality forcing its way into reality. The uncanny has become normal, and the fantastical has become the condition of our existence, Albers ranted, insistently – and all that Paul saw was an obstinate old woman crowned by white bangs.

She repeated herself. The fantastical has become the condition of our existence, Paul, she whispered on the phone. An impossibility that's suddenly become possible. I know, Albers, I saw you on TV, but I want you to take care of yourself a bit. The world's changed.

She was put under house arrest. For your own safety, they said. It would have been dangerous otherwise. An armed guard was placed in the lobby of the building and nobody was quite sure, really, whether it was to keep evil from coming in or to keep Albers from coming out.

✳

Paul knew every sob his daughter heaved; it was almost a language. This knowledge wasn't innate – on the contrary, he had spent his days and nights, in the first weeks, the first months, listening, deciphering her cries for a possible cause, a stimulus, an emotion; Albers said that he was a mother to the baby, she maintained that he was a seer, a diviner, she smiled but he suspected that she felt a faintly hidden resentment. His father didn't say anything. Don't you think your boy's something special, the old woman had asked without understanding that he didn't really talk about such things, that he didn't praise or mention anything, that he didn't discuss or compliment or criticise in general – it wasn't his style. But, put on the spot, he thought a bit and then said: He's a father. Nothing could have made Paul happier.

He knew those cries and those tears; the way everything sometimes combined, exhaustion, frustration, hunger, nightmares; a wet bed, a chill; the bedroom and hallways – which suddenly dilated so that she was alone, alone in the world, on a small damp mattress unmoored in the unknown like an island in darkness; until her father's familiar footsteps could be heard and all this emptiness around her reconfigured back into what it had been; a few seconds of waiting before the closeness, the warmth, the comforting words that she understood instinctively. Later on, he knew when she was ashamed, or when she was bored; he couldn't have said how, he just knew. The cost of this knowledge was becoming a light, fragile sleeper; he was now an animal ready to leap. And leaping was what he did one night, when Louise was about seven, and Paul's sleep was riven by a scream in which he recognised Louise's voice – although it was not like anything he had heard before; it sounded like no physical or psychical need she had ever expressed. What's that, he thought, literally feeling his hair stand on end, a sharp cry so acute that it reached into the inaudible, the ultrasonic, something that was not meant for the human ear to hear (but what ear, then?) and he had run into the child's room. Louise, sitting in her bed clutching her knees, an expression on her small face he had never seen before, was staring at a corner of the room, at the armchair where Paul had so often sat for a moment after reading her a story, before leaving his daughter for the night. Louise's arms were tight around her knees as she rocked back and forth. The window was open.

Paul hugged her, kissed her beloved head. What's wrong, my dear, what is it? And Louise didn't say anything, he thought maybe she was still dreaming, her eyes apparently open but turned inward, and he rocked her in his arms, warming her with his whole body through the small quilt, rather than first getting up to shut the window, and at the moment he finally felt her relaxing, at the moment when he himself was starting to nod off, Louise whispered in his ear:

The woman. He thought he had to be dreaming this time but he asked, What woman, my pet? The woman with fiery hair, Louise said, and Paul held her tight, There's nobody, sweetie, there's only you and me and we don't need anyone else, he whispered, but the truth was that he didn't dare to turn towards the armchair. He shut his eyes and did what he didn't know how to do because nobody had ever taught him: he prayed quickly, without realising that that was what he was doing. This is like a nightmare, he thought.

*

He never talked about Amelia. He said as little as he could about her, and hoped that would be enough. He looked at Louise, he watched her, she didn't seem to lack anything. But a child is not a bird. A child is not a cat. They played in the beautiful empty living room and Paul had terrible visions: a tall redhead walking through the walls and out the window, throwing herself down to the sidewalk below. Yes, a tall redhead, caught in the walls like a bullet shot many decades ago, a bullet which still pressed on, imperceptibly, coming from another point in time, but who could say, even so, that it wouldn't break through one day? Her fists and knees first, then her nose, her forehead, the rest. All the rest. And the final step, the jump through the window which wasn't even open, her fall a rain of glass, of shards in which the sky is momentarily reflected. This sky she hadn't known how to love. He suppressed his obsessions, pushed forward a small horse or pawn or other figurine meant to represent him within the game. Louise was having fun and he was incredulous and grateful beyond words for his daughter's innocence. Until the day when he caught her tapping the walls with a spoon in her hand. Hello, she said. Hello. And pretending to listen carefully. What are you doing, pumpkin, Paul had asked, a growing sensation of unreality in his chest, of unadulterated dread. I'm looking for Mummy, said Louise.

It's worse if you don't say anything. If you don't say anything, evil flows in and permeates, percolates through the heart of everything. Even so, he struggled to talk; what could he have revealed to Louise that she would have understood? That when the plants in the bathroom which he had bought because his daughter had begged for a jungle in which she could be a wild animal, when these *monstera deliciosa* and *monstera obliqua* trembled in a breeze he couldn't feel, it was like a sigh that he hadn't felt for years on his face, on his body? It's worse if you don't say anything. But what should he tell his daughter about a woman who, in the maternity ward, hadn't recognised them? A woman who hadn't loved them? And what should he tell her about his lovers, whom he brought home some nights, kissing them sometimes in the bathtub or against the sink, neither Paul's body nor those of these women leaving any trace, the surfaces retaining no memory of it, the debauchery slipping right off them, onto the pale-green tiles, onto the dark, gleaming leaves – or about what some of these women, these strangers, were feeling or claiming to have felt – some hostility, some presence?

He showed her some photos. In the one he liked best Amelia was wearing one of his shirts and Louise asked if she could have that one. We can frame it, if you'd like, he'd said, wondering what it would feel like to walk into his daughter's room and to see, each time, on the wall or by the bed, the sum of his failures. Not the photo, Daddy, the shirt, Louise said. How strange this child was! Not interested in images so much as in what was tangible. What could be touched, tracked, captured. At the museum she focused on the ground and the corners, blew on dust bunnies, loose strands of hair, everything that could come alive with a movement, intentionally or not. Come on now, Louise, look – the lady. The mountain. Look at the sky. But Louise said: That's not a lady, that's not a mountain. Pictures of skies upset her the most – she got angry, wrinkled her nose, slipped away, kicked off. Insects, by contrast, were a deliverance. You really are a little animal, he said. But he was charmed.

So Paul gave her a shirt that looked like the same one. For a few days, a few weeks, Louise wore it to sleep. Then it went back on a coat hanger, in the wardrobe, where it hung amongst the blues and greens of her childhood, at a slight remove, white and empty.

*

One cold spring day, he drove to the city where he had grown up to pick up Louise at his father's. He found them in a room that struck him as larger than usual, chillier too, until he saw what was missing: the birds. The birdcage was empty and his daughter and father radiated something, an electric feeling, a strange light (was that what had made him sick? He refused to believe it), they stared at him oddly, silent and energised.

Louise was ten and her face was starting to change, to slip towards that of a stranger; her nose, her mouth, were on their way to their final form; but to become who? He still wasn't sure – he simply saw what he saw, his father, his daughter, a new silence between them, an empty cage, the two of them glowing. Did you let them go? Paul asked, stupidly; they nodded together, and caught him off guard; he had thought that all this time they'd planned only to let them go when the birds were ready, which also meant, We'll let them go when *we're* ready. He thought that meant never. That no one is ever ready to let beauty out of one's life, no matter how unhappy that beauty might be. And he thought that it was still cold, too cold for colourful small birds in a drab city, and an image came to him – like the foreign ones that seemed to have come from somewhere outside of him: exotic birds – yellow, blue and green – raining down on the roads, unfit to survive in urban settings, tragically out of place.

And he who was the voice of reason, the family man, pushed away that image or vision or fear or desire to see colourful creatures plummeting, dead, onto windshields, onto umbrellas and balconies, pushed it away and kissed his daughter, then his father, and said: It's a bit chilly, maybe you could have waited a while longer, given yourself a bit more time, and they didn't say anything, didn't look at each other, but something changed, something imperceptible. And in that moment he understood. No, they couldn't have waited any longer, they couldn't have given themselves any more time, and they looked at him, his daughter and his father, without saying anything, and he knew that they knew, that they wouldn't say anything but that they knew, and less than a week later, without any warning, or seemingly without any warning, his father was dead.

*

Only then did he discover total loneliness, thorough isolation. He shut himself away in his strongrooms, in his clients' homes, he curled up on a bunk, reverted to the lost student who hadn't dared to leave his room because he didn't understand, wasn't sure he understood, how he should talk, should move. He wasn't sure he knew how to live. Louise could have consoled him, but no daughter should ever have to comfort her own father, he thought, and he didn't want her to be afflicted by his sadness which was far more than just sadness. He kept his distance. He spent hours and hours alone, not moving, not thinking about anything. An empty shell. He cried, but only in his sleep, and it wasn't clear whether he was crying for himself or for his father – nor did it matter which. You have to take care of yourself, Albers insisted to him, if you want to see your daughter again. He saw a therapist, a level-headed woman who worked on setting him to rights again, on making him a man amongst men again, a proper master of the universe again, and he listened to her obediently, but the whole time she was talking and he was answering, with difficulty, the same way a child might grasp at words, the way Louise grasped at French – the whole time, a part of him was bashing in the woman's face with a hammer.

He ended up getting a room in an Elisse hotel, their Elisse hotel, he insisted on room 313 with an authority he didn't feel. In the elevator everything came back to him, and in the hallway, and in front of this door where things had broken: voices, furniture, maybe bones; and certainly his heart. He fell onto the bed which couldn't possibly have been the same one, slipped between the sheets which couldn't possibly have been the same ones, and that night, at last, he felt a body against his consoling him about everything, the only one capable of saving him from himself. Living the madness turned out to be how he survived it.

Later, he wondered if it was that night, under the bedspread that had been sprayed, or maybe not, with flame retardants, in the night light's glow, in his hallucinations of a reunion, that he fell sick.

*

Like so many fathers, he tried to protect his daughter, and like so many fathers, in the end he failed. He couldn't shield her from everything. From cold, yes; from hunger, and illness, from some injustices and attacks, yes. From some images. And some ideas. But in the end, it wasn't enough. As always, there was still the unforeseeable. There was still art. There were still crimes. When she's sixteen, he repeated to himself, then she'll be ready. Which ought to have meant that he himself would be ready. But the world didn't wait. There was an unpleasant moment, after school, when he couldn't find Louise anywhere and heard someone saying, in a cheerful tone, that her mother had come to pick her up; and Paul had, in his rage and his fear, knocked over a table with one hand, as if it were nothing. You're scared of me, and you should be, he said, you don't know what I'm capable of. It turned out to be a misunderstanding; Louise – his Louise – was waiting for him outside, where the other kids were, at after-school sports practice.

He enrolled her in a prohibitively expensive private school where the students wore uniforms, and the first time he went to pick her up, in front of this flood of pleated skirts and jackets, mute anguish seized him: I won't be able to recognise her, I won't know which one she is; but he picked her out in a tight cluster of students – she had seen him already, had probably seen him a long while earlier; their eyes met and he had the impression of having passed a crucial test, unlike any other, as if, without his realising it, everything, absolutely everything he knew about love had been at stake. And then she smiled at him, from afar, and walked towards him, slowly, so as not to look, in front of her friends who were at once more and less than friends, like she was running to her father. But he saw her knees quivering a little with impatience, with love, while she made her way towards him. Finally the group of girls reached him, girls about to be women, who studied him silently – a prospect that terrified him – and Louise turned towards them with a shaky voice that, as he set his hand on her shoulder, she barely managed to control in saying: This is my father. The moment required all the solemnity she could summon, she, the new girl, the one who had to prove herself, earn their affection and admiration and appreciation, and Paul hated these girls judging his own, as ridiculous as it all seemed. But he declared, as seriously as he could for Louise's sake, Ladies, it's a pleasure. Call me Paul, please, and an electric shiver ran through the entire group – a shiver of what exactly he never did know, but the girls looked at Louise approvingly, and he saw her holding back a triumphant smile, a small pursing of her lips, he didn't understand anything about these creatures but he understood that the balance of power had shifted; and Louise gave him her schoolbag, and swiftly turned her back on these girls who were nothing and everything to her, saying: Come on, Paul, let's go home, this place sucks.

*

She asked questions about her mother and the answer was always the same; he had met her at college, in Albers's class (Albers was still Albers); they had fallen in love; she was dead. But what was she like? the child asked. It would have been better if I hadn't said anything, Paul thought. An adventurer, he said, an explorer. She was a traveller. Each time, Louise examined his face, and more than once he had the feeling that she wasn't listening to his words at all; she was scrutinising his face for tells, for signs that he was lying, trying to confirm doubts or suspicions.

*

And then she turned twelve and he could have sworn he saw the unmistakable strap of a bra suddenly disappearing in a drawer; suddenly, she shut her notebooks when he arrived, tilted away her phone's screen when he got close. A boy came over one day, a pale thing, half a head shorter than her, whom she peered at, through her lashes, adoringly. What! This wimp, this wilted creature who looks like he's never seen any sunlight, Paul thought; seriously, his ears are see-through, and that's just peach fuzz there! And his temples! So thin and blue that you could just squeeze them and push in his skull – like cardboard – that's him, that's *the thing* my daughter, my only daughter, with her powerful, indefatigable heart, can only look at with lowered eyelashes! And he watched them, helplessly, cloistering themselves not in her room – he would never have allowed that – but in the room he'd once thought his father would have moved into, the sitting room, and Louise shut the door so he had no way to be sure that they were just sitting; a brown curl hung over her face – strategically placed, Paul could have sworn. He who, suddenly a stranger in his own house, found himself prowling the hallway, his adjoining office. It's all a nightmare, he thought. I'm not going to listen at the door, he told himself, I'm not going to listen through the wall. He imagined himself holding the end of a stethoscope up to the plaster, or, worse, an ordinary drinking glass he'd press his ear against to amplify the sounds. That washed-out kid! He's got to be asthmatic, he thought, he's got to be unable to do anything, just getting an erection would kill him. Love was a matter of optics, unless it was a matter of worry or fear, in any case the strangest images kept cropping up; Paul had never thought he had so much imagination. Jealous of a

white-blond boy, just a kid – and yes, circling like a hawk. All
the same, I'm not going to be one of those men obsessed with
their daughter's virginity. He thought about calling Albers,
instead wondering what she would have done in his place.
He stepped into the sitting room that was suddenly no longer
for just anyone to use, with a plate of cookies in his left hand,
and the right one primed to pull the pipsqueak away from his
daughter's perfect body – and two small heads blindly turned
towards him, swaying under the weight of their virtual-reality
headsets. They were sitting on the couch a full three feet away
from each other – too far away for their hands to touch – held
vice-like in those machines. Paul was always terrified by how
such mechanical additions to a human body could hobble its
user, though of course he knew that inside that apparently
inert shell was another world, far vaster than any he could
dream up. He himself used it sometimes, for violent games
that he hid from Louise, games in which he broke necks with
his bare hands, games in which he showed the enemy no mercy
and in which the enemy showed him no mercy and in which
the blood spouting from a head wound tinged everything
with a reddish haze; and when he imagined himself, alone on
a couch, in the middle of the night, a non-existent weapon
in his fist, a non-existent knife between his teeth, jolting in
shock and excitement, he felt ashamed – but not nearly as
much as in this moment, one hand holding the snacks and
the other ready to strike, facing two pre-adolescents sitting
at a noticeable distance from each other, their eyes covered,
swaying under the weight of their artificial visions. Looking at

him without seeing him – unless, of course, the machines had an independent perception of him. Who knew whether those circuits weren't carrying thoughts of their own, unbeknownst to the children they encased. Who knew, in fact, who was playing with who.

Oh, sorry, Paul said.

He beat a hasty retreat, shamefacedly took refuge in the kitchen – and then started pacing back and forth. He was clinging too much to his fear, or his fear was clinging too much to him, and soon it took hold again – that vicious spiral of thought, But who knows what's going on down there? Who knows what's going on in that space that can't really be said to exist, but also can't really be said not to exist? What if she's stark naked in a bathtub and he is as well, and massive, and his erect penis reaching her lips? Who knows if that's how they have sex these days?

And, alarmed: What if she's chosen to be a redhead in that virtual space?

*

She turned fourteen and ran away, although it wasn't a flight so much as a misunderstanding, and to his utter surprise Paul found her in her grandfather's town. Now, Louise, couldn't you have called and let me know where you are? Louise was sitting at a bus stop, in a sleeveless top, eating a slice of pizza that looked bigger than her face and almost certainly was – at least she had a book in her hand, which almost never happened. Oh, come on, she said with her mouth full; in a

good mood, an excellent mood. I came to see if maybe I'd
see our parakeets again. But I think they're hiding, and Paul
wondered if, two years before the promise he'd made to himself would be due, she would come to understand the way
the world really worked, to understand what was possible
and what wasn't, that is, to understand violence and cruelty.
For the moment he didn't say anything. As usual, he didn't
say anything. He gave her his coat and she tucked the thin
volume in the pocket, where he would find it much later. It
was Nadia Dehr's *Life L*. He would reread it, his heart pounding, looking for the smoking gun, the poem that must have
inspired Amelia to leave, the first time around, all those years
earlier. The poem that had caused her to break his heart. If
literature could change the world, we'd know it by now, Nadia
Dehr had said, by way of explaining why she had walked away
from it all. In the end, she would turn out to be wrong; literature would indeed be capable of changing the world, since
it had broken Paul's heart, which is to say, Paul's world, and
had made him the man he would now be. The man sitting
in his kitchen, rereading verses older than himself, written
by a woman who had been dead for ages. What had ruined
Paul's life had redeemed Nadia Dehr's art. The smoking gun,
he would think stubbornly, that he would remember having
discovered in another kitchen, Albers's kitchen, so many years
earlier. *This boy is charming, he could be perfect for us – if only.*
He had thought it would kill him.

Yet the same strange thing would always happen no matter how many times he read the thin volume. He would leaf

through it, reread it, even shake it over the table as if art and crime could fall out of it like a flower that had been pressed and dried in it, but he wouldn't find, could never find the poem in question.

*

She was fifteen and stayed out until three o'clock, four o'clock in the morning, and he looked for her with the GPS, looked for the gleaming dot that was his daughter on the map, pinpointing her location in a part of the city where he hadn't gone in ages, in a club he didn't know and had no reason to know. He drove there, his gaze feverish, hovering, no matter how dangerous it was to drive so distractedly, on the blue dot that represented Louise and seemed to be static, but the closer he got the more detailed the scale became, as if he were swooping down on her, and the closer he got the more precise the dot became, and just before he reached the end point it seemed as if the dot were actually moving; it was swaying or rather turning upon itself, tracing an uninterrupted figure-of-eight that was, he thought, the movement of a young girl as she held out her arms to make-believe she was flying around the beach, or the movement of a young girl's hips as she made love in a bed, or even the whiplash movement of a young girl's head as she is being assaulted in a car park. He walked into the nightclub – Paul wasn't the sort bouncers said no to – and looked around for her, under the fluorescent lights, his heart pounding, and then spotted her at the bar, a glow-in-the-dark drinking straw in her hand, tracing incomprehensible patterns in the air, straddling the knees of a young man who watched her, his heel mindlessly spinning the stool on which they sat. A bit like me at the Elisse hotel front desk, Paul thought, and he felt very old. His daughter was swivelling: sometimes he saw her face, and sometimes he didn't, but whenever it was visible, she looked happy. A happiness that radiated from the child that she no longer was – it was beautiful to see, these two moments layered upon one another, the part of her life now ending and the one now beginning, and he watched a while longer, without making a fuss, then decided to simply head back. He waited in the car for her to come out into the fresh air; he watched her kiss this boy, unless it was already another one, because under the glowing lights and in the street they all looked the same; he saw her, her face lit up from below, ordering a car on her phone which came two minutes later, and, when she climbed in, he followed her. A driverless car, a young girl in the back seat; behind her, several metres away, a car with a driver, nobody in the back seat. Or so it seemed. He entered the apartment a few minutes after her but she was already in her bedroom; the empty rooms already had the atmosphere of a long sleep, and he wondered just how many things, in fact, he didn't know about her. More than yesterday, he told himself, and less than tomorrow. He did something he hadn't done in a very long time: he went to tuck her in. When he kissed her on her forehead, her lips smelled like mint but her hair smelled like night, a freedom and a passion that he, her father, could not be part of; all he could do was breathe in its remnants on her skin, her coats, the rim of her cups where she'd recently started leaving, here and there, traces of a lipstick that he never noticed on her lips.

✴

I smell her scarves, I smell her neck, the other day I actually found myself sniffing her toothbrush. Sometimes I feel like I'm a dog, he said to Amelia. It was ridiculous, after all this time he couldn't keep himself from talking to her. If she had been there they would have laughed, and each of them would have been relieved to see the other one confused. Sometimes, more surprisingly, Amelia answered. There are all sorts of ways, she said, to get from point A to point B. From inside to out-side, or from outside to inside, or from the heart to the head, or from the head to the heart, and finally to your hands. It's a matter of movement, Paul, go easy on yourself – and when she cut in he remembered how he'd loved her, as she had been when he was building his whole life, the one he was now living without her, to see her walk, just walk on by in the sun and in one of his shirts, barefoot on the floorboards. A moment, late afternoon, the light slanting, her hair ablaze. Something that she hadn't known or been able or been willing to see for what it was: commitment, kindness, the prospect of being a family.

Danger won't come from where you think it will, Paul thought. At the same time, danger will come from exactly, *exactly* where you expect.

✴

Girls disappeared, teenagers evaporated. One night they had been asleep in bed; the next morning, they were gone. Sometimes there was an open window. Rain fell into pink-and-white bedrooms, soaking the carpets – that was the first thing their fathers noticed, this fatal yet beautiful blurring between inside and outside. It was as if the girls themselves had turned into rain. Rain washed away everything. Curfews were instituted, with little effect on Louise's life with Paul. Girls were disappearing, an epidemic of kidnappings – but more likely they were runaways. Rarely were their personal belongings missing. They left with nothing but their coats.

I want you to come straight home, Paul said to his daughter; I don't like this, I don't like this at all. She rolled her eyes, and sometimes she looked so much like Amelia that it was unbearable, but never so much as when she pulled away. Daddy, stop. It's a rumour, not a crime.

It's not an art, either, he almost responded, but he caught himself. In the schools, it was all anyone talked about, frantically, to the point of near hysteria. Paul bombarded Louise with questions and Louise sized him up, as if she were wondering what he was even capable of knowing, what hearsay he was working with. Yes, she finally conceded. A woman, sometimes outside, sometimes inside – how she gets in, nobody knows – she's there, she doesn't do anything, she just watches you sleeping until, if we're to believe it, you disappear.

Have you actually seen her? he asked. With your own eyes?

Louise looked at him doubtfully for a long minute without answering.

Oh, Dad, she finally said. Come on. Don't be childish.

*

We believe we're protected, we believe we're outside all power relationships of which we ourselves are unaware. All the same, we ultimately have the better end of the bargain. In other words, the power we might actually be exercising – in fact, are likely exercising – is power we've been unaware of. Paul only realised this, belatedly, one morning, because he had never been afraid for his own sake but always for Louise's. Louise and her friends, Louise and her flimsy sham boyfriend, who by not being her actual boyfriend ended up winning Paul over despite his reluctance, despite his worries about the boy who seemed so withered a spark would set him on fire, so pale a spark would set him on fire, like a sun-starved plant growing deep in a basement. How could his parents let him out of the house, how could they let him do anything, even simply go from point A to point B – not to mention the protests they went to, these children who were no longer children, not really, and who now took part in these huge waves of human bodies that terrified Paul; of course, it was difficult, impossible to forbid them, although Paul tried all the same. These things always break down in the blink of an eye, Louise, it turns into a mess; and Louise, who barely came up to his shoulder, glared at him, witheringly, heartlessly; she smirked at him, yes, in an almost cruel way, which he felt was unjust, undeserved. He would only understand later, much later that *she* was the mess.

✳

He recognised her in one of those amateur videos where it seemed at first like he wouldn't see anything or that the only thing to be seen was the trembling of the cameraman's hand. Albers, he whined, it's making me seasick. She isn't there, I see a hat, a scarf covering a face; none of this proves that it's her; okay, there's a long arm, a thin strong arm and a gloved hand, and there's some kind of projectile. But he watched as it was thrown carefully and maybe even artfully – if throwing a ball is a sport and throwing a champagne bottle against a mirror is a pastime, then what should we make of those Molotov cocktails that strike a car and only then, as if by sheer force of will, of desire, explode and catch fire? Of course, he didn't say anything to anyone. Of course he talked to her about it, Now, Louise, what's wrong with you? Have you completely lost your mind? She shrugged. You're such a hypocrite, Louise replied, I can't believe you're trying to make me feel bad when you tore apart a luxury hotel. I saw you. And you were doing far worse things. Who's that slut you were fucking? That's your mother, Paul shot back. Louise slammed the door shut behind her. As soon as he could he tracked down those images, the proof that what had happened had really happened. He didn't recognise any of it. Their youth was all he could see, all that stood out. A preposterous, blinding, wild youth that he hadn't imagined he'd lived. But his body remembered. His body remembered everything.

✳

Paul pretended everything was fine. And he did well for himself. He hired one person, then five, then ten. On big screens and small screens, the world caught fire, the world broke up and split apart and one day Louise looked at him cheekily and said, Well, what's that, anyway, this Balkanisation everyone's talking about?

Louise and her friend David grew up in a terrified city, a city paralysed by its reflection in countless monitor screens, none of which, however, were enough to prevent the violent attacks, a truck driving into a crowd, a man setting someone on fire in a movie theatre. An explosion in the middle of the city – maybe a device placed there days, weeks earlier, during a short-term rental. Each incident taught these young people how to see, first and foremost, the threat that a new situation could pose, and so Paul and his daughter would eat dinner, fork in hand, and where the one saw a utensil the other saw a weapon. Yet newcomers continued to flood into this dangerous city, fleeing something further south that was worse, that was more tangible and dangerous, trading the certainty of an unspeakable death for, they came to realise, the uncertainty of an unspeakable life. Paul had been pursuing his ambitions, had been dreaming of Amelia Dehr, and all the while, as his mind had been elsewhere, the divisions in the city had deepened. On one side was what it had been and now struggled to be, forever a city of light, a capital of archaic opulence. And on the other side was a new city that was insubstantial and drifting and miserable and enduring, a strong-willed city determined to survive. A city underneath the city, in the cracks, the shadows, the rifts. Makeshift shelters. Mattresses under stairways, on rooftops. The city of cats become the city of desperate human beings, and yet it was still full of hope – hope that, too, was insubstantial and drifting and miserable and enduring, bric-a-brac architecture that was poor, fragile, but hardy. Headstrong. Site plans that changed every day, that marked where abandonment and violence broke out every night. Floor plans of broken promises. How strange it was that each of these two cities, of these two faces of the city, should fear the other and believe itself besieged by the other. And so the city turned upon itself. As if its left hand was breaking its right.

So Louise grew up in a state of emergency, although it was a vague, murky, unending emergency. Everything was a potential danger; identities and allegiances weren't fixed: it was all too easy for someone to be a citizen one day and an enemy the next. Authority was volatile, violence was volatile, police forces appeared and disappeared seamlessly; one day armed men were everywhere, in the streets, in front of the schools, and the next they had vanished only to re-emerge elsewhere. The weapons, too, were new, their lightness championed as a humane improvement when, in fact, they were simply evolving, adapting, becoming more precise and therefore more dangerous; and these new arms were tested on the population, on the city within the city, on the citizens within the city, increasingly adaptable water cannons brought out to disperse makeshift shelters by night and angry students by day; powerful jets drawn from the city's underground systems to subdue it, leaving bruises that subsequently turned yellow before disappearing; purportedly non-lethal arms with futuristic names, strange and poetic names: impulsive bullets, blasters, other weapons with names that nobody really used, that electrocuted their targets; but still, the armed forces' obsession with the infrastructure undergirding the city (water, electricity) drew them to weaponise it against the people it served or was supposed to serve – all these state-of-the-art conveniences were repurposed for repression. At least that was the gospel according to Albers.

These teenagers – Louise, her friend David, all the protesters – were pioneers. They were explorers: testing out their rights, their obligations, in search of a new world; like chemists. And like chemists during an accident in handling materials, during an encounter with the realities of power and emergency, it was their eyes and their hands that they lost most often, that they lost first, before losing everything. Eyes and hands were the most common injuries, the threats that kept Paul awake at night. Brittle bones – carpals, metacarpals – crushed under a boot, shattered by an expandable baton; retinas detached by the impact of non-metallic projectiles, corneas burned by riot gas. Eyes and hands: makeshift bombs thrown haphazardly, thrown too late, at a risky angle, some wounds and lives alike became casualties of mistakes. The first body parts to meet the world, the first organs to revolt were torn to shreds, drenched in blood. If thought resided in the mind and love in the heart, the hunger for justice and recognition in turn had their twinned and complementary seats in the eye and in the hand.

But they were innovators as well; they were reinventors; and the first tool, the first conquest, for these young, sad dreamers who were perhaps violent as well, was camouflage, elevated to scientific levels. The ways to cross a city under constant surveillance while going unnoticed: this was the focus of Louise's conversation, and her face was flush with youth and health; what inventiveness, Paul thought. Then it was invisibility as a fine art; what innocence, what childishness, he thought. He recalled the chip in his daughter's arm which he hadn't told her about, which she hadn't talked to him about, which she didn't know about.

She grew. He aged. Little by little the world he knew turned into one he didn't know.

*

If you see the camera, the camera sees you. It recognises your gaze, the space between your eyebrows, your nose, your mouth, Louise explained. So that means the simplest thing is still not to look it in the eye. The simplest thing is a plain old baseball cap, Louise said from beneath her own coral-toned one that boasted the words BALLROOM MARFA in light-blue ink – Paul made her take it off during meals, while Albers didn't. She had never been to Marfa in the West Texan desert, where there was no real ballroom to speak of, unless, of course, sidestepping scorpions and rattlesnakes counted as dancing. You shouldn't ever face the camera directly, you shouldn't ever meet it head-on, look it in the eye. Gramps taught me the same thing with some wild animals, said Louise, and Paul's heart twinged, he missed what his father had never told him. The simplest thing is plain old reflective sunglasses, Louise declared; on her nose was perched her own aviator-style pair – Albers made her take them off in the apartment, while Paul didn't. That way, the camera doesn't see you, it sees itself. It looks at itself, it loses itself, the camera doesn't know it's a camera and it falls in love with itself, Louise explained. And it's the same for drones. Gramps told me the same thing about demons, and Paul wished she would take off her sunglasses so he could see whether she was joking; he had the feeling she was, but all he could see was himself, strangely deformed, strangely distant, as though his right hand on the table, and the knife it held, bigger than his head, were thrust at the present, while all the rest of his person, his chest, his face (his heart, his head) swerved easily away into the past.

Gas masks are good for protests, obviously, because they're hygienic and anonymous, but the police check your bags so you have to strap them on under your clothes. Hoods are good, too, and in everyday life as well, Louise added two days later, as she pulled tight the drawstrings of her fleece hoodie; and Paul was delighted and charmed and a bit worried to notice that, near the hood's seams, right where the horns would have been if she had been, say, a gremlin, she had embroidered two blue circles within two white diamonds – spirals of thread, no, helices of thread; azure and nacre; inlaid shapes that could be just that, shapes, but which could also be eyes, wide open eyes, which rested or seemed to rest upon the devices that were now everywhere to be found between the sky and them. Like some fish, Paul thought. Like some birds. False eyes that hoodwinked their predators, made the animal seem bigger than it was, diverted their attention, protected the actual orbs. Camouflage is the weapon of choice for the smallest and most vulnerable creatures; his heart trembled, his heart never stopped trembling, nothing would be left of it in the end, he thought.

Clever, he said, trying to sound nonchalant, and the usual answer came: Not bad, huh? Gramps taught me how. How many lives, it occurred to Paul, can anyone live in a single life?

And then there were other things, silk scarves printed with the lower half of another face, like in that game for children where they combined and recombined different strips of paper ad infinitum to piece together faces of every variant of the human species with faces of animals, a fox or a bird; as if this whimsy was how mankind had been evolving, in fact, prepared for it; got ready to slip into what it wasn't, at least not just yet. And all of this, Paul told himself, was also a children's game, a childish game; Louise and the wimp and a few other friends were the next generation: those a few years older than them would have tried as hard as they could to inscribe themselves within the collective space of the cloud, to sublimate themselves into it, to disperse their presence through photos and selfies and videos, expertly and incessantly documenting their own lives. But these ones didn't. Their parents congratulated themselves for it at first.

*

And then she was sixteen and it was time. The faint whiffs she exuded started to change; she smelled like things he didn't know, unfamiliar mixtures of familiar liquors, clean-smelling chemical products that gave her a vacant air; now when she was late and they checked screens to reassure each other – just to reassure each other – she no longer showed up in bars or nightclubs but sometimes, strangely and perhaps even more worryingly, in public gardens that were closed, or in museums that were closed, or – I don't think this thing is working right, Albers said, waving her phone – in nameless areas that were wastelands, soon-to-be residential neighbourhoods, or buildings under construction which had never been opened. Listen, Paul said to Albers, let her be, because he remembered when he was sixteen, he, too, had been hanging out all the time, prowling, hopping over gates and scaling fences, exploring dangerous spots, and that had made his heart pound and he had liked the way his heart had been pounding – the truth was that transgression and Amelia Dehr were the only things that had made him feel truly alive, alive at long last. And Louise had her father's heart. Where's the little girl I used to know, Albers complained, she pops in, she pops out, it's like I'm looking at a stranger, and Paul gave a polite nod, but the truth was that he finally recognised himself – or so he thought – in his daughter.

Sometimes she came back smelling like saltwater, like dunes. The sea, however, was far away. Sometimes she came back and Paul could trace the sand slipping out of the soles of her trainers; and one time she came back and her mouth, covered in something that wasn't quite lipstick, was chapped, red, bruised, and her eyes were ringed in red, and she smelled like gas.

Come here, Louise, I want to talk to you. It was all there – he'd had sixteen years to find the right words, sixteen years to put everything in order, to pull together and sum up his whole life, to focus on just the basics, to invent it if needed. The funniest or oddest or saddest thing was that, after sixteen years, all that was left was a couple of sentences. Simple words that slipped past everyone's lips every day, or should have. Two sentences – but they were true. Paul knew this. The way he knew it was time.

Not now, Dad, said Louise, and she shut the door behind her.

*

The next day, she called him; he saw her name show up on the screen. She remembered that I wanted to talk to her, he thought, his fatherly heart filling with hope. He knew it was her, but all he heard was crying, simple and animalistic, Daddy. When he came, she was on her knees in front of Albers, soaked in blood, both of them soaked in blood. She had tried to save what Paul immediately saw could not, never could be saved. They had ordered takeaway but what had arrived was an interruption of reality, forcing its way through.

Unless it's the other way around, Paul thought, in his shock. Unless reality *is* precisely this: an old woman, a bullet hole in her stomach, a bullet hole in her forehead, and Louise covered in fresh blood.

Chaos breeds strange thoughts, and the thought that came to Paul, as he took his beloved daughter in his arms, as if a father could possibly save his child from all the horrors of the world, was: If she had looked more like her mother, even her lashes would be red, tinged with what nobody should ever see. So much blood. Poor dear Albers, that mind and that heart.

She'd spent her life wondering what could die in a city dying of fear.

*

Not long afterwards, he woke up in the middle of the night convinced that he could hear a woman's voice distinctly asking: Where is she, Paul, she's not back, something's wrong. He logged in to monitor his daughter, seized by a strange foreboding, almost certain that he wouldn't see anything, that there was nothing left to see. But no, the blue dot was right there, Louise was right there, at first he didn't understand what was out of the ordinary here, what explained the rush and panic. Look closer! it insisted, *open your eyes* – yes, he would come to think about this often, about this command, *open your eyes*, and that was what he did, he opened his eyes and looked. Then he saw what was wrong: his daughter – the blue dot that was his daughter – was moving across the city's map in a way that defied comprehension. She's walking through walls! Paul thought. It was the first thought that occurred to him and, at first, the only one. She's walking through walls. The blue dot was flouting streets, corners, their directions. Louise was cutting straight through the fabric of the city. Through buildings, even through strongrooms; walls didn't stop her, matter didn't stop her, she was going at full speed, this was his daughter, his splendid daughter who had conquered the city. Amazement overcame him. She's flying, he thought.

Louise had left with nothing but her coat, and he ended up finding the strange signal that was moving according to super-human or inhuman laws: a jay, a small bird with reddish-brown feathers and a black tail, although its wing was tipped with blue, a blue more beautiful and vibrant and complex than anything that could possibly appear on a phone screen. A species of field bird that, despite its fearfulness, had adapted to the city; birds that mated for life, but this one was alone – either it had lost its mate or had not yet found one – and Paul contemplated the fluttering creature in a tiny cage set on a desk at the private security company. Here, said the employee. And Paul, stunned, had gone, cage in hand, jacket thrown over it to shield the bird from the cold, from the weak lamplight – this is stupid, he thought while shivering, it's flown through the cold and the light, after all. This is stupid, he thought, but he still didn't pull the jacket back over his own shoulders.

In her wardrobe, under the clothes that had been too small for her for years now, he found a compress. On it was dried blood, rust-coloured stains in which the devastated father tried to find something, anything – a loving word, a promise, a treasure map – but none of those could be found. A slight smell of evaporated rubbing alcohol. She must have cut herself in the bathroom, mutely, taking care not to cry out; she must have felt with the tip of her knife for the foreign body, the parasite keeping her from being herself. Once she had found it, her good arm must have thrown it out the window. This was the most likely scenario, what he hoped for. That she had thrown it out the window. But when he closed his eyes, what Paul saw was that she had stuck her hand out in the night air and waited patiently until a small hungry creature had overcome its survival instinct, its sense of self-preservation, enough to come eat, out of her hand, this seed that the entire city had sprouted from, the city and its secret heart, Louise, and that nothing else would grow from now.

She had left with the others. With these long lines of sad young people who didn't recognise themselves in the world as it was, who took their coats one night and went, where to nobody knew. As vast as the world is, there's still no escaping it, and Paul thought about them, about his daughter amongst them, perhaps in forests, or almost certainly in cities, the cities of this century and the last, and his heart was torn but he counted on her to survive, counted on her indefatigable heart, her toned muscles, the knife he had never found because, he knew, she had had the presence of mind to take it with her, Louise who had left with nothing but her knife.

At night, in his sleep which no longer came, he knew the truth: Amelia had come for what she was owed. Her child, the girl he had tried in every way to keep away from her. He knew that was the way of the world. The way of the night.

Watch over her, he thought. That's all I ask of you: watch over her.

3

Louise remembered her childhood as a story in which some parts, important ones, might have been told to her in a foreign language or in her sleep; the scenes overlaid one another and sometimes contradicted one another. Chronology wasn't respected; she had never known her mother but was sure she had known her mother, and when she thought of those long, endless years that she had spent with Paul, she was sometimes reminded of a fairy tale – enchanting yet puzzlingly distant. There was danger there, a danger different from what you expected; a message that was thoroughly hidden; and this remarkable architecture, which kept little girls awake in their beds and fathers sitting at their bedside, this architecture that was a space within an indefinite time and era together (together in the forest! but also in her bed) – this architecture is perhaps, Louise came to think, a huge trick, a trap. Once upon a time there was a father and his daughter, once upon a time there was Paul and Louise, and their world, their wonderful world, was built on a threat, built around a central void, and she didn't know it or knew it without knowing it. However, she remembered everything.

She had grown up protected from the world. She had grown up in safety, said Paul – *in security*, Louise thought, because what her father didn't know, didn't understand, was that evil went around, that it crept in everywhere and struck the heart of everything. We don't need other people – we don't need anyone, Paul said, and for years Louise had repeated that. We don't need other people. Now she wasn't so sure. In the world as it was, all the rest counted just as much, all the others, because for the father and the daughter to be perfectly together, there needed to be justice and the outside needed, would have needed, not to be this dark and wild place that it had become or that it had always been. And the outside, too, crept in; a fatal blurring of inside and outside that was, for Louise, the strongroom between two walls, the room that was supposed to resist everything but that nobody went into, twenty square feet subtracted from the rest of the apartment and their lives, entirely devoted to catastrophe. From the hall-way there was no trace of it, but Louise knew it was there, and as in a fairy tale the secret room haunted her dreams. And as in a fairy tale she had to lose everything – her father, her city, and even her reflection; she had to travel the world over and venture into unstable places that ranked amongst the bloodi-est, to be able to push open a door that wasn't a door at all but a wall, one that she had grown up beside, that she could see from her bed. So she was not with the others, with this cohort of sad young people, those who dreamed of somewhere else. She would join them later – much later, if she survived her mission.

*

The cities of tomorrow, Albers used to say – Louise had been the only one who paid any attention to her at the end, this woman of superior intelligence, this generous woman who had spent her life, one might say, offering up her mind like food or spectacle to generation upon generation of students – the cities of tomorrow will be deserted and desert cities, cities where nobody goes out after dark and where, all the same, there are always surveillance cameras; or perhaps finished cities, built from the ground up in a matter of weeks – a commercial centre, residential neighbourhoods – but where nobody ever comes to live and the place only looks habitable: no water, no electricity, a project abandoned by developers, cropping up in the middle of nowhere and coming to nothing; or perhaps cities emptied by some toxic outbreak, killing all inhabitants or forcing them out; or perhaps drowned cities, wholly submerged within a reservoir or in an ocean that, due to global warming, due to melting glaciers, was rising, would go on rising. Or cities that were only cities in name because they'd been shelled, bombarded for so long that nothing living had a chance of subsisting there or dared to enter, except perhaps for drones gliding above ravaged roads and buildings and rooms to show us what a world without people looks like, which all the same is the world of people, wholly of their doing and their ill will.

This was what they hadn't understood, hadn't wanted to understand. The cities of tomorrow, Albers said, were ghost cities.

And it was towards one of these abandoned cities that Louise was headed. Her father had wanted to protect her from everything but there was one thing he hadn't understood, hadn't wanted to see: wherever she was, Louise had grown up amongst images of collapse and explosion, ruins and death, debris and flight. She had never been in a room without screens and seeing screens meant seeing destruction. Blank stares and blood-soaked faces, streets closed off like traps, vertical bombardments and horizontal charges – as vast as the world is, there's still no escaping it.

And now Louise was crossing the same borders as these men, women, and children fleeing something far worse than any war the world had ever known, beyond death itself, which one would have thought they knew and which revealed itself to be a more subtle state than that; long, desperate lines of the living in whose hearts something had died, or long, desperate lines of the dead in whose hearts something was alive. This ambiguity, the great discovery of the century or the great discovery of Louise who was crossing the same boundaries, the same borders that they were. But alone. And in the opposite direction.

*

She'd had to take two planes to get to this country where the frontiers shifted from day to day, expanding and contracting like a distraught heart. From cover to cover, Louise read the special issue of a popular science magazine – the sort that Paul liked. She read it attentively, page by page, as if performing a ritual of sorts. The magazine's theme was memory. It transpired that our memories are not unique. They live in several places, in the part of the brain that is here (and) now, but also in the part that is both the past and the future, which is the past for the future, and so each memory is two-fold. At least. Of course, such a discovery had required a certain violence, which took the form (Louise wasn't sure she quite understood) of electricity or even light, yes, maybe a simple ray of light aimed at grey matter, in any case intended for perfect darkness, deep within the skull's thick bone. Yes, it did seem that light, an immaterial pinprick of day, made it possible to activate, to deactivate certain memories; and in this way someone could, here (and) now, relive or resurrect particular shocks, particular brutalities, or forget them or force them to be forgotten, without damaging long-term memory. Thanks to this double positioning, this double life, she thought or hoped she understood, it was at once possible to remember and not to remember. What she, however, was sure she understood was that the memories in question, the ones that had allowed this beautiful, elegant breakthrough, were memories of fear. She wondered momentarily what the pioneers – the mice terrorised by electrocution and subsequently forced to relive this terror, reactivated in their brains by a ray of carefully aimed light – thought of it.

Why would she come here, why would she inflict that upon herself? A particularly elaborate mourning ritual, a barbaric exercise she would re-enact without realising it. She shut the magazine. Then her eyes. This wouldn't be in vain, because once these sorts of rites were completed, if they went well, it wouldn't be unlikely for the initiate to find some sort of presence. Some sort of peace or presence. Maybe those were the same thing. It wouldn't be any more unlikely for the initiate to die during these rites, she told herself, her eyes still shut, given how incomprehensible, how frequently violent these ceremonies are.

A very young woman in a war-torn country. A very young woman in a ghost town, looking for the mother she had always been told was dead.

*

My dear Paul,

Forgive me for writing to you. I believe we had agreed not to, but so many years and miles have made me wonder every so often about what I know happened. Every so often, beneath what happened, there seems to have been something else. I think that's what's called regret, but I've forgotten even that; words are falling from my mind like leaves from a tree, and I won't deny that it's a relief. It's possible to travel the whole world from Elisse hotel to Elisse hotel, without ever experiencing anything that even remotely resembles reality. At the Elisse hotel in Tokyo a maid told me the story, and I think it was true, of a receptionist who killed a guest and took her body out, folded up in her own suitcase. At the Elisse hotel in Mexico City I heard the same story, but this time she was the one who had killed him. All that is of course equally true or equally false. It's a matter of movement, that's the only thing I'm sure of. There are all sorts of ways to get from point A to point B. From inside to outside, or from outside to inside, or from the heart to the head, or from the head to the heart, and finally to your hands.

In short – I'm going around the world. Or against my old impulses. The memories I have are going every which way, too, going strong and then suddenly going rogue. I don't know whether they're disappearing or simply living some other life. Somewhere else.

I came back to Sarajevo because it's my city, at least that was what I thought; in fact, its war was my city, this war I came to too late, when it made me who I am. It shaped my identity, and, also, in a way, shaped the world we now live in, a world that is, in more than just name, a besieged city. I came back to Sarajevo and I didn't recognise anything of mine there. The markets were full of brass shell casings. Engraved on them were landscapes, sometimes in minute detail, sometimes with extraordinary skill, the familiar horizon of the city I was in and which had been the besieged city. These landscapes were distinctive specifically because they were depicted not on a canvas or on a page but on hollow metal, that is, emptied of its force, its death, which were one and the same thing: speed is what makes a projectile fatal. And where did that death, made physical in the form of powder, go? A fired bullet is also a journey. Simultaneously here and there, or almost – this almost which encompasses the duration of this journey is a word that, in fact, takes longer to say than to experience. A duration that's insignificant; barely a blink, a heartbeat, barely the difference between alive and dead.

Gleaming shell casings, in all sizes, all calibres – but at this point where was the death they had contained? Death, once contained inside, was now gone and, in a strange trade-off, replaced with an image on the outside. And strangest of all was that these things were everywhere to be found in the markets, that they had to have been made every day, manufactured in the surrounding mountains; or even, who knows, abroad. You see where I'm going here. Survivors or tourists. I don't see how it can be otherwise.

What delighted me were the starlings. Their migration routes have changed, because of global warming, I'm told, and when they're here, it's a rare and special thing. They take off in flocks, in mathematically perfect clouds. The sight is breathtaking. The world being the way it is, there's no reason for them not to fly up to Paris soon. Be careful, though, because they shit everywhere, the stench is terrible.

I'm going to follow them south, I'm going to look for downfall where it happens, I'm going to look for war where it happens: only in the face of risk am I not a danger. To myself. To others. As for the rest, don't worry; I'm not thinking about you (except when I forget not to think about you). As for the little girl, if I saw her tomorrow I wouldn't recognise her, or she wouldn't recognise me, and that is truly the greatest gift you could have given – to me, and to her.

I'm going to try not to write to you any more. You saved something in me that didn't deserve to be saved; I destroyed something in you that didn't deserve to be destroyed.

Take care,

Amelia.

*

Louise refolded the letter, which she stuck in her passport, as if it were a safeguard, a special authorisation, which in a way it was. The jeep's jolting kept her eyes from staying fixed on the lines, although it hardly mattered when she knew every word of it with her broken heart.

*

The building was rumoured to have served as the CIA's local headquarters, but Louise figured all that was just talk. With her short hair, dressed like a boy, she looked at the place and saw its naive, old-fashioned fairy-tale charm. In the seventies and eighties, its stance on hygiene and neutrality had made it the rallying point for a burgeoning population of itinerant businessmen, and, according to Albers, this neutrality resulted in desensitised, desensitising architectures – anaesthetising architectures where people ended up losing everything, from a sense of what was good and bad all the way down to their very identities. Paradoxically, those who were there were both safer and less so than they might have been elsewhere. Because of its declared imperialist complicity, since the seventies the Elisse franchise had been a source of resentment and a prominent target of what is still called fundamental anti-Americanism. Threats, bomb alerts, suicide attacks, and vehicle rammings had been recorded throughout the unstable Mediterranean area, and, of course, in the Middle East, where the hotel chain was quickly forced to abandon this unique prototype, an outpost left for local militia and the sand which had an almost supernatural way of slipping in everywhere. The sand was the first thing that Louise saw when she stepped inside, a beautiful, wild image, an American hotel with its name scrubbed away, its roof broken, in which an invisible wind traced shallow channels the colour of the light starting to wane outside, small dunes here and there under the modular furniture, its walls riddled with holes, and, down below, plants starting to overtake the space, quietly snaking up the edifice that their bulk alone would soon prevent from collapsing.

With her short hair, Louise looked like a boy, but this disguise wasn't meant to be one, not really; or rather, a strange thing was happening: the women she encountered recognised her for what she was, for one of their own – and kept quiet to protect her vulnerability. But all the men were fooled, and as it was their gaze she had to hide from, she was, as incredible as it might seem, safe, almost. But wasn't that what they – she and her pale, wilted friend, she and her belittled generation – had been working towards for so long? What she and David had been looking for was peace, a vision of the world built by men and by them deserted. What they had been looking for was the night; what the night did to the city, its parks, its museums. Everything was more mysterious then, everything seemed more honest. They wanted to be cats, shadows, they wanted to escape the constant gaze weighing on everything all the time and seeming to insist that they explain themselves, that they choose sides in battles they had no wish to fight.

The deeper she sank into the present-day heart of darkness, the wearier the men seemed to be, sand encrusted deep within the grooves of their foreheads, the folds of their skin, grains permanently lodged at the corners of their lips and their eyes, forming tears unable to fall, held captive by their eyelids. Mechanical yet perpetual and perpetually retained tears that could, in these desolate spaces, be an optical instrument. A tool for survival. And what becomes, Louise wondered, of the tears that do not fall? Of the sand that fills the smallest corner and clings to the slightest spot of dampness it finds, that of human bodies: fossils? pearls? And all these men were tired, and all of them were leaning on rifles they'd welded together from three different weapons.

At first she chose who she talked to based on their face, on something in their features that reminded her of the life she had abandoned, the warmth of the father she had loved more than anyone else in the world; or the way the sunlight made a lock of hair or the cartilage of an ear shine, reminding her of the friend she had had, the witness to her childhood, whom she'd once considered her other half. Then, by dint of unrolling her sleeping bag in the sand, by dint of saying words in a voice she wished were deeper and getting inconclusive answers, she changed. She transformed, she hardened, she let her father's face and her friend's face fade away, she stopped thinking about them, she came to trust them to find her at night, in her dreams. Just as this woman she was looking for had known to find her father, who groaned in his sleep then the way these men sometimes groaned now. Now it was their weapons she was using to choose who she talked to. Some rifles, she sensed, made their users wiser than others. A hand, set in a particular way on a rifle butt, could signal seriousness.

Trustworthiness. And finally, by forgetting everything she knew in the world, she progressed.

Her grandfather's language rose from her heart to her head and, here, proved to be her closest ally. She often cast her mind back to the long-gone man. To the line he'd uttered one day: In a forest, a good friend isn't half as good as a good knife.

She found herself wondering whether that could also be true in the desert.

She found herself wondering whether she could survive the life she had chosen for herself.

4

Six propellers and the world was hers. An arid, ragged world of mountains, stripped of any living soul – a world at war where even war hesitated to break out, and so remained abstract. No matter: hers.

At this point in her life, a period which was to be the last even though she could not possibly know it, Amelia could think of nothing better than hovering and flying. She spent a sizable part of her time mid-air, secluded in a bird's-eye view. Nothing existed and war existed: this combination, nothing and war, was the only place she felt at home. In risk, she came to love abstraction, and in abstraction, she came to love risk. She gave no thought to the life she'd abandoned. It wasn't inconceivable, however, that her life might be giving *her* some thought. She was doing better, far better than before, but this improvement was entrenched. This improvement entailed a relationship to the world that was more geometrical than human.

She liked excitement, but of one sort in particular: she liked being outside her own body. She liked seeing everything and nothing, she liked delegating, she liked these invincible extensions of her sight, that is, of herself. Where some were led by their heart, their dick, or their stomach, she was led by her optical nerve. Ever since leaving her family and her city, she had lived in these indeterminate grey areas of specified or unspecified conflict. Either she turned a blind eye to her own taste for violence, or violence, in its diffuse, uncertain, almost unavowed form, was now everywhere, in layers – at times hardly detectable and at others quite intense. It was possible to travel the world from one lawless area to the next, and it was possible to travel the world without ever experiencing anything that even remotely resembled peace.

That suited her.

Amelia drew on her expertise – she never talked about art – for the professional crews that called on her services for documentary missions. Amelia's eye was autonomous, airborne, wholly separate from her – the device's range was a quarter of a mile – and from any sight she might ever physically possess. The device was wholly freed from all human perspective. Through the drone, Amelia took in the landscape vertically. She only existed in states of extreme division, and this dislocation, this disseverance from herself, was both the symptom of what was wearing her down and the only thing keeping her alive. When the apparatus was mid-air, she guided it but she herself did not see much: only afterwards, once the drone was safely back, did she extract the photos. If she spent enough time at her computer, inspecting her aerial harvest, then it could be said that she spent most of her time in the air. That, too, suited her.

She had come here to the outskirts of an archaeological mission. Her job was to photograph sites that had hardly been documented, if at all, and were threatened by a potential, or imminent, outbreak of war. As difficult and seemingly inhospitable as it might be to any form of civilisation, the region had been consistently populated. Ignoring the traces of a continued human presence amounted, for those who had ventured here, to not wanting to see the peoples here. In talking about her work, Amelia said that she was working against two forms of destruction: temporal, and human. What her peaceable use of the drone didn't convey were the forms of destruction she was helping to accelerate, by propagating across lands and minds the idea of neutral, benign technology, the idea that her machine could serve what might commonly and naively be called the greater good. One thing was certain: her work helped to advance knowledge, which is to say – as the new generation would put it – an archive with so much uncertain potential – as shapeless, and with prospects as threatening or threatened as the areas where her work took her. Work that, furthermore, she would soon no longer have. Thanks to advancements in satellite photography and in automation, Amelia's purpose would soon be obsolete. Her popularised, devalued expertise would soon be in reach of all. Of all or of a machine, and she would be able to stay in her small apartment or in her hotel rooms, watching film after film, as she once did when she was very young, as she now did in the stretches between projects, unsure what these inane fictions would or wouldn't bring her, the curtains always drawn, always, because she was convinced she was being watched, without even any idea of who or what might be doing so. Danger won't come from where you think it will, Amelia thought. At the same time, danger will come from exactly, *exactly* where you expect.

The ruins, often, were invisible from the height of an average man, or woman, such as Amelia. To the naked eye, it was a mountainous desert, sand and rock, sand and dust, crags as far as the eye could see. How strange, the way a disappeared city also resembled a city about to emerge – nothing, a drawing in the dust, lines in the sand traced by the tip of a toe. A game. A wish. Still, archaeologists knew better, as did Amelia when she was piloting her machine, and it was only from above, from the sky, that the outlines of former cities took shape in pale lines rising out of the depths. They spoke of another time, of another relationship to peace and to water, both of which seemed to have always been lacking – but that, too, was incorrect; was an illusion. Amelia lived at some remove from the teams she worked with. She didn't build relationships, anything significant, except with the guides she depended upon, who were her interpreters and her drivers, her employees and her masters, because her dynamic with these men was one of almost total dependence; if she couldn't trust them blindly, she might as well have been walking blindfolded towards the horizon. Amelia and the guides, always men, lived together in peaceful efficiency, focused on piecing together this strange land registry that would allow them to keep track of the erasure. Sometimes they talked, sometimes they didn't. Sometimes they ended up laughing together, but then one or the other of them withdrew into an isolation that, owing to a lack of space, entailed reading a book or tinkering with the car.

Ever since abandoning her family, Amelia had felt light and somewhat absent, and everything had become easier, because she wasn't fighting, she had surrendered, she was living in a singular universe which she wasn't sharing with anyone else, she no longer resisted the strange visions that came over her in these practically lunar landscapes. She knew she was lost. She knew she'd lost everything, that the world she was moving within was entirely a result of what she hadn't wanted to see, hadn't wanted to know. She was living in the rubble of her rejected legacy, of documentary poetry, of the pathetic fragments trembling in the darkness of a decades-old box, of abjectly powerless words and lines, as only words and lines that have never existed to be read, never existed for the eyes, hearts or minds of anyone else could be; and yet they were all-powerful, secret prime directives; they bore dark, hidden truths, and, because she refused to engage with them, Amelia had had to submit to them. Because she knew nothing of Nadia Dehr, she had become Nadia Dehr, and this was the irony of her flight. And when, in a few months or a few years, she threw herself out of a window, to meet the concrete down below, she would finally know, without any question, what had become of this mother who had loved her poorly, badly, or not at all.

For the time being she lived suspended between sky and land, she lived through moments that seemed straight out of a dream or a nightmare, moments when the distant past ran headlong into what still seemed to her to be the future but in fact was the present, as if time were collapsing upon itself

– like today, when she saw her machine, the camera drone she had been flying, appear to hesitate for a minute in the air, saw it quiver – but of course it was Amelia's own trembling, so subtle it only manifested itself this way – and in the empty, darkening sky, a raptor descended upon the machine, its wings bewilderingly wide, its talons and beak primed for predatory capture – the pinnacle of evolution, in other words, of violence. She tried to summon back the machine but to no avail; it was as if she could feel it being borne away by something alive, something irresistible, an intelligence beyond language, single-mindedly focused on abducting its prey, and soon the bird was gone with, Amelia thought, her livelihood.

She described the scene to her guide, certain nobody would believe her, she mimed the aerial encounter with gestures similar to those he'd used to warn her against mines and explosives – they had several signs to communicate the totality of the world they shared, and strangely enough they understood one another well. English for what was said; hands for feelings, emotions, all that was unsaid. For danger, for the fears that choked their throats. He's going to think I'm insane, Amelia worried, but instead the guide, who was also the interpreter, the driver, the confidant, crossed his arms and sighed. He believed her easily enough – he explained that the region was known for its bird-catchers; not far from here were men and women and children who all spoke the raptors' language, thought the raptors' thoughts, lived with them as if they all belonged to the same species. What men? Amelia countered. What women? What children? She hadn't seen anybody. Not a soul in the inhospitable surroundings. But they, the guide replied, had seen her, they couldn't have missed her, the poor thing with red hair who thought she could have with her machine the relationship they'd always had with these living creatures – creatures that they saw being born and being fed, that they held tight in their sleep and innately understood in their sighs, and vice versa. But it was Amelia who sighed. Their birds are horribly rude, she said, who gave them an idea like that, to take my drone away from me? The machine's nothing but skin and bones! The guide took the crooked smile on her face for a curse being cast upon the men and women and children; but he was wrong. Actually, their birds are quite well-raised, he said (his hands added, she was still lost in translation sometimes), it's no accident, they took it hostage. The explanation caught Amelia so off guard that she let her arms fall. Any time you think you've understood something in the world we live in, you can rest assured that you actually don't know the half of it.

She finally asked: So what can we do? and what came next was even more surreal, it had been so long, years and years, but still she felt the urge every so often to talk to Paul, to tell him about these moments, and the guide shrugged his wide shoulders, unfolded his strong arms, traced something in the air – a cube? a box? No, a sheet of paper. We can draw a wanted notice. As if she had lost her dog. The ludicrousness of the whole situation was growing more and more apparent to Amelia. A wanted sign and a reward, which for her, in euros or dollars or convertible marks, would be nothing, or very little, and which for these invisible men and women and children who, no sooner than one war had ended, were already bracing themselves for the next, would constitute a real contribution to their individual or collective effort to survive.

For just a second she saw herself, there, in a beige anorak, a pink headscarf over her hair just starting to turn white; a pile of sheets in her hand, wanted signs for a machine with six propellers instead of a human or even an animal. For just a second the scene seemed patently absurd. As if she was looking at herself, or even one of her descendants, in the future. But this was the present. The guide, with his usual know-how, had written the text for these bulletins (but what walls were there to stick them to?) or these handouts (but what people were there to give them to in this vast, deserted expanse?). And the whole thing struck her as an outdated, slightly strange, almost touching vision of the future.

Nothing turned up in the days that followed, despite the reward promised in an alphabet she couldn't read, a substantial amount for this population that at times barely had anything to eat. Amelia didn't do anything. She waited. Little by little she sensed or thought she sensed the presence of hundreds of eyes in the mountain. Waiting had its merits. For her generation, waiting was a lost art. Finally, one night, a man presented himself, bearing a fragment of a flying machine, and Amelia's heart, which had been so cold, suddenly leapt – *was* it sensible to be so attached to a thing? – before she realised, a little surprised, that it wasn't hers.

In the following days other people came from all directions, and what they brought was often unidentifiable or unrecognisable; sometimes she could make out a few letters, or the insignia of the Luftwaffe, or some other distinguishing mark, fragments ranging from four inches to two feet long, all of which Amelia, in her incredulity, bought, letting the guide haggle on her behalf, because it was common courtesy to act as if these sums carried any real value, to make sure not to crush them with the realisation that the money over which they bickered was nothing to her. She bought all of them, so she could sort them by date or size or political bloc or presumed continent. Shards of flying machines, which she organised and reorganised in carefully arranged circles, and all around was the desert – but now she felt like she was at the centre of the world, and her apparent desertion was merely that: an appearance.

Idleness didn't suit Amelia. It set a fire in her head, a fire that spread to her joints, her ankles and her thin wrists, her reddened fingers. A slow-burning fire that dredged up the past. And all her mistakes. When she didn't have work to do, Amelia burned with all she hadn't said, all she hadn't done – a dangerous state for a woman who had turned her back on the world. But it came back, it crept in, through so many fragments she hadn't read, kisses she hadn't given. It nagged at Amelia: Did it blaze around her because it blazed within her, or the other way around? It was hard for her to believe but she knew it: some people lived in this world without having to fixate on so many questions. Waiting for someone to bring her the machine she depended on, all she had gathered was a pile of metal and circuits; broken devices, some of which were older than her, coming from lands or entire blocs that no longer existed – a political history of the region through its forgotten wars, through obsolescence and waste. Some of the fragments had been worn down by sand, polished, while others were still sharp-edged. Amelia waited. Her guide waited.

One day, in a somewhat hazy cloud of sand and dust – the empty space of desert air – a jeep came to the base. Where there's smoke there's fire, she thought as she rubbed her sore fingers. Because of the opaque cloud, nobody could make out the car, much less who was climbing out of it. Not yet. Who- ever it was started walking up the escarpment towards the camp. Amelia squinted. Well, well, she thought, and then her heart skipped a wild beat, because in the blink of an eye she was convinced she could see, further down, Paul. Paul as he had been at eighteen or twenty, thinner than that, weaker. Is that my fault as well, Amelia wondered. Her first thought wasn't a thought but a feeling, a surge of love that she tamped down, as she had for such a long time – reflexively, instinctively – until it was back where it belonged, which is to say, the smallest, least detectable spot possible; but it wouldn't disappear; it was like a clot she was terrified would some day be the death of her. Her second thought was that he was dead, and he had come back, the eighteen- or twenty-year-old man, to take her to task. Only then did she see that beneath the oversized anorak, below the short black curls, under the greyish burnous, was a young girl walking towards her. So it wasn't Paul, after all; Amelia was at once relieved and disappointed. She bore something of him, though. And Amelia immediately understood.

5

They didn't look like each other, and yet they looked like each other. Or rather, they didn't look like each other, and yet they looked at each other with recognition. This mother who wasn't a mother and this daughter who had no choice but to be a daughter talked and talked. Amelia didn't know how to speak to a child, and so she she talked to Louise the way she might talk to herself.

I didn't think you'd find me. I didn't even think you'd look for me. I thought you were smarter than that, I was afraid you'd be a redhead, but this is worse – you're as stupid as I am. I'd have liked for you to have your father's intelligence. Paul always knew how to protect himself from everything. Or was it Albers? Was she the one who filled your head with things? I know she died, Amelia said, she was killed, right? At her place? And Louise shuddered because she still remembered everything: the silenced, pneumatic blasts, the noise of the body she loved falling to the floor, and the blood, so much blood – her right hand had staunched the hole in her head, her left hand the one in her stomach, she hadn't dared to move until the body was cold – only then had she called her father, not before. But she did not say anything to this woman about that. It had to stay between her and Albers. And Paul, somewhat, too.

Was she cremated? I think that's what she wanted. But it's all so distant, Amelia said, and Louise said nothing, it was all close, too close in fact. None of this sat well with her. Well, Amelia Dehr continued, I was hoping you'd turn out differently. I did think about you every so often, especially for the first few years, I'd shut my eyes and believe I could see you, your first secrets, your first friends, your first boys. Yes, I believed I could see you from afar. It happened once or twice. I felt like I was back in that horrible apartment that he never let me leave, that I wondered if he'd really let me leave – and Louise thought about her childhood fears – and once or twice I woke up and I wasn't sure where I was any more, I'd dreamed that I'd been watching you sleeping and, I hope you can forgive me for saying this, it was the worst nightmare I'd ever had. It's true – it was by far the worst nightmare I've ever had in my life. I dreamed about him another time, I dreamed about him and me, and it was such a relief that we weren't at home, or rather, actually, we were at home, the very first home we'd had, my room when I lived at the hotel. He must have told you about that. That was the best. Everything after that was, to be absolutely honest, a terrible mistake, but what's done is done.

And Louise said nothing. She thought about Paul, who she sometimes thought she could hear groaning in his sleep – she would slip barefoot into his bedroom and try to figure out what he was saying, or try to wake him up, but in vain; in his bare room, in his ironed sheets, amongst the dark suits draped on the valet stand or a chair, her father was talking into the void, talking to the void; and all this seemed to her like the scene of an unseen crime.

I found your photo and some letters, Louise whispered. You kept writing to him anyway.

The letters. Those missives she had insisted on writing by hand, as in the last century. I did know I wasn't supposed to leave any traces. But I wasn't doing well. Later on, I stopped. Not writing them; I stopped sending them. There was no point, after all. I knew Paul inside and out, I shut my eyes and I saw him all decked out in his elegance, his principles, his ambition. I knew him inside and out, I was the voice that talked in his mind and told him things he didn't want to hear. I'd bet he's more like my own father these days. She sighed with a contempt that struck Louise as violently as a slap; her shock was evident, all the more so considering that Louise was equally as full of fury and spite. She wanted to tell her what her absence had been like; but Amelia wasn't listening, didn't want to listen, cut her off. There's nothing for you to do here, absolutely nothing at all, it's dangerous and ridiculous. Don't you have any friends? Don't you have any lovers? You must have dozens. Listen to me. You're beautiful. Of course you look like him. I'm sorry, that's why it's so hard for me to look at you.

But what did he do that was so terrible? Louise whispered. Her pride was all that kept her from crying like the child she no longer was. What did *we* do that was so terrible? Amelia shrugged. And this shrug was Louise's first encounter with a cruelty she'd never known existed, a cruelty her father had striven to shield her against. Just to say something, just to keep face, she asked: Well, then, what did you do all this time? Amelia looked at her and on her face her daughter saw that she was annoying her. Like a nightmare, Louise thought. I was told you liked art, she mumbled.

I liked Paul. And yes, I liked art. That was a long time ago. I left because I couldn't be a mother, I gave you to Paul in a way, in exchange for leaving. So, in a way, if it wasn't for you, I couldn't have left. I loved him but what good was that? We wore each other out, we wore each other down. Yes, I left. I lived here and there, Amelia said to this child she had refused to mother, and I ended up accepting my father's money. Like everyone else. Not much, but enough to taint me forever. You know where it came from, don't you? No? See, I made the right choice, Paul protected you after all. You got out safe, you don't know what my family is like. They're all leeches. But never mind that. The money came from sand. Sand for concrete. My father may not be one to brag, of course, but he's a robber, nothing short of a thief. He's still doing it, that's all he knows how to do. Tons and tons of sand. Three hundred for a house, thirty thousand for a highway. And now we're starting to run out of sand. It doesn't look like it, I know. Especially not here, it doesn't look like it. But the quarries have been drilled and excavated down to the bedrock, and one of the solutions my father and the others found was the ocean's depths. Massive boats, powerful pumps, thousands and thousands of litres sucked up blindly. All the plants and animals and coral were just collateral damage. The other solution, of course, is theft.

Massive trucks at dawn loading up on the beaches all around the world – Asia, India, Africa, America, Europe. And the result is that the coasts all around the world have been weakened. They're receding; the coasts and estuaries are this close to collapsing. They're breaking apart. Some Malaysian islands have almost completely disappeared. That's what my family does. And now it's your family – that'll teach you. But art . . . The way I see it, the future of art is the future of these coasts. What does it matter whether I like it or not? It'll disappear. Everything will disappear. All that's left will be the crimes. My father is like yours: a man constantly reinventing himself. The last few years, he's been building artificial islands in artificial shapes, and from overhead the outlines they form in the dead oceans, the dying oceans, are palm trees or stars or viruses, basic shapes for vulgar tastes. They're a mockery of what nature itself could offer; and even so, they're feats of engineering. Masterpieces. And the sea levels are rising. All this time the water's been rising and I think that soon enough all that'll be left on earth will be those islands, those horrid, horrible shapes, like a greedy kid's toys. I'm better off here, in the war, which at least is honest. I'm better off taking my photos. I put as little of myself as possible in them, but I still have the pathetic belief that it's better for there to be something than nothing. So that's what I do. I take aerial shots of what's disappeared or what's about to. In the unlikely case that worlds have to be reconstructed.

She's insane, Louise found herself thinking as she sipped some very hot tea with milk and sugar, Amelia's main fuel. She wondered if she really was – if it could be said that she really was, despite everything – her mother. She'd just arrived, she had sand everywhere: in her hair, under her nails, within the exquisite whorls of her ear. But what was upsetting her, what was getting in the way of this reunion, what was gumming up the delicate machinery of her dreams, was this abstract sand, this poetic (albeit darkly, despairingly poetic) sand that Amelia kept talking about.

Yes, I left it all because it was all corrupt. Your father, me, everything. The irony is that, as vast as the world is, there's still no escaping it; and that in trying to extricate myself from this corruption, I only ended up making it worse. I just wanted to protect you. I'm not sure I succeeded.

No, Louise said, not only did she not succeed, she actually failed outright. Because she never really left. Louise told her mother about her childhood touched by a spectre. A strange presence that wasn't continuous but dissociated, alternative, a visitation on some nights, and I wondered how that was possible, if I wasn't going insane. Amelia rolled her eyes. Was this woman a monster, Louise wondered, or was it just an act? For my benefit, the same way people crook their fingers to form a wolf's shadow on the wall of a child's room? She didn't let herself be intimidated, she went on the offensive, decided to be just as obstinate. Now I know it was my father. That he wanted you so much, that he thought about you so much, that he conjured you. It's not a matter of words or choice, it's a matter of love. And pain. It's possible to be contaminated by someone else's pain. Even when they never mention it. The funniest part is that I've wondered, always wondered, if the truth actually was that he had killed you. Can you imagine that? Him – a murderer? Louise laughed, but Amelia did not say anything. Amelia furrowed brows that the sun had bleached white. It's the opposite, I guess. He kept you alive. If you survived this long, if I thought I knew you even though we didn't talk about you, never talked about you, it's only because of him.

She looked at this stranger, a woman on the cusp of old age who somehow looked younger, no doubt because of the love she had refused to give – as if she had saved up a life or two this way. Could such things be just a matter of credits and debits? Have I gone the wrong way? Louise wondered, having given her all to get this far – but I didn't do it for her, or for my father. I did it for myself, myself alone, so I wouldn't have to eke out a living, or a dying, so I wouldn't have to live or die half-heartedly.

Louise's throat went dry; a bitterness choked her and seeped into her words, and all of a sudden, she felt tired, miserable, unable to speak. She'd come all this way, and in vain, why hadn't she stayed in the comfort of her own life, the one her father had kept her in like a cage – why hadn't she stayed back there, in that self-declared first world, which was ablaze all over, and in the blaze of which she had known friendship. Her freedom might have been illusory but her friendship on the other hand was wholly true; that much she could be sure of. In her deep disappointment, her mind turned to her friend. The one who'd never lied. Her sidekick, her confidant, the wan one, his arm linked in hers during the protests they had gone to almost religiously, as if rubbing together their shoulders and hips and dreams could ignite something, a spark, a kind of justice, a better world. How childish, she thought. And yet she missed those foolhardy risks she had thought she was taking, even though she had had no idea what danger, true danger, was. But it had built character. In one sense, they had all been children's games; in another, they had been an introduction to struggle. Two sides of the same coin, her head on David's lap as he had instilled fresh, soothing saline drops into her tear-gas-reddened eyes, artificial tears that rinsed her irises of all that they had seen; and they took turns, it was her job now, his head like a Roman statue's (but blunted, as if lost in the sand and found much, much later, after his name, his power, even his renown had been forgotten) on her lap, in a ritual of purification and solidarity. Another world.

Just say the word and I'll come with you. He spoke little but spoke well. He spoke the way he cut, he who hadn't shuddered while slicing her arm open to remove the chip. As if I were a cat! Louise declared, and David hadn't wavered. Just say the word and I'll come with you. But she had decided this trip was one she needed to make alone. Maybe she'd been right. Here she was, in a makeshift camp, beside a woman who was, had to be, insane. Louise got up. Night is falling, Amelia said, you should stay here, but she didn't really mean it, local custom put those words in her mouth. The young woman refused, she was going to head back to where she came from, unroll her sleeping bag under the wall of a hotel in ruins, it was just two hours away, she wouldn't have dreamed of lingering here, she was sure it would be the death of her if she did. No, better to go back where she had her bearings, amongst soldiers and deserters and mercenaries, some her age, David's age, which, come to think of it, was crazy.

*

Her sleep, in what was or wasn't a bedroom, was strange, her head swathed in a veil like a bride, to ward off leering eyes, mosquito stings, and the sand; and her dreams, too, were strange, like after-images of coral or urchins in this place where there had once, years before, been a sea, one that had since dried up and now haunted sleepers and lulled them.

*

The next day, however, Amelia came back to earth and came to her. For just a little while, she let go of her fixations, she was truly there, after two hours' drive, facing this young woman to whom, despite everything, she still owed something. She'd had trouble getting there, trouble talking, at first she walked around the abandoned hotel, sniffing like a lost animal, more puzzled than worried. Louise didn't say anything; she watched Amelia. She stayed perfectly still and the woman finally approached her. Sitting down, in the half-darkness, and simply saying: I'm listening. To you. And Louise began talking. Louise didn't know how to speak to a woman who, once, might have been her mother, and so she didn't talk to Amelia so much as she talked to herself. To the encroaching night. She said things she had never before managed to think; things that, having now been put into words, seemed to change state and even change essence, like a plant that looks nothing like the seed it grew from. Maybe this is what she'd come here to find. A voice of her own. And with this voice, Louise talked about the love she had for Paul. A love so strong that it weighed on her, that it blanketed her and slowly pushed out all the air she had, as she breathed in and out, turning the air she could breathe into its opposite, air that smothered her. She had never confessed this, not out loud, until now. He's lost just about all my respect, she said. I've had it with him. The world's on fire and he acts like nothing's wrong. He's been lying to me my whole life. He was lying to me when he tucked me in. When he was cooking. He lied to me in restaurants, at the pool. On the street. Everywhere. The only time he was honest was when he was asleep. Only then.

Amelia thought for a long while, so long it seemed she wasn't going to say anything. No words came to her. Just a quick, sharp breath. Then: You're being hard on your father. And to top it all off, you're wrong. Paul gave me his word when I left, he swore to me that he would never talk to you about me. So that you wouldn't have the childhood I had. I needed to be dead to you. I couldn't even be a bad mother; I couldn't be a mother at all. Look at me. See? See how awful I am? That's not what a child needs. The truth is, I was afraid. I was so afraid that I wouldn't know how to love you, that maybe I would look and find it in you as well, this awfulness that's swallowed me up, and the world as well. I have no idea whether I'm suffering from it or spreading it. Maybe both. What I do know, what I know without a shadow of a doubt, is that my mind isn't well.

It might be far-sighted, but it's not well. I'm not well. And I wanted to spare you. Paul has simply been respecting my one wish. My final wish, in a way; you might have noticed – but in the falling night, there's barely anything to see, barely anything at all – I'm living on borrowed time.

Listen carefully. Forget what I told you yesterday, and if you can't forget it at least don't take it to heart. I keep making the same mistakes. The truth is I've been thinking about Paul for years. I'm still thinking about us. Here, in the night, in the dark, my ideas are clearer, I can finally see. And what I see, in this scene moving further and further back in time even though it always feels like it's not long ago, but just far enough that I can't go back to it or touch it or take it in my arms – take you both in my arms – yet still close enough that I can lay my eyes on it – what I see is this: Paul saw me as I was, exactly as I was, and he loved me. And he still loves me. Maybe in spite of himself; at heart, whether or not he accepts it doesn't matter much. Any man capable of that, of knowing another human being exactly as she or he is and loving that human being, even when he's been betrayed, even when he's been abandoned, when he's been left all alone, that man deserves love, deserves respect, because his heart is beating against the times, because he's fighting like a swimmer against the current. You can't do anything for the world that's about to end or the world that's about to come if you can't see or understand that this man, as he is, is already the resistance.

Louise looked at this woman disappearing into the darkness and tears welled up in her eyes as her body reacted to something – violence? relief? – because this stranger, wholly cut off from her, wholly ensconced in her choices, maybe her madness or simply her nature, which she hadn't been able to ignore – this woman had just given her back her father, the only family she had. Maybe she's lying to me, Louise thought; I could spend the rest of my life trying to understand her. But then my life wouldn't be mine and she would have had two. No daughter should be haunted by her mother.

Night made its way into the ruined hotel, through the bullet holes, through the empty windows, with their glass shards lying all around them like treasure, invitingly, a fatal blurring between inside and outside. Night came in, night touched Louise who had never experienced such darkness, a perfect black, and yet even there, after a minute passed, she could see. Yes, she could see something there. They grew silent as the night fell and as the struggles to come took shape before them, came into focus. Louise made out or thought she could make out patterns, forms, like those connect-the-dots children's drawings, which in reality – here, in the desert, in the war she had come to realise was brewing – were an initiation into the sky and the night as it falls.

6

Paul's troubles began not long after his daughter left. It was the lights, he said, the light bothered him. It had a way of creeping in. He banished all the screens from his bedroom, down to the alarm clock, which he hid under the bed; even then, he complained, I can feel it, I can sense the blue LED, I know it's there, I know it's glowing, it's unbearable. Sylvia found him one of those aeroplane sleep masks. But even so the light somehow wormed its way to his optical nerve, it drove him crazy, he put up blackout curtains, darkroom curtains, shutting out the vague halo of street lights and the coloured beams that sometimes rose up from the *bateaux-mouches* on the Seine and which he had loved up to that point. It made no difference: pale dots swam everywhere on the underside of his eyelids. He couldn't escape. I think I'm sick, he finally said to Sylvia. He ended up stripped down to his underwear on a hospital bed, inhaling the vague smell of disinfectant, trying not to stare at the drab fluorescent lights above him. He did what he knew he shouldn't; he researched his symptoms himself, learned all about light pollution. Its effects on mammals, some forms of cancer resulting from working at night and from the blue, sickly blue light he'd been running away from ever since childhood. Its effects on the birds so disoriented that they lost their bearings, crashed into buildings and bridges.

He had tests done. So many questions; and when they asked him his age, the number he heard coming out of his mouth seemed unreal to him. Completely made-up. He was asked increasingly strange questions, about whether or not he had been exposed to particular substances. What do you mean, Paul asked, thinking of Amelia's smile, Louise's smile, was he paying for all that as well? Chemical substances, for example, have you to your knowledge been exposed to flame retardants? And this time he wasn't sure how to reply, he shrugged like his father had done. In the X-rays Paul saw a ribcage, an arm, a thigh, none of which he recognised as his. This shadow of his body had been invaded by luminous spots he suspected should not be there. He remembered having already seen similar images, if they were indeed images. He remembered having come up with the idea that it was light, luminous points, that had killed his mother, but all that seemed distant to him, buried in memories of a childhood he hadn't enjoyed and that he wasn't even connected to any more, apparently, as a result of forgetting. The truth was, before he had fallen ill, he had long since ceased to remember that there was something there to remember.

Is this how it all ends? he wondered. In this constant, wan light, which he had tried all his life to avoid, to outrun, and which was now eating at him from the inside out?

He was reluctant to go and get treated. David begged him, and finally convinced him. The young man seemed to have developed a strange fondness for him, unless he'd been explicitly given instructions to care for him. In Louise's absence he was the one who came and helped. He ran errands, seemed to know Paul's tastes and wishes without ever having to ask. At least stay for dinner, Paul said every time he showed up, and the young man apologised before excusing himself. One night, however, he did stay. Can I ask you something? Paul said, and after a moment's pause David nodded. He was a loyal being, utterly honest and wholly loyal, Paul thought, a little awestruck. What game were Louise and you playing the first time you came here? At first his visitor pretended not to remember but Paul pressed the question. With your video-game headsets. You know what I'm talking about. The pale boy – the young man – looked down; under his nearly white lashes he smiled. Promise not to make fun of us? Paul replied: I promise.

We were animals. Roaming around a city in ruins, flooded by water and overrun by trees, and in the ruins of what had been our school and was now just a caved-in roof, just twilight, we built our shelters. What animals? Paul asked. Oh, wild animals. Wolves, foxes. Sometimes birds. We saw the world through their eyes – sometimes it took a really long time to figure out where we were. In one of our homes, for example. Because grass had completely grown over the furniture and entire colonies of insects were living in the walls and under the floorboards. They were even crawling around in the books.

But why? Paul asked. What was the point of all that? Did you get anything out of it?

I don't know, David confessed. Just that we weren't the centre of the world, maybe. Maybe that it would all go on, even

265

without us. But I don't really know. He was quiet for a minute and added: It was just a game, you know. He often asked him what they were up to, and when he said *they* he meant Louise and him and the other self-effacing young people who had deserted everything Paul himself knew of the world. Everything he had coveted. David never gave him an answer. David, if I took a photo of you, would you show up in it? And David tried to stifle his smile, failed, broke out in laughter. It's been so long since I've tried. You know, that goes against our – and here Paul expected him to say *beliefs* – principles.

I'm tired, Paul confessed. I'm very tired. David looked him up and down calmly. What would help? he asked. I don't know, said Paul. Often he slept in his strongroom, a kind of tomb; yet even there, the lights still plagued him. The city still bothered him. What would help you, David asked, and Paul was touched that this young man would devote so much attention to someone he wasn't even related to. Not much, I'm afraid, said Paul the businessman, the man of power. Paul who at the same time was the abandoned lover, the abandoned father. Unless it's possible to restore the night to its original darkness, he sighed, and he wasn't sure any more whose line that was, his or someone else's; he was a bit ashamed of it; but David nodded solemnly, as if there was nothing more sensible in the world. And that was the last line Paul remembered, because after that the light swallowed up his entire field of vision, and he lost consciousness.

*

He woke up in what seemed to be a hotel room. It took him a minute to realise that it was a hospital. Through the window, a sealed pane of glass, he saw a tree – a poor, slightly awkward, slightly sickly tree; and, beyond, the gleaming city, poisonous but beautiful. Irresistible.

I knew, said a voice beside his head or within it, an entire neighbourhood driven mad by the light. People kept complaining about it. Their hair was falling out. Their teeth were falling out. They changed the lighting and everything went back to normal. Paul didn't dare to turn around – not right away. Somewhere else, it was the opposite, everything was going well until they changed the street lights and suddenly: car accidents. Suicides. Murders.

You're making it up, said Paul.

Not at all, she said.

She came closer, he heard her. Sat on the bed, lay down beside him, what would rubbing together their shoulders and hips and dreams ignite? A new spark, in a world already eaten away by light, blazing everywhere?

You again, said Paul.

Me again, said Amelia.

He took her hand. He felt her veins, her tendons, her thin fingers. He knew her age as he knew his own, but the numbers seemed unreal to them, they were younger than that, both of them were: they were only as old as their love. As what their love had become and which was now something else. A memory, a ghost, a still-unknown force field. A way out, perhaps. And a strange thing happened: the city, outside, suddenly switched

267

off. Not suddenly, but step by step, block by block, darkness spread. Night reasserted its dominion. And so tonight there was nothing left to behold but a shadowy, black rectangle.

The perfect image, said Amelia.

The perfect image, said Paul.

*

The day after the blackout, he felt better. And not just better – in fact, fully recovered. His doctors looked at him more oddly than when he was sick. Sylvia came to pick him up; she was beautiful and distraught and dressed in layers of thin fabrics already slipping off her shoulders and collarbones, not even covering the base of her throat; and this failure, in Paul's eyes, was art. She was wearing pink, burgundy, a creased silk skirt that showed some streaks of gold, the whole thing reminiscent of Rome, the city she had returned from. I couldn't get here yesterday, all the flights were cancelled, how did you recover so fast? Fully recovered! What happened? she asked a doctor, almost accusingly, and the doctor admitted that he'd be hard-pressed to answer that himself.

7

Paul was in bed with Sylvia the night he heard about Amelia Dehr's jump, Amelia Dehr's plunge. They had seen each other a few more times after she came back. They had gone to see Albers, that is, Albers's ashes, which they scattered together over the city she had theorised about, and loved, this city which had ended up rejecting her. That'll teach them, Amelia had said, they couldn't stand her. Well, they can just breathe her in now. A bit of Albers in their lungs. Paul, shocked and thrilled to be, had laughed. He found that preferable, in fact: more of Albers in him. In the world.

They had talked about Louise and about the world and Amelia's feeling had been that the former would fare better than the latter. She had talked about each as she might a concept, an abstract idea; but for Paul, his daughter's smile, her smell, her voice were of the essence. One thing I don't regret is that she looks like you, they had each said to the other. At the same time. Almost at the same time. That, too, had made Paul laugh. And all the while they were shyly keeping their distance from one another.

Maybe they could be friends, Paul had thought, but he knew perfectly well that was out of the question – that it had never been a matter of friendship between them. And no doubt Amelia felt that way, too, because shortly after that she jumped from her small apartment. The two witnesses talked about her smile and the strange, insane beauty of the scene, a tall woman barefoot, standing on a railing. Leaning nonchalantly against the wall – in the frame of that window like it was a door. Smiling, her hair still red, ablaze in the sun. Wearing a man's shirt. She had been smiling as if she expected to be seen, one of the witnesses said, his hands trembling; she smiled as if she needed an audience in order to take her life. But that wasn't it, the other witness said, she wasn't smiling at us, she was smiling at someone straight ahead, a head taller than her, but of course there was nothing in front of her, just the sky, the setting sun and its slanting light.

Then Paul understood that this was Amelia's only artwork, her form of artistry, her definitive and enduring way of making amends. It would be incomprehensible to everyone but him. A work meant for him alone. Paul knew it was him she had been smiling at.

Him, Paul, thirty years earlier, when he was asleep at his chair, at the front desk of the Elisse hotel, and he hadn't seen her leave.

Him, Paul, twenty years earlier, when he had bought that immense, empty apartment for the sole pleasure of seeing her in a ray of sunlight, barefoot, his shirt on her shoulders.

Him, Paul, when she had woken up in the maternity ward and she had seen him, with Louise in his arms, and she had contemplated them.

So she remembered, she remembered everything.

And so he finally knew that he was, and had been, loved.

Author's Acknowledgements

I would like to thank Mitzi Angel for bringing me to Faber and Emmie Francis for making it my home in the UK, and for her brilliant editing; my agent Laurence Laluyaux and the team at RCW; my French publisher Olivier Cohen and his collaborators at les éditions de L'Olivier, especially Violaine Faucon – and everyone who has, in their own way, helped me to write this novel, as well as the Centre National du Livre for the grant it awarded me, and the Villa Médicis, where this book was begun and abandoned, before being picked up again elsewhere, and finished at the Faber Residency in Catalonia. Many thanks to the French photographer Raphaël Dallaporta who shared his stories about drones, in connection with his *Ruins* series (2011). The lecture titled 'The Astronaut in the Rosebush', attributed to Amelia Dehr within these pages, is drawn from a text that was initially published in *Le Ciel vu de la terre* (Éditions Inculte, 2011), and includes a quotation from Tom Wolfe's *The Right Stuff* (Farrar, Straus and Giroux, 1979). Documentary poetry owes a great deal to my own mother and her work, and its continuation by other means. For the earliest writings of Nadia Dehr I took some inspiration from an article by the American art historian Jennifer L. Roberts titled 'Landscapes of Indifference: Robert Smithson and John

Lloyd Stephens in Yucatán' (*The Art Bulletin*, vol. 82, no. 3: Sept. 2000). Regarding the war in the former Yugoslavia, the works of Peter Andreas were an immense help during my writing of this novel. Most valuable of all were the direct and indirect accounts that were shared with me in Sarajevo during multiple trips.

Anton Albers is, of course, a fictional character; her life and her work comprise elements and notions adapted from intellectuals Giancarlo De Carlo, Jean Delumeau, Eric Hobsbawm, Saskia Sassen, and others. However, her spirit is a tribute to activist Mira L., without whom I might not have been born in Paris.

As for actual events that readers might be tempted to recognise in this story, it should be noted that they were frequently altered or amended intentionally. Consequently, any resemblance to actual persons, living or dead, is purely coincidental. Except perhaps when it concerns myself.

The Elisse hotel chain does not exist.

Translator's Acknowledgements

I owe a debt of gratitude to many friends and colleagues: to Clément Ribes, who first gave me the book, declaring that 'je suis sûr qu'il te plaira'; to David Ferrière, for his unflagging friendship and insight; to Laurence Laluyaux, who always has an ace up her sleeve; to Emmie Francis, Elodie Olson-Coons, Anne Owen and the fine team at Faber & Faber for keeping us all on an even keel; and, last but not least, to Jakuta herself.

Y036605

The item should be returned c · r~~
by the last date ~t~r ~ ~d ' ·

Cent 09.05.21